The Gentleman's Miscalculation

THE LOCKWOOD FAMILY

LAURA BEERS

Text copyright © 2025 by Laura Beers
Cover art copyright © 2025 by Laura Beers
Cover art by Blue Water Books

All rights reserved. No part of this publication may be reproduced, stored, copied or transmitted without the prior written permission of the copyright owner. This is a work of fiction. Names, characters, places and incidents either are the product of the author's imagination or are used fictitiously. Any resemblance to actual persons, living or dead, business establishments, events or locales is entirely coincidental.

Chapter One

England, 1813

Lord Winston Lockwood was not in a jovial type of mood. He sat at the long, rectangular table in the dining room of Brockhall Manor as a luncheon was being held in honor of his brother's marriage to Delphine. He was truly happy for them, despite feeling a pang of jealousy at the love that they so clearly had for one another.

Winston knew that he had every reason to be happy, but he wasn't. And that was what irked him the most. Why couldn't he just be content with his blasted life? He had established himself as a barrister in London, and he owned a sheep farm. However, no matter what he did, he still felt like an utter failure.

What was worse was that he knew nothing about sheep, but when the opportunity had presented itself, he had decided to take the risk. He wanted to prove to others—and himself— that he could do more than what was expected of him.

His eyes drifted towards Miss Bawden, the fiery red-haired young woman who irritated him to no end. She was undeniably beautiful, but she was far too opinionated for his tastes. She seemed to have an opinion on everything and anything. It was rather vexing. He had learned that he could only take her in small doses or else he would go mad.

It had been this way for many years. Their interactions were a series of endless debates and squabbles, each one trying to outdo the other. As they grew older, they found it was best to avoid one another altogether, despite her always being underfoot when she visited his sisters.

Miss Bawden turned her head and met his gaze. Rather than look away or show any hint of embarrassment at being caught staring, he tipped his head in acknowledgement. Her eyes sparkled with annoyance, as they always did when she looked upon him. At least she was consistent.

His mother clinked her fork against her glass, drawing everyone's attention. "We are most fortunate to come together to celebrate Bennett and Delphine's wedding, but it is time for them to depart for Scotland," she announced. "Let us gather outside to say our final goodbyes."

Winston shoved back his chair and rose. He couldn't wait until this was over so he could retreat to the solitude of his bedchamber. He wanted to be alone. It was much more comfortable than being surrounded by happy people who seemed to have no idea of the burdens he carried.

As he walked towards the entry hall, his sister, Melody, came to walk next to him. "You were remarkably quiet during the luncheon," she said. "Is everything all right?"

"Everything is fine," he responded in a short, dismissive tone, hoping to end this line of questioning.

She gave him a look that implied she didn't believe him. "What troubles you? And I would prefer the truth, if you don't mind."

Winston should have known that his sister would see right through him. She was remarkably astute for being eight and ten years. "We can discuss it later," he replied.

The Gentleman's Miscalculation

This was not a conversation that he wanted to have in passing.

"Very well," Melody said, "but do not think I will forget. I have the memory of a hawk."

Feeling an overwhelming need to tease her, he asked, "How do you know that hawks have a good memory?"

"Hawks have been used as messengers for hundreds of years," Melody replied.

"No, you are thinking of carrier pigeons," Winston said. "Typically, falcons are trained to retrieve prey."

Melody grinned. "Perhaps, but hawks are much more intimidating than pigeons. So, I contend I am more like a hawk."

He chuckled. "You, my dear sister, are anything but intimidating, at least to me." With her blonde hair, blue eyes and fair skin, he had no doubt that she would cause a stir amongst the *ton*. But there was a quiet strength she possessed that set her apart. It was what she wasn't saying that had always given him pause. There was a world of unspoken thoughts and feelings behind those blue eyes, and it made him wonder how much she kept to herself.

Elodie, Melody's twin, chimed in from behind them. "What are you two discussing?"

"The kind of bird that Melody would be if she were a bird," Winston replied, glancing back at her.

Elodie joined them, wearing a pensive expression. "She would definitely be a nightingale since she has such a beautiful singing voice."

"But I am clever like a hawk," Melody contended.

"Are hawks clever?" Elodie asked with a lifted brow.

Melody nodded firmly. "They have to be, being predators and all."

"Not all predators are smart," Winston contested. "Look at cats, for instance."

Elodie's eyes widened in disbelief. "Cats are incredibly

clever and make the best pets," she declared. "They have so for thousands of years."

Winston smirked. "They mostly lounge around, sleeping and grooming themselves," he said. "Occasionally catching a mouse does not prove their intelligence."

"You just don't like cats," Elodie accused.

"It is true," Winston replied. "I never quite understood why our grandmother kept so many in her manor. I think I counted ten at one point."

"The cats kept her company, especially in her later days," Elodie remarked. She didn't appear to be bothered by the fact that their grandmother's manor had been overrun with cats, but it had greatly bothered him. He couldn't explain why, but perhaps it had something to do with his belief that cats belonged in a barn rather than an elegantly furnished manor.

As they followed the line of guests outside, Winston watched as Bennett and Delphine said their final farewells.

Bennett caught his eyes and approached, speaking in a low voice, "Are you certain my absence won't be noticed for a fortnight?"

Winston understood his unspoken concern. Bennett was worried about their Aunt Sarah's safety since her husband was still searching for her.

Placing a hand on his brother's shoulder, Winston assured him, "Enjoy your time with your wife. All will be well here. I promise."

"If you are sure…" Bennett's words trailed off.

Winston flashed a confident smile. "I am," he insisted, casting a glance at Grady, the Bow Street Runner posing as a footman.

Delphine came to stand next to her husband, placing a hand on his back. "We should depart soon so we can arrive before dark."

"Yes, Dearest," Bennett said, exchanging a look full of love with his wife, before leading her to the coach.

While the coach drove off, Winston felt immense relief that he could now retreat to his bedchamber. To be alone.

Turning, he found himself face to face with Miss Bawden. Not bothering to muster up a smile, he greeted her with a curt, "Miss Bawden." There was no need for pretenses. They both knew they detested each other.

Miss Bawden pursed her lips together, as if she had just eaten something that had disagreed with her. "Lord Winston," she replied tersely.

They stood in an uncomfortable silence, their mutual animosity palpable. Winston could not help but wonder how someone so beautiful could be so utterly disagreeable. He even suspected that Miss Bawden's steely gaze was capable of frightening small children.

Winston had no desire to spend another moment in Miss Bawden's presence. "Excuse me—"

His words were interrupted when his mother approached, gracefully inserting herself into the conversation. "Mattie, it is always a pleasure to see you," she greeted warmly. "I was hoping that you might join us for dinner this evening."

Miss Bawden's eyes flickered towards Winston, uncertainty evident in her expression. He suspected she had as little desire to dine with him as he did with her. "That is most kind of you, Lady Dallington, but I… uh…"

Looping arms with her, Elodie pleaded, "You must come to dine with us."

"I suppose I can," Miss Bawden responded, shifting her gaze to Elodie. "But I do not wish to be a bother."

Elodie smiled broadly. "Do not be ridiculous. We all enjoy spending time with you. Isn't that right, Winston?"

Botheration.

His sister was goading him.

Fortunately, Winston was a trained barrister and no stranger to such social maneuverings. With practiced ease, he maintained his polite façade. "Indeed, Elodie," he replied smoothly, "Miss Bawden is always welcome in our home."

He could practically hear Miss Bawden roll her eyes at his words. But she was too much of a genteel woman to let her emotions lay bare. Instead, she returned his smile. "That is most kind of you to say, my lord."

To the neutral observer, it looked as if they were having a pleasant conversation, but they both knew better. It was a delicate dance of civility they were performing for the sake of others.

Winston's mother spoke up. "Did you not bring a coach?" she asked, addressing Miss Bawden.

"I did, but my father had to depart from the luncheon early. No doubt someone needed him from the parish," Miss Bawden said, taking a step back from the group.

"Perhaps you could even join us for games afterwards," Elodie suggested cheerfully.

Miss Bawden briefly smiled. "I shall see if I am able," she said before dropping into a graceful curtsy.

As Winston watched Miss Bawden walk away, he couldn't help but mutter under his breath, "Games? Truly, Elodie?"

Elodie feigned innocence. "Is there a problem, Brother?"

Winston couldn't resist a wry smile. "No, but I fear Miss Bawden might cast a spell of darkness over our manor."

His mother let out a soft sigh. "I have never understood the animosity that you have towards Mattie. She is a delightful young woman, and I do so enjoy having her in our home."

"We shall have to agree to disagree, Mother," Winston said, leaning in to kiss her on the cheek. "Now, if you will excuse me, I have work that I must see to."

"In your bedchamber, with a bottle of whiskey?" she asked knowingly.

Winston did not want to have this conversation. He was tired and he wanted to be alone. "Goodbye, Mother."

His mother's expression hinted at disappointment, but she

refrained from pushing further. "Promise me that you will join us for dinner," she implored.

Winston had no desire to spend the evening with Miss Bawden. Her voice grated on his ears, rendering every conversation with her unbearable. Nonetheless, he relented with a resigned nod.

"Very well, you may go now," his mother said. "But I shall see you tonight."

Spinning on his heel, he retreated inside before his mother changed her mind. Why couldn't his family see the true nature of Miss Bawden? Despite their praises, he alone glimpsed the darkness within her heart. It had changed him, and not for the better.

As Miss Mattie Bawden walked away from Brockhall Manor, she was grateful for every step that distanced her from the infuriating Lord Winston. He was someone she wished to spend as little time as possible with. Never had she met a man so vexing.

She still couldn't quite believe they had kissed once. It had been a sheer moment of madness on her part, and she wondered if Lord Winston ever thought about that kiss. Because she most certainly did not. Nor did she remember how he had gently held her in his arms, as if he'd cherished her.

It had been entirely unexpected. Winston's usual stern demeanor had softened for that brief moment, and she had glimpsed a side of him she hadn't thought existed. It was a side she both loathed and longed to see again.

Mattie shook her head, trying to clear her thoughts. She had more important matters to attend to than pondering the complexities of a kiss that never should have happened.

In the distance, she caught sight of her grandfather's crested coach parked in front of their modest cottage. Which was odd, given that last she had heard he was in India with her uncle and aunt, overseeing their business dealings.

But she was not about to complain. It had been far too long since she had seen her grandfather, and she welcomed the visit.

She quickened her steps until she reached the cottage, where she found her younger cousin sitting on a bench under the covered porch. Francesca's expression was downcast, her eyes tinged with red, indicating she had been crying.

What was her cousin doing here? She had never come unannounced to visit them before.

A feeling of dread washed over her.

Something had happened.

Mattie sat down next to her cousin and nudged the girl's shoulder with hers. "Why are you here, Franny?"

Franny continued to stare at the ground, a tear rolling down her cheek, but she made no effort to wipe it away.

Unsure of what was causing Franny such pain, Mattie wrapped her arms around the girl and her cousin crumpled into the embrace.

"Will you not tell me what is wrong so I may fix it?" Mattie asked, hoping her cousin trusted her enough to confide in her.

In response, Franny let out a loud cry, sobbing into her arms.

Mattie could not remember a time when Franny had ever cried in front of her. Despite her age of five and ten years, Franny had always held herself with remarkable grace and decorum. What could have happened to cause such a heart-wrenching reaction?

The door opened, and their white-haired housekeeper, Mrs. Watson, let out a sigh of relief at the sight of her. "Your father is requesting to speak to you," she informed Mattie.

Mattie hesitated, torn between comforting her cousin and going to speak to her father. "Can it not wait?" she asked.

Mrs. Watson shook her head. "I'm afraid not. He seemed rather adamant," she responded. "Go. I will see to your cousin."

Reluctantly, Mattie dropped her arms and said, "Franny, I have to see what my father needs. I will return shortly."

Franny sniffled in response, but still she said nothing.

Rising, Mattie offered a look of appreciation to Mrs. Watson before she headed into the cottage. Her father's study was in the front and was a small, square room barely able to fit a desk and two chairs. Despite its size, he had managed to fill it with piles of books in nearly every corner.

Mattie approached the study and saw the door was partially closed. She could hear hushed voices coming from within.

She stopped just outside the door and knocked, making her presence known.

The voices stopped.

"Enter," her father ordered.

Mattie pushed the door open and stepped inside. Her father, a stout figure behind the desk, seemed worn down, burdened by the weight of responsibilities. His slumped shoulders betrayed his fatigue, his weariness evident in every line of his face.

A tall, lanky man stood near the window, his expression solemn as he watched Mattie enter the room.

"You wished to see me, Father?" Mattie said, feeling a palpable tension in the room.

With a gentle sweep of his hand, her father gestured towards one of the chairs that faced his cluttered desk. "Yes, please sit. We have much to discuss." His voice was cordial, but a slight inflection at the end of his words gave her pause.

Mattie did as she was told and sat down, giving her father an expectant look.

Her father returned to his seat and sighed. "I'm afraid I have some awful news to share with you." He hesitated. "Your uncle and aunt have succumbed to the fever while visiting India."

She sucked in a breath at that horrific news. "They are dead?" she asked. "What of Grandfather? Was he not with them?"

A pained look came into her father's eyes. "He is still alive, for now," he shared, "but he has grown increasingly weak from the effects of the fever. The doctors are worried if he attempts to travel home, he will die on the ship."

The tears started flooding her eyes as she attempted to blink them back. She had heard her father's words, but they seemed so wrong. So unbelievable. Her uncle was the strongest man that she knew. How had he succumbed to the fever?

Her father's eyes were moist, and she had little doubt he was trying to be strong for her sake. "I know this is a shock, but I think it is best that we give Franny some time to recover before we travel to Darlington Abbey. Furthermore, it will give the parish some time to find a new vicar. I do not wish to leave them without one."

Mattie's gaze remained fixed on her father as he delivered the unexpected news. "We are leaving our home?" she inquired, her words heavy with disbelief. This had been the only home she had ever known.

His eyes softened with understanding. "I am now my father's heir, and I am expected to ensure the estate is profitable in his absence. This is not what I had envisioned for us, but it is my duty," he explained, his voice resigned.

The weight of his words settled heavily on Mattie's shoulders, her chest tightening with the realization of the implications. She was no longer just a vicar's daughter. Her father was a viscount and heir to an earldom. One day she would become a titled lady.

The Gentleman's Miscalculation

Mattie didn't know what to feel at this precise moment. It most definitely wasn't joy for her elevation in status. She cared little about that. All she could think about was how devastated her cousin must be at losing her parents.

Her father continued, "I have sent for Emma at her boarding school, and I do hope she will return shortly."

Mattie's mind started racing with all of the things that needed to be done. "We should go into mourning at once."

"Yes, we should," her father agreed. "As the lady of the house, I will expect you to handle such things."

This wasn't the first time that her father had called her that. Her mother had died during childbirth and Mattie had been taking care of the household from a young age. Although it was not overly complicated since her father was a vicar and they lived in a modest cottage next to the chapel.

Mattie rose and clasped her hands together. She was determined to remain strong and not fall apart. Her whole life had just been upended but her father needed her now more than ever. "Do we have the funds to purchase new gowns?"

The tall man, who had been quiet the entire time, spoke up. "Lord Wythburn will have access to whatever funds he deems necessary."

Her father gestured towards the man. "Forgive me, but I failed to mention that Mr. Johnson is your grandfather's solicitor. He traveled with Francesca since I am now her appointed guardian."

Mr. Johnson nodded respectfully at her father. "I was instructed to assist in any way that I could during this difficult time, my lord."

"Thank you," her father acknowledged before redirecting his attention to Mattie. "I know I am asking a lot from you…"

Mattie put her hand up, halting his words. "I am more than capable, Father."

"I have no doubt, but that doesn't mean I do not feel remorse for it," he admitted. "I am saddened by the fact that you were forced to grow up far too early after your mother's passing."

There was some truth to her father's words. She had taken on more responsibilities at the young age of two and ten years old, but she did not resent it.

Squaring her shoulders, she assured him, "You need not worry about me. I am prepared to take on whatever responsibilities come our way, just as Mother would have wanted."

As her father's gaze lingered on her, Mattie sensed his unspoken worry but remained determined to reassure him of her strength and resolve.

Mattie offered him a faint smile. She could do this. She *had* to do this. But first, she needed a moment alone to collect her thoughts. "Excuse me for a moment," she said before she swiftly departed from the study.

Alone in the corridor, she rested her back against the wall and allowed the tears to come freely. Her heart ached for the loss of her aunt and uncle, who had always treated her with such kindness. Now, she was in a position to return the favor by ensuring Franny was always loved and cared for.

Mattie reached up and swiped at the tears streaming down her face. She didn't have time for this. She needed to speak to the dressmaker about commissioning mourning gowns. Until then, she could dye a few of her gowns black.

A thought occurred to her.

Lady Dallington would be able to assist Mattie since she had only recently stopped mourning her brother-in-law, the late Lord Dallington. Mattie knew calling upon others was discouraged during the mourning period, but she hoped Lady Dallington wouldn't chide her for it. She doubted she would, as she almost considered the marchioness a second mother, having spent so much time around her and her family.

Mattie thought about Franny, wondering if she should go to her instead of escaping to Brockhall Manor. But what was the point? She couldn't fix this, no matter how hard she tried.

And she needed advice on how to best help herself and Franny.

Coming to a decision, Mattie resolved to seek Lady Dallington's counsel. She needed guidance and support, not just for herself but for Franny as well. She departed from the rear of the cottage and, with purposeful strides, approached Brockhall Manor. She stepped up to the door and knocked.

The door promptly opened and the solemn butler greeted her. "Good afternoon, Miss Bawden," White said, standing to the side to allow her entry. "Do come in."

"Is Lady Dallington available to receive callers?" Mattie asked.

White's eyes crinkled around the edges. "Wait here, Miss," he replied.

As the butler walked off, Mattie caught a glimpse of herself in the mirror. Red-rimmed eyes stared back at her and stray locks of red hair had escaped her carefully arranged coiffure, framing her face in disarray.

Taking a moment to compose herself, Mattie inhaled deeply, her chest rising and falling with the effort to steady her nerves. Lady Dallington had always been a pillar of strength and wisdom, and Mattie found solace in the thought of seeking her counsel. The weight of her newfound responsibilities bore down on her, but she was determined to bear it with grace.

Did she even have a choice not to?

Chapter Two

Winston was descending the grand stairs when he saw Miss Bawden staring at her reflection in the mirror. He huffed. Why in the blazes was she here? It wasn't time for dinner. Could she not read a clock?

He would rather chew glass than deal with Miss Bawden. He had picked a lousy time to sneak down to the kitchen for a biscuit. Perhaps if he walked swiftly, Miss Bawden wouldn't notice him.

But as he stepped onto the marble floor, she turned her head, and he saw something unexpected. Miss Bawden's eyes were red-lined and hairs from her elegant coiffure had escaped, cascading down her back. She looked disheveled and sad, which surprised him. He had always believed she was incapable of such emotion.

She turned her head and her eyes widened slightly. "Lord Winston," she greeted, her words lacking any warmth.

"Miss Bawden," he acknowledged.

Winston wanted nothing more than to be far away from her, but he had been raised to be a gentleman. And a gentleman did not ignore a young woman in distress, no matter how maddening she might be.

With compassion in his voice, he asked, "Is there something you are in need of, Miss Bawden?"

He expected a curt response, but to his surprise, she shook her head. "No, thank you, my lord," she replied without the slightest hint of annoyance.

Now he was worried.

Miss Bawden was not one to be polite to him—for any reason. Yet, she spoke to him in a civil tone, as if they didn't dislike one another.

Did he press her? It wasn't his place, but something stirred deep within him. He almost felt bad for her... almost. After all, he was still working on the assumption that she was the spawn of the devil.

Miss Bawden reached up and tucked a piece of errant hair behind her ear. "Will you stop looking at me like that?" she asked.

He furrowed his brows. "How, pray tell, am I looking at you?"

"With pity," she said, tilting her chin. "I don't need—or want—your pity." Her words held the curtness that he was familiar with.

"Good, because I do not pity you," Winston replied. "I am just merely curious as to why you look..." He stopped, unsure of what he could say that wouldn't make this situation any worse than it already was.

Miss Bawden visibly stiffened. "How do I look?" she asked, her words holding a warning. It was evident that she was waiting to be insulted.

But he didn't want to become too predictable.

Winston took a step closer to her, but still maintained a proper distance. "You look troubled," he settled on.

"I am fine," she rushed out.

"Just fine?" Winston pressed.

With pursed lips, Miss Bawden regarded him. "May I ask why you care, my lord?"

The Gentleman's Miscalculation

Why did he care? That was an excellent question. He had been at odds with Miss Bawden for so long, except for that one weak moment when he had kissed her. But that was over a year ago, and he was different now because of it.

Knowing Miss Bawden was still waiting for a response, he said, "Contrary to your low opinion of me, I do not wish ill will to fall upon you."

"That is incredibly thoughtful of you," Miss Bawden responded dryly. "I can now die happily knowing you care for me."

Winston didn't know why he bothered. Miss Bawden only regarded him with contempt, and here he was, trying to do the right thing. Botheration. How he hated being a gentleman at times, especially around Miss Bawden.

"I am trying to be nice," Winston said, his voice filled with exasperation.

"Well, don't be," Miss Bawden snapped back. "Furthermore, I came to speak to your mother, not you."

Winston bowed slightly. "Do not let me stop you then."

"Thank you," Miss Bawden replied.

He should go, but there was something that was telling him to stay. And that nagging feeling is what worried him. Why should he remain in Miss Bawden's presence? She clearly did not want him there, and he would rather be eating a biscuit than engaging in this pointless exchange.

But as he watched her, disheveled and distressed, he couldn't shake the urge to dig deeper. There was a vulnerability about her that he had never seen before, a crack in her usually impenetrable façade. It stirred something within him, something that compelled him to stay and try to understand what had caused her such evident pain.

"Are you sure that there is nothing I can do to help?" he asked, surprising even himself with the gentleness in his voice.

Miss Bawden's eyes flickered up to meet his, her annoyance giving way to something softer, almost like surprise. For a moment, she seemed to hesitate, as if weighing the sincerity of his offer.

"Just… leave me be, Lord Winston," she finally said, her voice quieter now, almost pleading.

Winston nodded, feeling a strange mix of frustration and concern. He turned to leave but couldn't help but glance back, hoping that, perhaps, she might change her mind and let him in, just a little.

His mother stepped into the entry hall and her eyes landed on Miss Bawden. "Oh, my dear, what is wrong?" she asked, closing the distance between them.

As his mother's arms wrapped around Miss Bawden, she fell into her embrace and let out a sob. "My aunt and uncle died," Miss Bawden said between sobs.

Winston felt like an interloper in his own home. Not entirely sure of what he should be doing in this moment, he removed his handkerchief from his jacket pocket and extended it towards Miss Bawden.

She accepted it and stepped out of his mother's embrace. Wiping her face with the handkerchief, she said, "I do apologize for the display of my emotions."

"That is utter nonsense. Don't be ashamed to cry, especially when your wounded heart needs it," his mother declared. "Come, let's continue this conversation in the drawing room over a cup of tea."

"Tea would be nice." Miss Bawden turned to face him. "Thank you for the handkerchief, my lord."

He smiled in response. "You are welcome."

His mother slipped her arm over Miss Bawden's shoulders and started leading her towards the drawing room. For some inexplicable reason, he felt compelled to follow them. It wasn't because he wanted to, but rather because he felt it was the right thing to do. Which was odd. Why did he want to be a part of this conversation? He didn't. He just wanted a blasted biscuit.

The Gentleman's Miscalculation

But his biscuit could wait, at least until he could offer some comfort to Miss Bawden.

As he stepped into the drawing room, he found a chair adjacent to the settee where they were both sitting. His mother cast him a questioning look, but refrained from asking him why he was there. Despite being at odds with Miss Bawden, he couldn't bear to see someone in pain without offering some form of comfort.

His mother spoke up. "Tell me everything that has happened."

Miss Bawden took a deep breath, no doubt in an attempt to compose herself. "My grandfather, aunt and uncle traveled to India to oversee their business dealings, leaving behind their daughter, Francesca," she shared. "And we just received word that my aunt and uncle died from the fever and my grandfather is still recovering."

"That is terrible news," his mother murmured. "How may I help you at this most difficult time?"

Miss Bawden ran a hand down her gown. "We need to go into mourning, but I am at a loss of what I should do."

His mother offered her an understanding smile. "You have come to the right place, Dear," she said. "You will need to get mourning gowns and accessories and a black armband for your father."

His mother continued, "The dressmaker in the village will know what fabric to use, but typically bombazine is most often used in the countryside. Since you are mourning an uncle and aunt, I would recommend you go into mourning for at least three months. But I would strongly encourage that your cousin mourns her parents for six months."

"I intend to dye a gown or two until we can commission our mourning gowns," Miss Bawden said.

"I would advise against that since you can afford to buy mourning gowns. Dyeing gowns is more for the people who lack funds to do so," his mother explained. "And you are now the daughter of a viscount. You must act the part, always."

A maid stepped into the drawing room with a tea service in her hands. She placed it down on the table in front of his mother. "Would you care for me to pour, my lady?"

"No, thank you," his mother replied as she reached for the teapot. She poured three cups of tea and extended them to the group.

Miss Bawden took a sip of her tea before asking, "What of notifying our relatives of my uncle's and aunt's deaths?"

His mother placed her teacup down onto the tray. "The announcements will need to be trimmed in black, and some people send black gloves along."

"Are the black gloves necessary?" Miss Bawden asked.

"Not in my opinion," his mother replied. "I would recommend a hatchment to be placed over the front door for at least six months."

Miss Bawden nodded. "I believe we still have the mourning wreath from when my mother passed away."

"That is good," his mother said. "Just try to remember to breathe. Many people will have opinions on how you should mourn, but it is much more relaxed in the countryside."

Tears welled up in Miss Bawden's eyes. "I can't believe my aunt and uncle died. It just seems unreal to me."

Lady Dallington reached for her hand. "I am sorry for your loss, and I want to express my deepest sympathy to you and your family."

"Thank you," Miss Bawden murmured. "I shall pass along your condolences to my father. I know he will appreciate them."

Winston observed the genuine sorrow in Miss Bawden's eyes. Despite their differences, he couldn't help but feel a twinge of empathy for her, considering he had only lost his uncle five months ago.

But what could he possibly do to ease her pain? And did he even want to?

His mother's voice cut through the stillness. "Do you wish to borrow any mourning jewelry?" she asked.

Miss Bawden put her hand up. "That is not necessary," she replied. "I do not anticipate going to any social events while I am in mourning."

"Normally, I would recommend you delaying your debut if your father or sister died, but I do not think it is necessary in this case, considering it was an uncle and his second wife," his mother shared. "Based upon your elevation in status, I think it is wholly appropriate for you to be presented to Court this Season."

Miss Bawden looked at his mother in disbelief, as if she couldn't quite believe the words that were being said. "I have never considered attending a Season before because of our humble circumstances, but everything has changed."

His mother leaned forward, her expression softening. "It has," she said. "And I would be happy to host you, right alongside Elodie and Melody, assuming your father has no objections."

Miss Bawden's breath caught. "Do you mean it?" she asked, her voice barely above a whisper.

His mother patted her hand. "Yes, it would be my honor."

Miss Bawden grew silent, and Winston's gaze drifted to the window where rain streaked the glass. Conflict churned within him. He had a mix of sympathy for Miss Bawden's circumstances and a selfish desire to keep her away. If his mother hosted her for a Season, he would never get Miss Bawden out from underfoot. She would always be there, waiting to torment him, just by her mere presence alone.

Mattie couldn't quite believe the situation she found herself in. She had never considered the Season before due to her family's humble circumstances. But everything had changed now that her father was the Viscount of Wythburn. It was as if fate had shifted the pieces on the chessboard, granting her a move she hadn't anticipated.

But her heart grew heavy. Could she truly participate in the Season, knowing her cousin was still mourning her parents deeply?

"If you don't mind, may I think on the Season?" she asked. "I am not quite sure if I am ready for such a thing."

Lady Dallington's eyes held understanding. "Of course. Take all the time you need," she said.

Elodie's voice came from the doorway. "Oh, Mattie!" she exclaimed. "You simply must come to Town with us. We would have such fun."

Winston chuckled as he rose to address his sister. "I see that your habit of eavesdropping on private conversations has not gone away."

"If you wanted it private, you should have closed the door," Elodie said with a shrug. "It was hardly my fault."

"Do you mean to insinuate that you consciously waiting at the door to overhear conversations is somehow our fault?" Winston asked.

Elodie didn't look the least bit ashamed by her actions. "Perhaps we both share some of the blame."

Winston shook his head. "If you will excuse me, I have some things I must see to." He bowed. "Ladies."

Mattie gripped the white handkerchief in her hand as she resisted the urge to thank Winston for his kindness. No good would come from that, she thought. Winston was already so full of himself. He didn't need any further encouragement to swell his ego.

Yet, despite everything, he had shown her a moment of

genuine kindness and perhaps it was only fair to acknowledge that.

In a steady voice, Mattie called out, "Lord Winston."

He paused near the door and turned to face her, his eyes questioning. "Yes, Miss Bawden?"

"Thank you for the use of your handkerchief. I shall wash it and return it to you at once," Mattie said.

For a moment, the corners of his mouth lifted ever so slightly, creating the faintest hint of a smile. It was such a fleeting expression that she almost thought she had imagined it. "You may keep the handkerchief," he replied. "My sisters keep me well stocked in them."

Mattie noted the warmth in his eyes, a stark contrast to the usual coldness she was accustomed to. "Oh, that is most kind of you," she responded.

Winston tipped his head in acknowledgement. "Take care, Miss Bawden," he said softly.

As she watched him depart from the room, Mattie sat back, her thoughts swirling. She found herself momentarily distracted from her grief, pondering the unexpected gentleness she had witnessed in Winston.

Elodie must have noticed Winston's unusual behavior as well. "That was unnerving," she remarked. "You two are usually at odds with one another."

"I know, but I wouldn't read too much into it," Mattie said.

"You are right," Elodie responded as she walked over to the chair that Winston had just vacated. "Regardless, I heard everything, so you don't need to explain anything."

Lady Dallington cleared her throat. "Is there something you wish to say to Mattie?"

Elodie nodded. "Yes, I am deeply sorry for your loss," she said, her tone filled with genuine sympathy. "How are you faring?"

"I suppose I am as well as can be expected," Mattie replied with a small, weary smile.

"Well, then, we must give you something else to think about to distract you," Elodie declared. "Just think of what fun we shall have this Season!"

Lady Dallington gave her daughter a pointed look. "Truly, Child. You need to learn to be more sympathetic."

"It is all right," Mattie assured her. "I doubt that Elodie was acquainted with my aunt or uncle."

With a shake of her head, Elodie replied, "I knew of your uncle, Lord Wythburn, but I had never met him or any of his wives."

"Well, he had only two wives," Mattie said, knowing her friend was just trying to lighten the conversation, for which she was most grateful. "The first one died within their first few years of marriage and then he married my Aunt Edith."

Elodie sat down and reached for a biscuit on the tray. "If I ever choose to marry, I think I would like to haunt my husband, assuming I died, and he remarried."

Mattie giggled. "Why would you haunt your husband?"

"For fun," Elodie replied with a mischievous glint in her eyes. "After all, surely I will be bored in the afterlife. What else would I be doing but haunting someone?"

Lady Dallington did not look amused. "I am pleased that you have resigned yourself to the fact that you will marry… at least someday."

Elodie waved her hand dismissively in front of her. "If I do marry—and do not hold me to that—it will be for love, just as Delphine and Bennett have."

"May I ask what changed your mind?" Lady Dallington asked, her tone softening with curiosity.

Elodie paused, a thoughtful look on her expression. "Seeing Delphine and Bennett together, witnessing their genuine affection and partnership, made me realize that love is not a weakness. It can bring two vastly different people together and bind them together in unison."

Lady Dallington smiled in approval. "Love is indeed a powerful incentive. I am glad that you recognize its importance."

"Well, I suppose if I'm going to be bound to someone for life, it might as well be someone I love," Elodie declared. "But don't expect me to get married anytime soon. I did, however, compile a list of attributes that I want in a husband."

Lady Dallington sighed. "Dear heavens," she muttered.

Mattie couldn't help but ask, "What is on that list?"

Elodie retrieved the paper from the folds of her gown and held it up. "The usual attributes, I suppose. I want him to be tall, dark and handsome."

"That sounds rather vague," Mattie said.

Elodie continued to read the paper. "I will not tolerate someone with bad breath, overindulging in alcohol or nonstop chattering."

"But you tend to chatter constantly," Mattie pointed out.

"Yes, but it is a fine quality to have in a woman, not a man," Elodie countered. "Everyone knows that."

Mattie puckered her brow, knowing the list was rather straightforward and her friend was anything but predictable. "Any other unusual traits that we need to be aware of?"

"Oh, yes," Elodie replied. "I cannot tolerate a slow blinker or someone that eats their peas one at a time. Both are non-negotiable."

Lady Dallington gave her daughter a long, disbelieving stare. "Where did I go wrong with you, Child?"

Unfazed, Elodie responded, "Marriage is not something that I am going to happen upon. It will only happen after serious contemplation."

"Love is not something you can plan," Lady Dallington argued. "It just happens."

"Nothing happens by chance," Elodie asserted.

Lady Dallington frowned. "We shall continue this conversation later. Right now, we need to console Mattie. Her life has changed considerably."

Mattie glanced between the two women, a small smile forming. "You do not need to worry about me. This conversation has been most riveting and has helped me forget my troubles—if only for a moment."

"You are most kind, but Elodie should put that list away and focus on ensuring our guest feels welcome," Lady Dallington insisted.

Elodie returned the paper to the folds of her gown. "Done," she said, her eyes drifting over to the window. "I think a game of pall-mall might lift Mattie's spirits."

"As much as I would love that, shouldn't I be in mourning?" Mattie asked.

Lady Dallington's eyes held compassion. "It might be just the distraction you need," she replied. "Besides, we would never tell anyone."

Mattie carefully considered Lady Dallington's words. They were in the countryside, so the mourning requirements were far less stringent. And it would be nice to be outside.

Coming to a decision, Mattie said, "I think I would like to play a game of pall-mall."

Elodie clapped her hands together. "Wonderful!" she exclaimed. "We will have to ask Winston to join us to even out our numbers."

Mattie weighed her words carefully. "Do we have to invite Lord Winston?" she asked.

"Is there a problem with Winston?" Elodie asked, feigning innocence.

"It is just that… playing pall-mall with Lord Winston hasn't always been the most enjoyable experience," she admitted. "He has a tendency to cheat."

Elodie raised an eyebrow, a knowing smile playing on her

lips. "You two both have a very different recollection of what happened during that particular game."

Mattie pointed at her forehead. "I have a memory like a hawk."

"A hawk?" Lady Dallington asked. "I haven't heard that expression before."

"Melody came up with that expression and I do think it fits," Mattie shared as she rose. "Thank you for the reprieve, but I do think it is time that I return home and start on my tasks at hand."

Rising, Elodie asked, "Is there anything that I can help you with?"

"You are kind, but I have to do these things on my own," Mattie replied. "At times like this, I especially miss my mother."

Elodie placed a hand on Mattie's sleeve. "No matter what happens, you will always have us."

"Unless I become a slow blinker," Mattie quipped.

"Well, that goes without saying," Elodie countered with a grin. "Come, I will walk with you to the door."

As they made their way towards the main door, Mattie felt grateful for her visit to Brockhall Manor. Lady Dallington and Elodie had briefly made her forget her troubles. It still baffled her that they were related to the ornery Lord Winston. Although he had surprised her on this visit. He had shown a depth of compassion that she didn't think was possible for him.

Standing at the door, Elodie gave her a final, reassuring embrace. "Remember, Mattie, we are always here for you."

Mattie felt a small but genuine smile form on her lips. "Thank you, Elodie. I will remember." With that, she stepped out into the fresh air, ready to face the tasks awaiting her at home.

Chapter Three

A white mist hung low to the ground as Winston charged his horse forward, savoring the solitude of the early morning. The stillness wrapped around him like a comforting shroud, and he relished the reprieve from his burdensome life. At this hour, he was alone, free from the chatter and expectations of others, which was a rare and precious gift.

Yet, a familiar feeling of guilt gnawed at him. Despite having everything he had ever wanted, he felt weighed down by expectations and fears. What if he never made something of himself? What if he forever lived in the shadow of his father, or worse, his brother?

His father was a marquess and Bennett was the golden child, the heir. Winston was merely the spare, the one who had to leave home and find a profession that suited him. And he had done just that. He had become a barrister and found great satisfaction in his work—until that one blasted case.

The memory of Johnny haunted him. The boy, no older than ten, had stood in front of the platform where his mother had been hanged. Her crime had been thievery, but she hadn't deserved to die. And yet, Winston's actions had led to her execution. He could still see Johnny's tear-streaked face, the raw pain in his eyes.

Winston slowed his horse to a trot, the mist swirling around them. He could no longer escape the reality of his choices or the consequences that followed.

He had thought becoming a barrister would bring him purpose and fulfillment, but that case had shattered his illusions. Now, he was left grappling with guilt and a profound sense of inadequacy. How could he ever hope to live up to his own high expectations when his conscience was so heavily burdened?

As he led his horse into the woodlands, Winston wanted to rediscover the happiness that he once felt, though he doubted it was truly possible. The notion that he even deserved happiness was questionable. He had taken Johnny's mother from him, leaving him alone. How could he ever reconcile that fact?

Ahead, the steady murmur of the stream reached his ears before he saw it. The sound was comforting, and this was his sanctuary, his place for a moment of peace. But as he turned the corner, he realized he wasn't alone.

Miss Bawden.

What in the blazes was she doing here? This was his place of solitude, not hers. Besides, it was his family's land, and she was trespassing.

Winston reined in his horse, the sound of hooves muffled by the soft ground. He dismounted quietly, not wanting to startle her, but his presence had already been noticed.

Miss Bawden looked up from her seat on a large rock, surprise flickering in her eyes. "Lord Winston," she acknowledged, her tone more civil than he was expecting. "I didn't expect to see anyone here, at least not at this early morning hour."

"This is my father's land," he said, struggling to keep his voice even. He didn't want Miss Bawden here anymore than he wanted to contend with a wild boar. Both were ornery and left a stink in the air.

She stood, brushing off her skirts. "I apologize, but I needed a place to think. Edwina showed me this place once."

Winston sighed at the mention of his cousin. "Yes, well, Edwina is no longer residing here, and you are trespassing."

Miss Bawden seemed unconcerned by his remarks nor was she making any attempt to leave. "It is such a peaceful spot. It almost feels… untouched."

For a moment, they stood in silence, the stream's gentle babble being the only sound between them. Winston felt a pang of empathy. He had come here to escape his own demons, and it seemed Miss Bawden was running from her own grief as well.

"Is everything all right?" he asked, the question surprising even himself. Why had he asked such a thing? He wanted her to leave, not stay and participate in idle chit-chat.

Miss Bawden hesitated, then shook her head. "No, not really. However, it is not something you need to concern yourself with."

"Perhaps I can help," he offered, surprising himself again. "Sometimes talking to someone, especially someone who is not involved, can make things clearer."

She regarded him cautiously, as if weighing his sincerity. Finally, she revealed, "It is my cousin, Franny. She lost both of her parents, and I don't know how to help her."

Winston nodded, understanding more than she knew. "When my uncle died, I took it rather hard. He had been a man that I had always looked up to, and secretly aspired to be like," he shared. "My only advice is that sometimes just being there is enough. Offering support, even when you feel helpless, can mean the world to someone in pain."

Miss Bawden's eyes softened. "Thank you, my lord. I just wish I could do more than be there."

He cocked his head, considering her words. "When your

mother died, what helped you the most to navigate through the grief?"

"Time," Miss Bawden replied. "I still miss my mother every day, but it gets a little easier with time. Well, time and friends that baked us food. Loads of food. We couldn't even eat everything that had been provided to us."

"Then perhaps you should bake your cousin something," Winston suggested.

Miss Bawden made a face. "I like my cousin. I wouldn't wish to make her sadder by eating my cooking."

Winston chuckled. "I take it that Mrs. Watson still doesn't let you cook."

"No, she insists I stay far, far away when she prepares our meals," Miss Bawden said. "However, she has recently let me start boiling the water again."

"That seems like an easy enough task."

Miss Bawden grinned. "You would think, but one time I was reading, and the water spilled over, extinguishing the flame."

"I see how that could be a problem."

"So now I am not allowed to read while watching the water boil," Miss Bawden said. "Have you ever watched water boil?"

Winston shook his head. "I have not."

"It is not the least bit enjoyable," Miss Bawden said.

Winston found himself smiling. "It seems cooking is not your forte. Perhaps you can find another way to support your cousin."

Her grin faded slightly, replaced by a thoughtful expression. "I just want to help her feel less alone."

Hearing the sadness in Miss Bawden's voice made him wonder if she was speaking only about her cousin. "Do you feel alone?" he prodded.

Miss Bawden ducked her head. "I do, at times," she

admitted. "My father is busy being the vicar, my sister is at boarding school, and I am a spinster."

"You are hardly a spinster."

"I am one and twenty years old," Miss Bawden replied. "And I haven't even had a Season yet."

Winston led his horse to the stream to drink. "I thought my mother was hosting you for the upcoming Season."

Miss Bawden winced. "I haven't yet found the courage to ask my father about that," she admitted. "I do not think he will be pleased."

"Whyever not?"

"My father needs me at home," Miss Bawden said.

Winston lifted his brow. "I daresay that was before he became a viscount and heir to an earldom. He will now have a team of people around him, ensuring the estate is thriving, as well as a household staff."

Miss Bawden lowered her gaze. "I suppose you are right, but I still feel responsible. I have always managed the house on my own. It is hard to let go of that."

"Change is never easy, but your father will understand," Winston said. "Do you not think he would want you to find your own path and happiness?"

She brought her gaze up. "You are right. He would," she replied. "Thank you. Your words mean more than you know."

Winston nodded. "Be careful, Miss Bawden," he urged. "If we continue on as we have been, we might even become friends one day."

"That would take a miracle," Miss Bawden responded, softening her words with a smile. "Besides, it will just take one game of pall-mall before we are at odds once more."

Reaching up, Winston rubbed the shoulder which had been hit by a mallet Miss Bawden had once thrown at him during an intense game of pall-mall. "You make a valid point," he said.

They fell into another comfortable silence, the shared moment of vulnerability bridging the gap between them.

Botheration.

He shook his head, trying to clear his thoughts. There would be no good that came out of them becoming friends since they had been at odds with one another for so long. It was familiar. Comfortable. And he didn't want to let Miss Bawden in, knowing she had a propensity for making his life miserable.

Yet, the unexpected connection they had just shared gnawed at him. He had always found solace in their bickering, a predictable routine that required no emotional investment. But now, seeing her vulnerable, struggling with her own burdens, complicated things. He didn't need this kind of complexity in his life.

"Miss Bawden," he began, his voice harsher than he intended, "I think it is best if we—"

"Yes, my lord?" she interrupted, looking at him with a curious, almost hopeful expression.

Winston's resolve wavered. He could see the uncertainty in her eyes, the fragility she rarely let show. He clenched his jaw, forcing himself to continue. "It is best if we maintain our… usual distance. We each have our roles to play, and it is much simpler that way."

She blinked, the hope in her eyes dimming. "Of course," she replied. "I do think that would be easier… for both of us."

He nodded curtly, feeling a twinge of guilt. It was better this way, he told himself. Better to stick to what they knew, to avoid entanglements that could lead to further complications, such as another kiss.

His back grew rigid at that thought. No, he wouldn't kiss Miss Bawden ever again. It had just been a moment of weakness, a lapse in judgment. He had always wondered what it would be like to kiss Miss Bawden, imagining it as a way to dispel the strange tension between them.

He had half-hoped that it would be dull, but instead, it had sparked a desire for more. He would not—could not—give in to that temptation once more.

"Take care, Miss Bawden," he said, turning to leave.

"And you, my lord," she replied.

He stopped himself and turned back around. "You are welcome to stay here as long as you would like," he said. "It is a place for peace, after all."

Miss Bawden smiled faintly. "Thank you. That is very kind of you."

As he mounted his horse and rode away, Winston couldn't help but feel that he had just made a mistake. But why would he want to be friends with Miss Bawden? No good would come from that. Of that, he was sure. Yet, a nagging doubt gnawed at him as he rode through the misty woodlands. Perhaps he had been too hasty.

Mattie took a shortcut through the woodlands. As she approached her family's cottage, the faint smell of freshly baked bread wafted through the air, a comforting scent of home. This was her sanctuary, the place she had always known, and soon she would be leaving it so her father could assume his new title.

She understood the reasoning behind the move—duty, family legacy, the responsibilities that came with their newfound status. But understanding didn't equate to liking it. She would be leaving behind her friends, including the Lockwood family, who had always shown her genuine kindness. Well, except for Lord Winston. He had always managed to aggravate her to no end with his insufferable arrogance.

Yet, despite his cocky exterior, Mattie had caught glimpses of the man behind the mask he wore. There were moments when his guard slipped, revealing a depth and vulnerability that intrigued her. She often wondered what drove him to maintain such a façade. What was he hiding from? What burdens did he carry that necessitated such a mask?

As she pondered these questions, she knew one thing for certain: despite the changes ahead, she would miss the familiarity of her life here, and perhaps even the sparring matches with Lord Winston.

The door of the cottage flew open and her father stepped out onto the covered porch, frustration etched in his face. "Where have you been, young lady?" he demanded.

Young lady?

Her father only used that term when he was truly upset with her.

Mattie came to a stop in front of him. "I was just taking a walk through the woodlands," she said. "Is everything all right?"

Tossing up his hands in exasperation, her father replied, "No, everything is not all right. Franny is crying… again."

"That is not unexpected," Mattie said gently, "considering she just lost her parents."

"I know, but she was crying into her bread," her father replied, his shoulders slumping slightly. "I don't know what to do to help her. She is inconsolable."

Mattie placed a comforting hand on his sleeve, offering a small, reassuring smile. "Shall I join you for breakfast? Perhaps together we can manage to coax a smile out of Franny."

Her father's eyes were sad. "I spent many years as a vicar consoling others, drawing upon my own experience after losing your mother. But I was not prepared for the loss of my brother," he admitted, his voice breaking slightly.

"We will get through this," Mattie encouraged. "One step at a time. Let us start with breakfast and see if we can bring a little bit of comfort to Franny."

Her father nodded, taking a deep breath to steady himself. "Thank you, Mattie. I do not know how I would manage if you weren't here."

"You would do just fine," she assured him.

"No, you are special, Child," her father said. "Mother would be very proud of the young woman that you have become. I know that I am."

Mattie was touched by her father's words and blinked back the tears that were threatening to form. "Thank you, Father," she responded. "Come. Let us go to the kitchen and eat our breakfast."

Together, they walked into the cottage and headed towards the kitchen in the rear. Mattie's heart sank when she saw Franny hunched over in a chair, tears streaming down her face.

In a soft voice, Mattie said, "Good morning, Franny."

Franny gave her the briefest of glances before her gaze dropped back to the table.

Mattie wasn't about to give up. Not yet. She sat down next to Franny and asked, "Have you eaten breakfast?"

Franny shook her head silently.

Mrs. Watson stepped closer and handed Mattie a plate of food. Mattie placed it gently in front of her cousin. "You need to eat and keep your strength up," she encouraged.

In a barely audible voice, Franny asked, "What is the point? My parents are dead, and they are never coming back."

Mattie's heart lurched at the raw pain in her cousin's voice. "You may think that your life is over, but it is not. You will have to discover a new normal."

Franny sobbed into a white handkerchief. "I am all alone now," she declared.

"You are not alone. You have us," Mattie assured her. The fact that Franny was speaking proved that they were making some progress. Healing this wound would take some time.

"I want to go home," Franny said, her voice breaking.

Her father stepped closer, his voice gentle yet firm. "In due time. Once a new vicar is brought on, we can depart for Darlington Abbey. Until then, let us grieve together without household staff being underfoot."

Franny lifted her tear-stained cheeks, her expression one of pure anguish. "What is the point?" she asked. "I will never stop grieving."

"Give it time…" her father began.

Jumping up from her seat, Franny shouted, "No! My parents left me behind. I was supposed to go on that trip to India, but they felt it was best if I stayed behind. I should have died right alongside them."

Mattie went to place a hand on her sleeve, but Franny yanked back her arm. "I want to go home! I don't want to live in this dilapidated cottage!" she shouted. "I want my bed, my friends and my old life back."

With a hand covering her mouth, Franny ran from the kitchen. A moment later, the sound of a door slamming echoed through the cottage.

Her father's eyes remained fixed on the empty doorway. "Poor Franny. She is taking this rather hard."

Mattie accepted a plate of food from Mrs. Watson. "We must give her the space she needs."

"Do you truly believe that will make a difference?" her father asked, his voice tinged with doubt.

She sighed. "It is not just space she needs. She needs time, understanding and the reassurance that she's not alone. We can't replace what she has lost, but we can help her find her way back to some semblance of normalcy."

Her father nodded slowly. "You are right," he said. "Perhaps you would like to give my next sermon."

"Do you still intend to work as a vicar?"

"Yes, but only until they find my replacement," her father replied. "I must admit that I am getting a little tired of people calling me 'my lord,' and it has only been a day since I have heard the news."

Mattie smiled. "You have a lifetime to get used to that."

"Do not remind me," her father said, sitting down next to her. "How are you faring with everything?"

Her smile dimmed. "I am doing the best that I can," she said. "I called upon Lady Dallington yesterday and that truly lifted my spirits."

"I think very highly of Lady Dallington. She was the first to offer condolences when your mother passed away," her father revealed, his eyes growing reflective. "They were in Town, visiting the late Lord Dallington, and she even ordered the cook to bring us food for weeks."

Mattie picked up her fork and knife and took a bite of her breakfast, the familiar taste bringing a small measure of comfort. "Lady Dallington has offered to host me for the Season," she shared.

Her father stared back at her. "This upcoming Season?"

"Yes, the upcoming Season."

He frowned deeply. "Absolutely not! We are in mourning," he declared. "It would be unacceptable for you to participate in such frivolous social events."

Mattie pushed the food around her plate with her fork. "I am one and twenty years old and I have never had a Season."

"That is because we couldn't afford one," her father said.

"I know, but our circumstances are different," Mattie pressed. "We haven't discussed it yet but I am hoping I am in possession of a dowry now."

Her father leaned forward in his seat. "Yes, you have a dowry of fifteen thousand pounds, as does your sister, and Franny."

Mattie's heart took flight at that news. "Fifteen thousand pounds?" she repeated. "That is a fortune."

"It is, but I am not ready for you to attend a Season," her

father insisted. "You are needed at home to care for Franny and your sister."

"It is only for a few months, Father, and…"

Her father started rubbing his temples, a sure sign that he was growing upset. "I know, but I just worry about you. This transition has been difficult enough without the added pressure of societal expectations."

"I will be careful," she promised. "And I will return home whenever you need me. But please, do not discount Lady Dallington's offer so quickly."

He studied her face for a long moment before bobbing his head. "Very well. I will consider it, but that doesn't mean I will agree to it. It just means I will give it additional thought."

"Thank you, Father," Mattie said.

"Do not thank me yet," her father responded as he rose from his seat. "If you will excuse me, I have a meeting with Mr. Johnson soon about the state of my father's estate."

After her father departed from the kitchen, Mrs. Watson claimed the seat he had just vacated.

"I do hope your father will come around," Mrs. Watson said. "You deserve to have a Season, especially after all the sacrifices that you have made for this family."

Mattie shrugged one shoulder, dismissing her praise. "I have done only what is expected of me."

"More, if you ask me," Mrs. Watson declared, giving her a pointed look. "Aside from your terrible cooking abilities, you have kept this house running."

"I daresay you are giving me far too much credit since you do all the work," Mattie said. "Besides, I am not sure if the dressmaker will have time to create elaborate gowns for the Season, much less all the other accessories I will require. Perhaps it is just a wishful fantasy on my part."

Mrs. Watson grew thoughtful. "What of your mother's gowns?" she asked. "You have yet to look through them in all these years."

"I am sure that they are terribly outdated."

"No doubt, but that doesn't mean you can't use the fabric to create a reticule or use them to line a bonnet," the housekeeper suggested.

Mattie smiled at that thought. "I shall look at the gowns later and see if any of the fabric is salvageable."

Mrs. Watson's eyes sparkled with enthusiasm. "You should do more than just look. Imagine what you can create with those fabrics." She rose. "Come, let us fetch that trunk from the attic."

Mattie's excitement grew as she followed Mrs. Watson up the narrow stairs to the attic. It had been far too long since she had gone through her mother's things.

As they reached the attic, Mattie looked around the dust-covered treasures from the past. Mrs. Watson pointed to a large trunk in the corner, and together they lifted the lid. Inside were her mother's gowns, each one a piece of history and a connection to the woman she dearly missed.

Carefully, Mattie unfolded the first gown, its fabric delicate yet vibrant despite the years. "These are beautiful," she murmured, running her fingers over the intricate embroidery. "I had forgotten how lovely they were."

Determined, Mattie began sorting through the gowns, envisioning what she could create with these fabrics. But the first step, and the most important, was convincing her father to allow her to have a Season.

This was her chance to step out of the shadows of duty and into the light of possibility. And she would not let it slip away.

Chapter Four

Winston exited the stables and walked towards Brockhall Manor. He was hungry but was in no mood to engage in conversation. He just wanted to eat in peace in the dining room and retreat to his bedchamber.

Under normal circumstances, he would already be back in London, attending to his affairs. However, the situation with his Aunt Sarah and her son had demanded his presence here, especially since Bennett was away in Scotland.

How he hated waiting around, twiddling his thumbs and hoping all would be well. Weeks had passed with no sign of Isaac. Winston hoped, perhaps naively, that Isaac had decided to abandon his pursuit of Sarah and their child. But deep down, he knew better. Isaac was likely lying low, waiting for the perfect moment to strike when they were least prepared.

The measures Winston had taken to protect his aunt were extensive. He had hired a Bow Street Runner to oversee her safety and relocated her to a secret location. Even he wasn't privy to her exact whereabouts, thanks to Jasper's discretion. This arrangement ensured that if Isaac did come sniffing around the manor, they could genuinely claim ignorance of her location.

Winston stepped into the manor and made his way towards the dining room. Once he arrived, he let out a sigh of relief. The room was empty, just as he had hoped it would be.

He took a seat, and a footman promptly placed a plate of food in front of him. As he ate, he enjoyed the silence.

But his solitude did not last long.

Elodie breezed into the room, her voice far too cheery for the early hour. "Good morning, Brother."

Winston looked up, trying to mask his irritation. "What are you doing awake at this hour?" he asked.

Coming to sit across from him, Elodie replied, "I couldn't sleep any longer. I thought I would seize the day."

Winston took a bite of his food, hoping Elodie would take the hint and refrain from idle chit-chat.

His hope was short-lived.

Elodie leaned to the side as a footman placed a cup of chocolate in front of her. She reached for it and asked, "How are you this fine morning?"

"I am well," he replied briskly.

"Did you go for a ride this morning?" she inquired, undeterred.

"Yes," he said, keeping his responses short.

Elodie took a sip of her drink. "That is a shame. I was hoping you would want to go riding after breakfast."

Winston placed his fork and knife onto his now-empty plate, indicating he was finished. "I have work that I need to see to," he stated. He was already tired of this conversation, and he had a feeling that it had only just begun.

"Are you working on one of your cases?" Elodie asked in a hushed voice.

"Yes," he replied curtly, his patience wearing thin.

"Can you tell me what the case is about?" she asked, her eyes wide with expectation.

Winston shook his head. "I'm afraid I cannot."

Elodie's face fell slightly at his response. "You are no fun," she said lightly.

Shoving back his chair, Winston stood up. "And with that, I shall leave you to your breakfast," he said, eager to escape.

"Will you not stay and keep me company?" Elodie asked.

Winston paused, feeling a pang of guilt. He had responsibilities, and they weighed heavily on him. However, nothing was pressing at the moment, and he could spend some time with his sister.

Coming to a decision, he returned to his seat. "I shall stay for a few more moments," he said.

Elodie's face lit up. "Wonderful," she declared. "What shall we discuss? Religion? Politics? The state of our economy?"

"What do you know of those things?" he asked.

"More than I should," Elodie replied with a smile.

Winston should have known his sister would want to discuss topics that were more serious in nature, but he had no wish to be chided by his mother for doing so. "Perhaps we should discuss something that won't get either of us in trouble with Mother."

"It is vexing that women aren't allowed to speak on things of true importance," Elodie said, her shoulders slumping slightly.

"That is not true."

Elodie shot him a frustrated look. "Do you truly care about ribbons and whatnot?"

"I could be made to care," he attempted.

"Very well," Elodie said with a wave of her hand. "What are your thoughts on the latest fashions?"

Winston kept his face expressionless, knowing that Elodie was calling his bluff. "I like them," he responded vaguely.

"Can you be more specific?"

With a defeated sigh, he replied, "No, I can't. I must admit that I care little for fashion."

Elodie's smile grew. "I knew it," she replied. "Yet that is what young women must discuss. That, or the weather."

Melody entered the room and said, "Do not forget that we can speak on embroidery and all the different kinds of stitches that we use."

"I don't know how you can jest about this," Elodie remarked. "I would rather speak about the weather than embroidery."

Taking a seat next to her sister, Melody responded, "You must not be doing it right, then."

"I am pretty sure there is only one way to talk about embroidery, and it is boring," Elodie joked.

Turning her attention towards Winston, Melody gave him a pointed look. "We could always discuss Aunt Sarah, and when, and if, we will ever meet her."

Winston shifted uncomfortably in his seat. "You know about Aunt Sarah?"

Elodie spoke up. "We have known for some time now, but what we don't know is why no one will talk about it with us."

"It is for your own safety," Winston said.

"How so?" Elodie inquired.

Winston glanced at the footmen in the room and ordered, "Leave us." If he was going to have this conversation, he wanted to do so in private.

After the footmen departed from the room, closing the door behind them, he turned his gaze back towards his sisters. "Aunt Sarah and her son are somewhere safe. That is all you need to know."

"Why are they not residing with us?" Melody asked. "Would it not be safer than hiding out somewhere else?"

"Aunt Sarah was terribly abused by her husband, Isaac, and she only had the courage to leave when he turned his heavy hand on their son," Winston informed them. "Since Father was estranged from his sister, we thought it would be best to keep up the charade until Isaac no longer posed a threat."

"How do you know that Aunt Sarah is safe?" Melody pressed.

Winston reached for his glass and took a sip. "A Bow Street Runner is ensuring her protection."

Elodie's eyes widened. "I have always wanted to meet a Bow Street Runner. Just think of the stories they could share."

"You are not going to meet this particular Bow Street Runner," Winston said. "He is remaining close to Aunt Sarah for the time being."

Melody grew solemn. "What can we do?"

"For now, just go on as normal, and with any hope, Isaac will not dare attempt to approach Father about his wife's whereabouts," Winston responded.

"Do you think that is likely?" Melody prodded.

Winston grimaced. He didn't want to worry his sisters, but he didn't want to lie to them either. He felt that they deserved the truth. "No, I do not," he admitted. "I think it is only a matter of time before Isaac shows up on our doorstep."

Elodie held up a knife in the air. "Then we shall fight to protect our own!" she exclaimed with dramatic flair.

"That is wholly unnecessary," Winston said with a shake of his head. "We will just inform Isaac that we do not know where Aunt Sarah is, and he will leave."

"And if he doesn't leave, then we fight!" Elodie declared.

Winston glanced skyward in exasperation. "Good gads, there will be no fighting, at least not with knives. We can solve this problem with our words."

Melody laughed. "Elodie is always looking for a fight."

Placing the knife down, Elodie said, "But Isaac stands to lose out on Aunt Sarah's inheritance if he doesn't find her. That is the motivation for him not to leave quietly."

Winston groaned. "How did you know about Aunt Sarah's inheritance?"

Not looking the least bit ashamed, Elodie replied, "You might want to close the doors when you speak to Father."

"Eavesdropping is a terrible habit to have," Winston chided, giving his sister a stern look. "But Elodie is correct. Aunt Sarah is to receive one hundred pounds per annum. In order for Isaac to collect the money, he must have his wife present. Uncle Richard stipulated that requirement in his will."

"Do you think Uncle Richard knew Isaac was hurting Aunt Sarah?" Melody asked.

"I don't know, considering Father had no idea," Winston said. "He hadn't spoken to his sister since she had eloped to Gretna Green with Isaac."

Elodie lifted her brow. "When do you think we can meet Aunt Sarah and our cousin?"

"Not until this is all over," Winston replied.

As he uttered his words, his mother stepped into the room and announced, "I am calling a family meeting."

Winston eyed his mother curiously. "Should we not have Father present during this family meeting?" he asked.

His mother waved her hand in front of her. "I will relay what we discuss with him. Do not worry," she replied. "But I am worried about Mattie. As you all know, I have offered to host her for the upcoming Season, and I think we must help prepare her for what is to come."

Winston rose. "And that is my cue to leave."

"Sit down," his mother ordered. "This is a family meeting, and no one leaves until I give you permission to do so."

"But I have nothing to contribute to this meeting," Winston attempted as he returned to his seat. He truly didn't wish to speak about Mattie. He had more important things to do with his time.

"Au contraire, Son," his mother said. "You are an integral part of this plan."

"What plan?" Winston asked with dread in his voice.

What did his mother have planned? And why did he need to be a part of it?

His mother smiled as she walked further into the room, making him feel even more unsettled. "I would like you to take Mattie on a carriage ride this afternoon."

Winston could not have been more surprised by what his mother was asking. "Why me?" he blurted out.

"Because you have known Mattie for years and you two are comfortable around each other," his mother responded.

"We hate each other," Winston muttered.

"Hate and admiration go hand in hand," his mother countered.

Winston huffed. "Not in our case."

His mother's smile grew. "It is one carriage ride. I am not asking you to marry the girl," she said. "And I will expect you to behave like a gentleman."

"Again, why me?" Winston asked, his voice much harsher than he intended. "Surely you can convince another gentleman in the village to do so."

"Mattie is in mourning, but it is perfectly acceptable for a friend of the family to console her by taking her on a carriage ride," his mother replied.

Rising, Winston declared, "We are not friends, and I am a grown man. I will decide who I take on a carriage ride."

His mother approached him and patted his cheek. "Of course, my dear. But it is just one carriage ride, and I ask so little of you," she said.

"Mother…" he sighed, "I am a trained barrister. Your tricks are not going to work on me."

"You are right," his mother said as she turned towards Elodie. "How would you like to drive a carriage?"

Winston frowned. "Surely you jest. Father would be furious if Elodie drove one of the carriages."

"Would he?" his mother asked, feigning innocence.

He knew precisely what his mother was doing and it vexed

him to no end. But he wasn't about to let Elodie drive a carriage. What would people think if they saw her? He did not wish to open their family up to gossip. "Fine," he mumbled. "I will do it."

His mother met his gaze. "What was that, Dear?"

With a clenched jaw, he said, "You win. I will take Miss Bawden on a carriage ride, assuming she even wants to go on one."

She clapped her hands together. "Wonderful. I will see to the carriage being brought around front," she said before departing from the room.

Elodie giggled. "That was entertaining to watch."

Melody bobbed her head in agreement. "Mother would have made an excellent barrister," she said.

Winston dropped down onto his seat. The last thing he wanted to do was spend time with Miss Bawden but he had been outplayed by his own mother.

Mattie stood in the drawing room of her cottage, her eyes fixed on her mother's dresses spread out before her. The sight filled her with a sense of overwhelming frustration. Each dress, though once elegant, now seemed hopelessly outdated. A small part of her had hoped she could alter one of her mother's gowns for the Season, but that would be an impossible feat. It would take far more effort than she had anticipated to transform even one of these gowns into something suitable for high Society.

A loud knock echoed through the cottage, breaking her concentration. Mattie barely acknowledged it, assuming Mrs. Watson would see to it. After all, no one ever visited her, and it was more likely that someone was seeking out her father.

With a sigh, she crouched down and picked up a pink

gown, examining it closely. The fabric was still beautiful, and she thought about repurposing the material to line the inside of her bonnets or even her reticule.

The knock came again, this time more insistent. Mattie called out, "Mrs. Watson!" but received no reply. Annoyed, she placed the pink gown back among the others on the floor. This was absurd. She was capable of answering the door herself, even if Mrs. Watson believed it was beneath her station.

Determined, Mattie walked briskly to the door, prepared to face whoever was on the other side.

As she opened the door, Mattie was greeted by the sight of Lord Winston, his face etched with annoyance.

"Good gads!" he exclaimed. "You are answering the door? Do you have no shame, Woman?"

Mattie mustered up a polite smile. "Did you come all this way to insult me, my lord? If so, what a delightful treat."

"No, that was not my intention," he said, his tone softening slightly.

"Then what was your intention?" she asked, halfway considering slamming the door in his face.

Lord Winston peered over her shoulder into the house. "Shouldn't Mrs. Watson be answering the door?"

"I am perfectly capable of opening a door."

"But you are the daughter of a viscount now," he pointed out, his brow furrowing.

Mattie sighed, a touch of weariness in her voice. "Thank you for reminding me," she said. "Will that be all?" She began to close the door.

Lord Winston quickly placed his hand against it, preventing it from closing. "I have a purpose for being here."

"Do you, now?" she asked, her interest waning.

Lowering his voice, he mumbled, "Would you like to…" His words trailed off, making him seem even more uncomfortable.

Mattie arched an eyebrow. "I'm sorry. Can you speak up? I couldn't hear you."

Looking rather pained, Lord Winston cleared his throat. "Would you care to go on a carriage ride with me?" he asked.

No.

Absolutely not!

That is what she wanted to say, but instead she found herself asking, "Why?"

He dragged his fingers through his dark hair, clearly frustrated. "It is a nice day for a carriage ride. Is it not?" he asked, his eyes darting everywhere but at her.

Realization dawned on her, knowing there would only be one reason why Lord Winston would ask her to go on an outing such as this. "Your mother asked you to take me on a carriage ride. Did she not?" she asked.

Finally, he met her gaze. "She did," he replied.

Now Mattie was intrigued. She no more wanted to go on a carriage ride with Lord Winston than eat a shoe for dinner. But the fact that the prospect made him so uncomfortable made her want to go even more.

"A carriage ride sounds nice," Mattie found herself saying.

Lord Winston's expression fell, a look of mild panic flashing across his face. "Are you sure? There must be something else you want to do with your time."

Mattie smiled, and this time it was genuine. "There is no other place I would rather be." Just seeing Lord Winston's reaction made it that much more worth it.

"Wonderful," Lord Winston said through gritted teeth.

Opening the door wide, Mattie asked, "Would you care to come in while I collect a hat for our carriage ride?"

Lord Winston reluctantly stepped into the entry hall, stopping just in front of her. "You are enjoying this, aren't you?" he asked, his tone laced with exasperation.

Her smile widened. "Very much, my lord."

His eyes narrowed slightly, but he remained quiet.

As she moved towards the drawing room, Lord Winston followed closely behind. "What are all these dresses doing in here?" he asked, gesturing to the array of gowns.

"They were my mother's," she explained, turning to face him. "I had been half-hoping to create a new gown with the fabric for this Season."

Lord Winston's eyes roamed over the gowns, a look of incredulity on his face. "Surely, you jest. A woman of your station does not make her own clothes."

"You seem to forget that my father only just inherited his title," Mattie said. "I have been making my own clothes for years as the daughter of a vicar."

"But the life that you once knew is over," Lord Winston remarked, meeting her gaze. "Have you even spoken to a dressmaker?"

Mattie nodded. "Yes, she is making us mourning gowns, but it will be months before I can commission new gowns."

"Well, you can't wear these," he declared with a dismissive wave of his hand.

Placing a hand on her hip, she asked, "And why not… Lord Whineston?"

Lord Winston visibly tensed. "You have not called me that since we were children," he said, his voice strained. "I do not miss it."

"Well, you walked into my home and started dictating what I should be doing," Mattie said, her tone sharp.

"I am trying to help you," he insisted.

Mattie dropped her arm to her side. "I never asked for your help."

Lord Winston took a deep breath. "You are impossible to get along with."

"I could say the same about you, my lord," Mattie countered.

After she retrieved a blue bonnet from the corridor, she

returned to the drawing room and saw Lord Winston standing by the window, his hands clasped behind him.

For a moment, she allowed herself to admire him. It didn't help that he was handsome, with his broad shoulders, dark hair and strong jawline. And when he smiled—truly smiled—it had the power to make her heart race. But he must never know that.

"I have my hat," she announced, breaking the silence.

Turning to face her, his eyes studied her. "Good, I was worried," he said in a mocking tone.

Mattie pressed her lips together, debating if this carriage ride was a good idea. No doubt they would spend the entire time arguing. However, the thought of his discomfort brought a wicked sense of satisfaction.

She placed the bonnet on her head and tied the strings with precise movements. "Shall we?" she asked.

Lord Winston put his hand out, gesturing that she should go first.

As they approached the door, Mattie turned abruptly, almost colliding with his chest. His hands came up to steady her, his touch sending a shiver down her spine. "Careful, Miss Bawden," he murmured, his voice unexpectedly gentle.

Being this close to him reminded her of the night that they had kissed. The way he had looked at her had caused her heart to beat only for him. It was the most magical of nights, one that she would remember forever.

"Miss Bawden?" Lord Winston's gruff voice snapped her out of her reverie.

She blinked and took a step back out of his arms. "My apologies," she said, flustered. "I was woolgathering."

Lord Winston gave her a look of disapproval. "Well, I do not have all afternoon to wait on you."

"Out of curiosity, how much time have you allocated for this carriage ride?" she asked. "I wouldn't wish to deprive you out of a moment to spend time alone in your bedchamber."

"Why do you care what I do with my time?" he retorted.

Mattie shrugged. "I don't," she replied. "I am just attempting polite conversation."

"You will have to do better than that when you are mingling with people of the *ton*," Lord Winston stated.

"I assure you, I can be quite pleasant when the situation warrants it."

"And this situation does not warrant it?"

A dry laugh escaped her lips. "Of course not, my lord," she declared. "You are only taking me on a carriage ride because your mother asked you to."

Lord Winston clucked his tongue, his annoyance barely concealed. "I suggest that we call a truce, for now."

"A truce?"

"Yes, we attempt to be civil to one another on the carriage ride, and when it is over, we both go our separate ways."

Mattie considered him for a moment, her eyes searching his for sincerity. "And the truce is only for the carriage ride?"

"Yes," Lord Winston confirmed.

"Very well," she agreed. "A truce it is."

With that agreement, they stepped outside and approached the waiting carriage. Mattie couldn't help but feel a sense of anticipation at the prospect of spending time with Lord Winston under a fragile truce. It was both daunting and intriguing.

Lord Winston came to a stop next to the carriage and offered his hand. Mattie placed her hand into his and allowed him to assist her up. His grip was firm and steady, and she couldn't help but feel a spark at his touch.

Once she was situated, Lord Winston came around the other side and settled beside her, their legs brushing against one another in the confined space.

He reached for the reins and urged the team forward, his gaze straight ahead. "It is a fine day we are having, is it not?"

The weather. That was a safe topic. "Yes, it is quite lovely."

"Do you think it will rain?"

Mattie glanced up at the cloudless sky. "I do not think so, but it is England. It always rains, does it not?"

Lord Winston nodded. "It does."

Mattie wasn't quite sure which was worse: arguing with Lord Winston or discussing a mundane topic such as the weather. Both seemed equally tedious. She decided she would much rather have a frank conversation with Lord Winston and hoped that he felt the same.

"I have read about your cases in the newssheets," she said, turning slightly towards him. "You must be proud of your accomplishments."

Instantly, she knew she had struck the wrong chord.

Lord Winston's back grew rigid. "Proud?" he repeated, a bitter edge to his voice. "No, that is not the word I would use to describe it."

"Then what word would you use to describe it?" she pressed, genuinely curious.

Mattie noticed the hard stare. The clenched jaw. And realized that whatever she had said had upset Lord Winston. His usual confident demeanor was replaced with something darker, more troubled. The reins tightened in his grip, and his knuckles whitened.

"Obligated," he said, his voice low and tight. "I do what is necessary, not for pride or recognition, but because it must be done."

She paused as she carefully considered her next words. "That sounds… burdensome."

"It is," he admitted, his gaze still fixed on the road ahead. "But such is the weight of responsibility."

Mattie studied him for a moment, hearing what he wasn't saying. Lord Winston had wanted to be a barrister for as long as she had known him. So why did he seem so troubled? Most people in his position would be boastful. But not him. Why? It led her to only one conclusion. "I'm sorry," she said.

"For what?" he asked.

She placed a hand on his sleeve. "For whatever it is that has happened to you."

He turned his gaze towards her, his eyes hard and searching. "Why do you suppose something has happened to me?" he half-asked, half-demanded.

"Am I wrong?" she asked softly.

Lord Winston's chest heaved as if he were trying to control a storm of emotions. He dropped her gaze and returned to staring straight ahead, the reins slackening slightly in his grip.

The silence between them stretched, heavy with unspoken words. Mattie could see the internal battle waging within him, the vulnerability he so desperately tried to hide. She had never seen him like this, so raw and exposed. It made her heart ache for him in a way she hadn't anticipated.

Chapter Five

Winston did not want to have this conversation with anyone, much less Miss Bawden. He had regretted agreeing to this carriage ride the moment he had laid eyes on her. Despite their truce, he found this situation unbearable.

The very thought of her presuming to understand him, or what he had been through, filled him with irritation. How dare Miss Bawden assume she knew anything about him? She knew nothing of his struggles, yet she looked at him with compassion, or worse, with pity. No. He didn't want her pity.

He was a successful barrister, achieving something significant in his life. He wouldn't allow her to minimize his burdens or reduce him to someone deserving of sympathy. The anger bubbled inside of him at that thought.

What was worse, though, was that her hand was still on his sleeve, and he didn't want her to remove it. The touch was comforting, reminding him of a time when they weren't so at odds with one another. A time when they had shared more than just insulting words and icy glares.

But she had rejected him.

The memory of that night, when he had laid his heart bare only for her to turn away, was still fresh in his mind.

Winston couldn't let her back in, not for any reason. His heart became impenetrable, fortified against the likes of Miss Bawden. He couldn't afford to be vulnerable again, especially not with her.

Miss Bawden removed her hand from his sleeve and glanced up at the sky. "The sun is relentless today," she said. "Perhaps we should turn back around."

"As you wish," Winston said as he turned the team around.

In a soft voice, Miss Bawden asked, "Did I say something wrong, my lord?"

Yes.

Everything out of her mouth was maddening.

Taking a deep breath, he forced himself to remain civil, acknowledging the truce that they had between them. "Your concern is noted, but unnecessary. I assure you, I am quite capable of managing my affairs."

Her eyes widened slightly. "I wasn't implying otherwise," she replied. "I merely wished to offer a listening ear, should you need it."

Winston's jaw tightened. "I do not require your pity or your concern. My burdens are mine alone to bear."

"Pity?" she repeated, a touch of indignation in her voice. "You misunderstood me. I never meant to imply that you were incapable. I only wanted to…"

"To what?" he interrupted, his tone harsh. "To comfort me? To make me feel better? You cannot possibly understand what I have been through."

A tense silence followed his words.

After a long moment, Miss Bawden said, "Perhaps not, but that doesn't mean I don't care."

"Care?" he huffed. "Are you capable of caring?"

Miss Bawden stiffened. "I thought we had a truce between us," she muttered.

For a moment, Winston felt a pang of regret, but he

quickly buried it. He couldn't afford to let his guard down, not again. "I appreciate your concern, but it is unnecessary," he said, his voice holding the usual cold detachment that he used for Miss Bawden. "Quite frankly, I think it might be best if we rode in silence."

Miss Bawden nodded, her expression resigned. "As you wish, my lord."

As the team traveled down the road, Winston kept his gaze straight ahead, determined to keep his emotions in check. He had built walls around his heart for a reason, and he wouldn't allow anyone—especially not Miss Bawden—to breach them.

Miss Bawden's eyes remained fixed on the woodlands as she spoke, her voice tense. "I just saw a man in the woodlands, watching us."

Winston glanced at her skeptically. "I doubt that," he responded. "Perhaps you saw a tree and mistook it for a person."

She rolled her eyes. "I think I can tell the difference between a man and a tree."

"Can you?" he retorted, a hint of mockery in his voice.

"Why do I even bother trying to speak to you?" she asked.

He shrugged nonchalantly. "I agree that it is a pointless endeavor."

Miss Bawden shifted in her seat, turning to look back at the passing woodlands, her eyes narrowed in concentration.

"What are you doing?" he asked, curious despite himself.

"I told you, I saw a man watching us from the woodlands, but he is gone now," she informed him.

Winston knew he was going to regret asking this, but he asked it, nevertheless. "What did this 'man' look like?"

"He appeared tall, with a stout build, and had dark hair," she replied with certainty. "What if he was a poacher?"

"I doubt it, since our gamekeeper keeps a close eye on these woodlands. We would know if a poacher was on our lands," Winston said dismissively.

Miss Bawden turned her gaze forward again, her chin tilted defiantly. "I know what I saw," she stated firmly.

Winston felt the urge to get another jab in, even though he knew he should keep his mouth shut. "It wouldn't be the first time you were wrong," he said, a smirk playing on his lips. "After all, when we were younger, you and Elodie insisted that unicorns were real."

"That was when I was ten," she shot back.

"Yes, but you claimed you saw a unicorn running through the woodlands," Winston pointed out.

"True, but you had to go back eleven years to prove a point," she said. "Whereas you have been proven wrong on a daily basis."

Winston lifted his brow. "When, pray tell, have I been wrong?"

"Just moments ago, you claimed I couldn't tell the difference between a tree and a man," Miss Bawden said. "And I know what I saw."

"Yes, but I did not see a man," Winston argued, his tone clipped. "I only saw trees."

"Why can't you just take my word for it?" Miss Bawden asked.

Winston gave her a pointed look. "I deal in facts, and I rarely take someone's word for anything. That is how you lose cases."

Miss Bawden fingered the strings of her bonnet. "But I am not one of your cases or clients, for that matter."

"No, you are not," he agreed. But what she was, he couldn't quite define. They had known each other most of their lives, and at times, albeit briefly, they had been friends. Yet now, they seemed perpetually at odds.

In a curious voice, Miss Bawden asked, "How is it that even with a truce in place we still find things to argue about?"

Winston's expression softened slightly. "It is far more familiar to me."

Miss Bawden lowered her hands to her lap. "I suppose you are right," she said.

The carriage jolted slightly as it rolled over a bump in the path, causing them both to sway. Winston took a moment to steady the reins, his mind racing. He glanced at Miss Bawden and sighed.

"There was a time," Winston began, surprising himself with his candor, "when we weren't always at each other's throats."

A small smile played on Miss Bawden's lips. "I remember," she said. "Whenever you would visit Brockhall Manor, we used to play together in the gardens, before…"

"Before everything changed," Winston said, finishing her thoughts.

"Why did it change?" she asked.

Winston hesitated, grappling with his emotions. "I suppose… life happened. Expectations. Responsibilities. We grew up and became different people."

Miss Bawden nodded slowly. "I miss those days," she admitted. "When things were simpler."

"Do you?" Winston asked. "I always thought you relished our arguments."

She laughed. "Perhaps I do, in a way. They are a part of who we are now. But sometimes I wish…" Her voice trailed off.

"What do you wish?" Winston prompted, his heart beating a little faster.

"That we could find a way to be friends again," she said, her gaze meeting his. "Without the insults and arguments. Just… friends."

Winston felt a lump form in his throat. He had not expected this conversation, nor the emotions it stirred within him. "I would like that, too," he admitted. "Perhaps we can start anew."

Miss Bawden smiled, a genuine, warm smile that reached

her eyes. "I would like that, as well," she said. "But how do we accomplish such a feat?"

"That is an excellent question," Winston said. "I think we start by being nice to one another."

"That is easier said than done, my lord."

Winston chuckled. "Why don't we offer each other a sincere compliment?" he asked. "Surely we can do that."

"I suppose so, but you go first," Miss Bawden said.

"All right, I will try," Winston replied as he considered her for a moment. There were many things that he admired about her, from her intelligence to her fierce independence, but he didn't dare voice those thoughts. If he did, she might suspect that he harbored feelings for her—which he did not. He decided it would be best if his compliment was vague and unassuming.

"I like your red hair. It suits you," he said.

Miss Bawden's lips quirked into a half-smile. "That was a terrible compliment."

"I thought it was more than adequate," Winston defended, his tone light.

"You can do better than that, surely," she teased.

Winston knew she was right. "Fine. I admire your tenacity. You never back down from a challenge… ever. You would rather fall on your own sword than be proved wrong."

Miss Bawden's smile grew. "Thank you," she said. "And for my part, I admire your dedication to your work. You have become quite accomplished as a barrister, and it is evident that you care deeply about what you do."

Winston felt warmth spread through him at her words. "I appreciate your kind words," he said.

"This isn't so difficult, after all," she remarked.

"No, it isn't," Winston agreed. "Perhaps, if you are not opposed, we can keep this up."

Miss Bawden winced, but her eyes held a mischievous glint. "Yes, but it might be best if we forgo complimenting each other all the time. People might become suspicious if we are too familiar with one another."

"Agreed," Winston said. "We do not want people to start talking about us."

"Do you suppose we should start calling each other by our given names once more?" she asked, her voice tentative. "You used to call me Mattie when we were younger. It only changed after…" Her words came to an abrupt stop, her cheeks flushing slightly.

The kiss.

Everything changed after that moment.

Winston cleared his throat, trying to ignore the sudden rush of memories. "I have no objections to calling you Mattie, but you must call me Winston. And no more 'my lording' me. It is grating on my ears."

"I would like that, Winston," she said.

The way she said his name made his heart pound in his chest. He hoped that she couldn't hear it. The memory of their kiss lingered between them, an unspoken tension that neither wanted to address directly.

"Well, then, Mattie," Winston said, trying to keep his voice steady, "we are almost to your cottage."

"Yes, we are," she agreed. "Do you remember when we used to play in these woodlands as children?"

"I do, particularly the time when we played in poison oak, not knowing any better," Winston remarked.

Mattie giggled. "We were both so miserable after that. I had never experienced such a painful rash before."

"Yes, but we learned our lesson the first time," Winston said.

As they neared Mattie's cottage, Winston stole a glance at her. The strands of red hair that framed her face caught the sunlight, giving her an almost ethereal glow. He didn't dare tell her that red was his favorite color because of her, nor that he had never met a more beautiful girl than her. These were things he could never tell Mattie. The barriers he had built around his heart were too strong, too necessary, to let such truths escape.

The coach came to a gentle stop in front of the cottage. Winston jumped down and walked around to Mattie's side, offering his hand to help her dismount. She took it, his touch sending warmth through her. He steadied her as she stepped down, causing their faces to be close enough that she could see flecks of gold in his blue eyes.

"Thank you for the ride, Winston," Mattie said, her voice soft but sincere.

He smiled. "You are welcome, Mattie," he replied. "I am glad that we came to a new agreement."

"So am I," she admitted. "It was nice to talk without the usual arguments, even if only for a moment or two."

Winston nodded. "Perhaps we can do this again when we are in Town for the Season," he suggested.

"I would like that," she responded.

As she turned to walk to her cottage, Mattie felt a sudden, overwhelming urge to say something—anything—that might delay his departure. But the words stuck in her throat, held back by the memory of the pain he had caused her.

She reached the door and turned back to give him one last smile before entering the cottage.

As she stepped inside, she saw Mrs. Watson pacing in the drawing room. "Good, you are back," the housekeeper declared. "I don't know what to do with your cousin. She has refused to eat all day."

"Would you like me to speak to her?" Mattie suggested.

Mrs. Watson stopped pacing. "If you don't mind," she responded. "She is in her bedchamber."

Mattie approached the white-haired housekeeper. "We need to give Franny the space to grieve on her own."

"She is so young to lose her parents, but not as young as you when you lost your mother," Mrs. Watson said. "You both handled the grief so differently."

"People do not grieve the same, and that is all right," Mattie remarked. "Frankly, there is no right way to grieve."

Mrs. Watson offered her a weak smile. "Go speak to your cousin, and then I want to hear all about your carriage ride with Lord Winston."

"There is nothing to tell," Mattie said. "He asked me to go on a carriage ride and I went."

"But, why now?"

Mattie smiled her understanding. "Lady Dallington asked him to take me on a carriage ride and she can be quite persuasive when she wants to be," she explained. "We have come to a new understanding."

Mrs. Watson's brow shot up. "An understanding?"

She shook her head. "Not that type of understanding," she insisted. "We are going to attempt to be friends."

"Attempt?"

"Well, Lord Winston does manage to say the most infuriating things," Mattie said. "I can only hold my tongue so much."

Mrs. Watson laughed. "I have never quite understood why you two are at odds with one another. You used to be childhood friends."

"People grow up and change," Mattie remarked. "But I should go see to Franny."

"You can run, but you can't hide from this conversation," Mrs. Watson joked. "The cottage is not that big."

Mattie placed a hand on the housekeeper's sleeve. "I promise we will talk later," she assured her. "I am hoping to coax Franny out of her bedchamber and bring her to the kitchen for some food."

"I wish you luck."

Turning on her heel, Mattie headed up the stairs and down the corridor that led to Franny's bedchamber.

She came to a stop in front of the door and knocked.

No response.

The next time, she knocked and opened the door. "Franny?"

As she stepped into the room, she saw her cousin was lying in bed, staring up at the ceiling.

"How are you faring today?" Mattie asked, taking a seat beside her on the bed.

Franny turned her head, her eyes filled with sadness. "I'm not quite sure how to feel," she admitted, her voice trembling with emotion.

Mattie reached for her hand. "There is no right way to feel."

Tears welled up in Franny's eyes as she confessed, "I am angry, and sad, and lonely..." Her voice trailed off, a sense of despair creeping into her tone. "Will it ever get any easier?"

"I wish I could tell you that it does, but I won't lie to you," Mattie replied. "You have to go through the hard part before you can come out on the other side."

"I'm not sure if I can," Franny said weakly.

Mattie squeezed her hand reassuringly. "You are a Bawden. I know you are capable of doing things that are unbelievably hard."

A tear escaped Franny's eye and rolled down her cheek. "I am tired of crying, but I don't know what else to do."

"To begin with, you should eat, at least enough to keep your strength up," Mattie encouraged.

"I'm not hungry."

Mattie nodded. "I understand, but you can't lose too much weight or else you won't fit into the mourning gowns that we ordered," she said.

Franny turned her head to look back up at the ceiling.

"Sometimes, I wish that I would wake up from this terrible nightmare and my life would be the same as it was before. My parents would be alive and we would be back at our country estate."

The plea in Franny's voice made Mattie's eyes fill with tears, knowing she had felt the same way when her mother had died. The fear of living without her mother was crippling, but she had waded through the grief. Now she just had to help Franny do the same.

"I may have only lost my mother, but I understand what you are going through," Mattie said. "But lying in bed is not going to help. You need to learn to live without your parents."

Franny sighed deeply. "I am tired of looking at these four papered walls," she admitted, her voice weary.

Mattie released her hand and stood up. "Then let us go to the kitchen and get you something to eat."

As if on cue, Franny's stomach growled, and she gave her a shy smile. "Perhaps I am hungrier than I realized."

"If you are not opposed, we could go on a walk after you eat," Mattie suggested, trying to sound encouraging.

Franny sat up and swung her feet over the side of the bed. "Let's not get ahead of ourselves," she said, rising. "I am not sure if I am ready to go outside and encounter other people just yet."

Mattie laughed. "You won't have to worry about that. We live by the chapel, and only members of the parish come by to visit my father. It would be entirely different if we lived in the village."

"Your village is so quaint," Franny remarked as they walked.

"I would imagine it is rather small compared to the one by your country estate," Mattie replied.

Franny grew quiet, a shadow crossing her face. "It is your country estate now, is it not?"

Mattie looped her arm through her cousin's. "It will

always be your home, no matter what happens," she stated firmly.

"I am just an orphan now," Franny declared, her voice heavy with sorrow.

"You are my father's ward and a very loved member of this family," Mattie said as she guided her towards the door. "I do not want you to think otherwise."

They departed the bedchamber and headed towards the kitchen on the main level. Once they arrived, Mattie saw Mrs. Watson bustling around the kitchen, her apron dusted with flour.

The housekeeper stopped when her eyes landed on them. "Ladies," she greeted warmly. "Please sit and I will bring you both food."

Mattie dropped her arm and sat down at the table. She was pleased when Franny claimed the seat next to her.

Mrs. Watson brought over two plates with food on them and placed them down in front of the young women. "Would you two care for something to drink?" she asked. "I just made a pitcher of lemonade."

"Yes, please," Mattie responded, glancing at Franny, who nodded in agreement.

While Mrs. Watson went to retrieve the lemonade, Franny started eating the sandwich that was in front of her.

After a few bites, Franny said, "Thank you, Mattie."

"We are family," Mattie replied with a gentle smile. "We take care of each other, always."

Franny continued to eat as Mrs. Watson placed glasses of lemonade down on the table. "Drink up," she encouraged before she started tidying up the kitchen.

As Mattie reached for the glass, her father stepped into the room with a weary expression. His brow was furrowed, and his eyes carried the weight of a long day.

"Good, we are all here. I have an announcement to make," her father said. "I just received word that they found a vicar to replace me. He will arrive in a fortnight."

Mattie grew silent, a whirlwind of emotions swirling within her. Her whole life was here. She was tied to this parish and its people. The thought of leaving was unsettling, but she knew it was inevitable.

Her father interrupted her musings. "We will depart for Darlington Abbey once the vicar arrives and we spend a day or two discussing the parish."

"That is wonderful news, my lord." Mrs. Watson retrieved a plate and placed it onto the table for her father. "Go on, you must eat before your next meeting."

As her father began to eat, a thought suddenly occurred to Mattie. "What will Mrs. Watson's new position be when we move to Darlington Abbey?" she asked. "After all, I must assume there is already a housekeeper."

Her father cleared his throat. "About that…" He hesitated, exchanging a poignant look with the housekeeper. "We discussed it, and Mrs. Watson has decided to remain here to help the new vicar ease into his position. Furthermore, her son lives in the village and she wants to remain close to him."

Mattie blinked, taken aback by what her father had just revealed. She felt a pang of sadness and loss. Mrs. Watson had been more than a housekeeper. She was a friend. A confidante. The thought of leaving her behind was unbearable.

Her father must have sensed her concern because he gave her a discerning look. "This is Mrs. Watson's decision, and we must respect it."

Mrs. Watson came to stand by Mattie and placed a reassuring hand on her shoulder. "I know this may come as a bit of a shock for you, but you will have a whole household staff at Darlington Abbey to tend to your every whim."

Franny bobbed her head. "It is true," she replied. "You will love Mrs. Devan, our housekeeper. She has always been so nice to me."

Mattie lowered her gaze to the table. It didn't matter that there was a whole household staff at Darlington Abbey. She just wanted Mrs. Watson to remain with them. She hated change, especially this kind.

"Mattie..." Mrs. Watson started, "I will come to visit you and I will be able to see your new home."

Mattie looked up as she fought back the tears. "But it won't be the same. You have always been there for me."

"And I will always be here for you, even if we are apart," Mrs. Watson said, her eyes softening. "You will forever hold a special place in my heart."

Reaching up, Mattie placed her hand over Mrs. Watson's and gave her a grateful smile. She could never fully repay the housekeeper's kindness, but knew she was better because of her.

Her father pushed his plate away from him. "I am meeting with Lord Dallington soon, and I was wondering if you would like to come with me to Brockhall Manor." He glanced between Mattie and Franny. "Both of you."

Franny shook her head. "I do not think that is wise. I do not know them, and I am in mourning."

"I think it might be good for you," Mattie encouraged gently.

"What if I say or do the wrong thing?" Franny asked. "My mother hadn't started taking me to call upon her friends yet."

Mattie gave her an understanding look. "It will be all right. I promise. The Lockwood family has always shown me kindness, and I am sure they will do the same for you."

Franny paused, uncertainty in her eyes. She then lowered her gaze and took a deep breath. "I think it will be best if I remain here. I wouldn't want to burden anyone with my problems."

"Are you sure?" Mattie pressed.

"I am," Franny replied. This time, she sounded much more confident. "I need more time to myself."

Her father met Mattie's gaze. "Shall we depart?" he asked, rising from his seat.

Mattie nodded. "We won't be long," she assured her cousin.

As they prepared to leave, Mattie felt a tinge of sadness for her cousin. She understood Franny's need to be alone, but she also wished her cousin could find some comfort in their company.

Chapter Six

Winston sat on the settee in his bedchamber, a bottle of whiskey in his hand. It was so tempting to drink and forget his burdens. But no matter how much he drank, he couldn't forget Johnny and the look that was on his face when his mother was hanging right in front of him.

Why had he ever agreed to take that blasted case?

He already knew the reasons. He was trying to establish himself as a barrister, and it seemed like a straightforward case. Yet, his actions caused the taking of someone's life.

Winston tilted the bottle towards him. He wanted to forget. No, he *needed* to forget. Ever since that fateful day, he found himself retreating from the life that he once knew. He felt as if he didn't deserve all the accolades that he had been given.

The room was silent except for the ticking of the clock on the mantel. Winston stared at the amber liquid in the bottle, his thoughts drifting back to the courtroom. The memory of Clara's trial haunted him. The evidence seemed clear, leaving no doubt of her guilt. But now, in the dim light of his room, every detail felt twisted, every decision wrong. He had trusted the judicial system, but he had destroyed a boy's life in the process.

The guilt gnawed at him, a relentless ache that no amount of whiskey could dull. He had always prided himself on his ability to separate his work from his emotions, to remain detached and objective. But this case had shattered that illusion.

The idea of leaving it all behind and focusing on his sheep farm was a tempting escape. He could envision the simplicity of that life, which was a stark contrast to the demanding world of law. But even as he considered it, he knew it wasn't a solution. Running away wouldn't change the past or absolve him of his mistakes.

He sighed, placing the bottle on the table beside him. Winston's thoughts turned again to Mattie. She had always been there, a thorn in his side and yet a source of comfort. Their relationship was complicated, filled with banter and disagreements, but beneath it all, there was a connection he couldn't deny.

Despite her exasperating ways, he was drawn to Mattie. He remembered the way she had looked at him on their carriage ride, her eyes full of determination and understanding. She had a way of seeing through his defenses and reaching the parts of him that he tried to keep hidden.

Winston knew he couldn't hide from his past or his responsibilities. He had to confront his demons, face the consequences of his choices, and find a way to make amends.

But where did he even start?

With a heavy heart, he rose from the settee and crossed the room to the window. The afternoon sun burned brightly, filling the room with an uncomfortable contrast to his inner turmoil. All he wanted to feel was darkness surrounding him. That was what he deserved.

A knock came at the door.

"Enter," he ordered.

The door was opened, and Grady stepped into the room. "A word, my lord?" he asked, not bothering to wait for a reply before closing the door behind him.

Winston found himself curious as to why the Bow Street Runner had sought him out, knowing it came at great risk to his disguise as a footman.

Grady walked further into the room. "I received word from Jasper."

Turning to face the Bow Street Runner, Winston asked, "Is my Aunt Sarah all right?"

The Bow Street Runner nodded. "Yes, but a man fitting Isaac's description has been seen in the village. We must be extra vigilant at this time."

Winston felt a cold dread settle in his stomach. Isaac's presence could only mean trouble for them. "I will inform my father that Isaac might be calling upon him soon."

Grady looked serious. "From what Jasper told me about Isaac, he does not seem like a man that will go away without a fight."

"Let us hope that isn't the case," Winston said. "I will inform White of this development and insist the footmen are prepared for whatever may come."

"Very good," Grady responded as he headed towards the door. He stopped and turned back around. "I thought you might be interested in knowing that Miss Bawden has arrived with her father. They are currently in the drawing room."

Winston attempted to keep his face expressionless. "Why would that concern me?" he asked.

Grady looked amused. "My apologies, my lord," he said, not seeming very repentant at all.

As Grady departed from the room, Winston was left alone with his thoughts. He couldn't deny the sudden flutter of anticipation at the news of Mattie's arrival. Despite the grave situation with Isaac, the thought of seeing Mattie brought a flicker of warmth to his otherwise troubled heart.

With a deep breath, he made his way to the drawing room. He had only seen Mattie a short time ago when they had gone on the carriage ride, but that hardly mattered to him, especially with their new understanding. They were going to attempt to be friends once more. Was that even possible?

Winston paused briefly at the drawing room door, composing himself before entering. When he stepped inside, his gaze immediately sought out Mattie.

"Mattie," he greeted. "I was made to understand that your father had accompanied you here."

She smiled, and now the room was brighter because of it. "He is meeting with your father," she explained.

"Ah, that would make sense," Winston said, suddenly feeling very foolish for coming down to greet Mattie. "I am sure my mother will be here shortly."

"I expect so, as well," Mattie responded.

Winston felt nervous, and he was never nervous. Not around Mattie or anyone. Why was she causing such a reaction in him? "It is a nice day we are having, is it not?"

Mattie bobbed her head. "Yes, quite nice."

Winston found himself at a loss for words as an awkward silence stretched between them. He took a step closer, searching for something meaningful to say. "I trust you found the journey pleasant?"

"It was uneventful, which I suppose is a good thing," she replied. "I would have preferred to walk, but my father was insistent that we take the coach."

"As he well should, since he is a viscount now," Winston said.

Mattie's smile dimmed. "Do not remind me."

Winston cocked his head. "Did I say something wrong?" he asked.

She waved a dismissive hand in front of her. "I do not wish to burden you with my troubles."

"It is no trouble at all," Winston replied. "I thought we were going to at least attempt to be friends."

A look of uncertainty crossed Mattie's features before she shared, "I recently learned that my housekeeper, Mrs. Watson, will not be joining us at Darlington Abbey. She is going to remain behind and tend to the cottage for the new vicar."

"Does Darlington Abbey not have its own housekeeper?" he asked.

Mattie clasped her hands in front of her, the gesture betraying her emotions. "Yes, but I have known Mrs. Watson for most of my life. She is more than a servant to me. She is a dear friend."

"I can only imagine how difficult that must be for you," Winston acknowledged.

Letting out a deep sigh, Mattie continued, her voice tinged with sorrow. "To add to my misery, I am not quite sure how to help my younger cousin. She is struggling since losing her parents."

"All while you are still grieving their loss as well," Winston observed.

"Yes, but my grief seems inconsequential compared to Franny's," Mattie shared.

Winston took a step closer to her, but still maintained a proper distance. "Why is that?"

Mattie's brows knitted together. "Franny lost both of her parents," she replied. "I merely lost an aunt and uncle."

"I hadn't realized that it was a contest on who had a right to grieve more," Winston responded gently.

"It's not, but..." Her words trailed off, her gaze dropping to the ground. "I can't seem to focus on my own grief, knowing how much pain Franny is in."

Winston crossed his arms over his chest. "Why does that burden fall upon you?"

"Because my father is dealing with the loss of his brother and the daunting prospect of running an estate," Mattie said, her voice heavy with responsibility. "I do not wish to burden him any more than he already is."

"What of your sister, Miss Emma?" he inquired.

Mattie huffed. "I fear that Emma will only make the situation worse since she is rather self-absorbed," she said. "She should be arriving tomorrow."

Winston studied her, noting the weariness in her eyes and the rigidness in her stance. "I have known you for a long time, and I have no doubt that you will weather this storm and do so spectacularly."

Mattie gave him a small, rueful smile. "You are far too confident in my abilities."

"I have always admired your strength, Mattie," he admitted earnestly. "You are not one to sit by and let life pass you by. You are determined to live your life, on your terms, even if that means you throw a mallet or two."

She laughed, a genuine sound that did inconvenient things to his heart. "I have only thrown a mallet at you before."

"So you admit that you were aiming at me?" he asked with a teasing smile.

Not looking the least bit repentant, she replied, "I was, but that is only because you cheated at pall-mall."

Winston let out an exasperated sigh. "Not this again," he said. "We were not playing a game when I moved my ball."

"I didn't move mine," Mattie remarked, her tone playful.

"You didn't need to," Winston pointed out. "Regardless, it might be best, for the sake of our friendship, if we let that matter drop and agree that we did not see eye to eye."

Mattie considered him for a long moment, her eyes searching his. "I will agree, but only because I would very much like to be friends with you again."

"Good, because I think we are better as friends," Winston

said. "And I do not want to be hit by a mallet again. It rather hurt."

She laughed again, the sound softening the tension between them. "I promise I will not throw a mallet at you ever again… even if you deserve it," she responded, her eyes dancing with mischief.

Winston grinned. "Thank you. That is very reassuring."

They stood there for a moment, watching each other, but Winston was not in a hurry to fill the silence with useless chatter. In Mattie's presence, he felt something he hadn't felt in a long time—reprieve. The weight of his burdens seemed to lighten, if only for a moment. It was as if Mattie had the power to chase away the shadows that had been plaguing him.

An adorable blush crept up Mattie's cheeks, and she dropped her gaze. "I wonder what is keeping your mother," she offered.

"I shall go find out."

"Thank you," she responded.

As he walked to the door, he stopped and turned back around. "Mattie, I… I want you to know that I am here for you," he said. "Whatever you need, whatever support I can offer, you have it."

Mattie met his gaze. "That is most kind of you to say, Winston."

He held her gaze for a moment longer than what was considered proper before he departed from the drawing room. He didn't know what had transpired between them, but he felt it was a promising step towards rekindling their friendship.

As he stepped into the entry hall, he saw Elodie was standing by the door. He lifted his brow. "Dare I ask what you are doing?"

Elodie smiled broadly, her expression far too mischievous to be innocent. "I was just standing here, doing nothing in particular," she said. "And I most assuredly was not listening to your conversation with Mattie."

Winston shook his head at his sister's antics as he went in search of his mother.

Mattie dropped down onto the settee, her mind swirling with confusion over what had just transpired between her and Winston. He was starting to be vulnerable around her once more, and that worried her. He was showing her a side that he rarely showed. It was the side that she had once fallen for and kissed.

But no good would come from kissing Winston ever again.

They were attempting to be friends, and she found she needed a friend now more than ever.

Elodie entered the room with a bemused look. "What, pray tell, is going on between you and my brother?"

"Nothing," Mattie said, attempting to sound nonchalant. "Why do you ask?"

Walking closer to the settee, Elodie replied, "Well, I was standing outside the door listening…"

"That is a fancy way of saying you were eavesdropping."

"… yes, I was, but I heard the most distressing thing." Elodie paused dramatically. "Winston complimented you."

Mattie laughed. "Is that all?"

Elodie's brow shot up in disbelief. "Is that all?" she repeated. "You two hate one another."

"Hate is such a strong word."

"Well, am I wrong?" Elodie pressed.

Mattie straightened in her seat, taking a deep breath. "It is true we disliked one another, but we decided to call a truce," she explained. "We are attempting to become friends once more."

"Friends?" Elodie repeated, her tone incredulous. "Surely

you jest. You two could hardly be in the same room just a few days ago."

"You make a good argument, but we have found all the fighting to be rather tiresome," Mattie replied.

Elodie started pacing, her steps quick and agitated. "I do not like this. Not one bit."

Mattie was afraid she wasn't going to like the answer, but she decided to ask anyways. "Why is that?"

"You and Winston not liking one another was constant. I could plan on it," Elodie said, her pacing never ceasing. "But you two being friends, that is not good."

"Why is it not good? Shouldn't you be happy that we are trying to get along?" Mattie asked.

Elodie stopped pacing and faced Mattie, her expression serious and full of concern. "Because if you two become friends, or worse, something more, it could complicate everything."

Mattie shook her head. "We are just trying to be friends. Nothing more."

"I hope that is true, for both of your sakes," Elodie stated. "I don't want either of you two to get hurt."

"You are overthinking this, Elodie," Mattie insisted.

Elodie tossed her hands up. "Or you are *under*thinking this!"

Mattie rose from her seat and approached her friend. "I appreciate your concern, but it is unfounded," she said. "Winston and I have a long way to go just to be friends."

"You certainly appeared friendly only a moment ago," Elodie muttered.

"Appearances can be deceiving, especially when you are eavesdropping," Mattie teased. "Winston was only trying to comfort me during this difficult time."

Elodie didn't look convinced. "It seemed more than that, but I shall take you at your word."

"Thank you," Mattie said.

As she uttered her words, Lady Dallington stepped into the room with Melody trailing behind.

"I do apologize for the delay, but Melody and I were looking over the new gowns that we had commissioned for the Season," Lady Dallington said. "Mrs. Harper has outdone herself."

Mattie ran a hand down her gray gown. "I am still waiting for the mourning gowns to be delivered, so I wore the darkest-colored dress I own."

"I have no doubt that Mrs. Harper and her seamstresses are working on them this very minute," Lady Dallington assured her.

"I do hope so," Mattie said. "I do not want anyone to think that we are forgoing the mourning period."

"I do not think anyone is concerned with that, considering the news is only just spreading around the village," Lady Dallington remarked. "Everyone knows it takes time for gowns to be made."

Melody walked across the room and sat down on the settee. "When is Emma set to arrive?"

"She should be arriving tomorrow," Mattie replied. "Father intends to hire a governess to see to Emma's education once we arrive at Darlington Abbey."

Lady Dallington nodded in approval. "As she is a daughter of a viscount, it is expected that he should retain a governess."

"I do hope the governess can handle Emma," Mattie said. "She can be rather headstrong and obstinate."

Elodie giggled. "That does sound like someone we know," she remarked with a knowing look at Mattie.

Mattie smiled. "Yes, well, I do have strong opinions, but my sister seems to have delusions of grandeur."

"Then she will fit in well amongst high Society," Lady Dallington remarked.

A maid stepped into the room with a tea service, setting it

carefully on the table in front of Melody. "Would you like me to pour, my lady?"

Melody offered her a kind smile. "No, thank you. I shall pour." She leaned forward to retrieve the teapot. As she began to pour the tea, she asked, "How old is Emma now?"

"Emma is six and ten years old," Mattie responded.

"I do not know why she cannot return to her boarding school until she is presented at Court," Melody suggested. "We remained at our boarding school, despite Father inheriting his title."

Lady Dallington settled gracefully into a chair beside Melody. "That was only because you had four months left of your schooling and you both refused to return home."

Elodie bobbed her head. "I am grateful that we went away to boarding school rather than be taught by a stuffy governess."

"Not all governesses are stuffy," Lady Dallington countered. "It is imperative to find the right fit."

Melody poured four cups of tea and distributed them with practiced ease. "I made many long-lasting friendships from my time at our boarding school."

"Yes, including Josephine," Lady Dallington said. "You two are prolific writers to one another."

Elodie furrowed her brow. "Who is Josephine?"

Melody waved a dismissive hand in front of her. "You remember Josephine. She was there for our first year but left shortly thereafter."

"No, I don't recall her," Elodie responded. "What did she look like?"

"She was tall, with dark hair, and unassuming," Melody said. "I am not surprised you don't remember her since she kept to herself."

Elodie took a thoughtful sip of her tea. "That is odd, considering we spent so much time with one another."

Melody did not appear concerned. "I'm sure you will remember her when we see her during the Season."

"I guess so," Elodie muttered.

Turning towards Mattie, Melody said, "We are being completely rude to our guest. We haven't even asked her how she is faring."

Mattie lowered the teacup to her lap. "I am well, but I am struggling to find a way to help my cousin. She is distraught over the death of her parents."

"Give her time, lots of love and understanding," Lady Dallington recommended.

Elodie brought her cup up to her lips as she remarked, "Winston said something similar when he was discussing this very same thing with Mattie. Isn't that right?"

Mattie tipped her head in acknowledgement. "Yes, Lord Winston was very insightful on the situation," she acknowledged.

"That does not surprise me," Lady Dallington said. "Out of all my children, Winston is the one that feels the most deeply."

"I feel deeply," Elodie argued.

Lady Dallington gave her daughter a pointed look. "Perhaps, but you are much more vocal about your feelings. Winston holds them in, and they no doubt gnaw at him."

Elodie placed her empty teacup onto the tray. "I wonder if that is why he is such a successful barrister."

"I cannot speak to that, but I do worry about him," Lady Dallington remarked.

Winston's voice came from the doorway. "There is no reason to worry about me, Mother," he said, stepping into the room with a determined stride.

Turning her attention towards him, Lady Dallington responded, "I am a mother. It is my job to worry about my children."

He went to stand next to Elodie. "I am seven and twenty years old. I can handle my own affairs."

"Yet you are not married," Lady Dallington reminded him.

Winston crossed his arms over his chest. "Yes, and that is by choice. A wife would just complicate my life."

"A wife is a blessing," Lady Dallington countered. "Look at how happy Bennett and Delphine are. Their happiness seems to radiate off them."

Mattie noticed that Winston grew rigid at the mention of a wife. Interesting, she thought. What was it about taking on a wife that bothered him so greatly?

In a gruff voice, Winston said, "Not everyone has Bennett's good fortune."

"Sometimes one must forge ahead, making their own path, and not rely on good fortune," Lady Dallington advised.

Winston uncrossed his arms, letting them fall to his sides. "Do we truly have to discuss this now, considering we have a guest?"

Lady Dallington shifted her gaze to Mattie, her eyes warm and kind. "I daresay that Mattie is more than a guest. I consider her as family."

Mattie offered Lady Dallington a grateful smile. "Thank you, my lady," she acknowledged. "I feel the same way."

As she reached for the teapot, Melody addressed her brother with a playful grin. "May I offer you some tea while Mother is interrogating you?"

"Tea would be wonderful," Winston replied, his tone softening.

Melody went about pouring a cup of tea and extended the cup and saucer to Winston. He took it with a nod of thanks.

Lady Dallington placed her teacup onto the table. "I want what every mother wants, and that is for all of my children to be happily wed."

"Getting married does not ensure our happiness," Melody

argued. "Even if we were most fortunate to find love, which is rare and elusive in high Society, we still must live our lives, which have no guarantees of being carefree."

Winston took a sip of his tea, his gaze thoughtful. "Melody is right. Happiness is not guaranteed by marriage alone."

Lady Dallington sighed softly. "I understand, but my marriage to your father has brought me immense joy. That is what I want for each one of you, especially since life is difficult."

Mattie watched the exchange with interest, recognizing the deep bond between them all, one she was grateful to be a part of despite their disagreements.

Elodie spoke up, her tone decisive. "I doubt I will ever get married. I see no point in losing my freedoms for a chance at love."

"I support your decision, Sister," Winston stated. "Perhaps you can help me run my sheep farm."

Perking up, Elodie declared, "I would greatly enjoy running a sheep farm."

Lady Dallington let out a heavy sigh. "You two are incorrigible," she stated with exasperation in her voice. "I do not know what I am going to do with either of you."

Finding herself curious, Mattie asked Elodie, "Do you know anything about sheep?"

Elodie's eyes sparkled with enthusiasm. "I know if you see a sheep on its back that you must roll it to its side," she replied. "Other than that, I am at a loss. But I can learn."

"Why don't you focus on the upcoming Season first?" Lady Dallington asked. "You never know, you may enjoy all the social events that London has to offer."

"I truly doubt that," Elodie responded.

Lady Dallington turned her attention towards Mattie. "Did you speak to your father about my offer to host you for the Season?"

"I did, and he is still mulling it over," Mattie said. She

didn't wish to reveal that he hadn't been keen on the idea, but she hoped he would reconsider—for her sake.

With a reassuring smile, Lady Dallington remarked, "I am sure he will see the wisdom in it. It would be a wonderful opportunity for you."

Mattie returned her smile, albeit a bit forced. "I hope so," she said, though doubt lingered in her mind.

Fortunately, Elodie must have sensed the tension because she interjected, "Well, if you don't attend the Season, you could always help run the sheep farm with us."

Winston chuckled. "Indeed, the more the merrier."

Chapter Seven

Winston took a sip of his tea as he listened to the conversation going on around him. He knew his mother meant well in wishing that he should marry, but it wasn't that simple. He had made the mistake of being vulnerable with Mattie, and she had betrayed him. The pain of that experience had left him resolute in his decision: it was better to be alone.

Quite frankly, he deserved that after what he had done with his life. He didn't deserve to be happy.

Grady stepped into the drawing room, his usually composed face shadowed with an uncharacteristic solemnity. He caught Winston's eyes. "May I speak to you for a moment, my lord?" he requested, his tone grave.

Winston nodded, placing his teacup back on the tray. "Yes, of course," he replied. "Excuse me, ladies." He rose and followed Grady into the entry hall, his mind racing. For the Bow Street Runner to interrupt him like this, something significant must have occurred.

Once they were alone, Grady turned to him, keeping his voice low. "Isaac is in the study, waiting on Lord Dallington, but his lordship is in a meeting with the vicar and the solicitor of the village."

"I shall handle it, then," Winston stated.

Without waiting for a response, Winston strode towards the study, determination in every step. He would confront Isaac and speak his mind, father or no father. Just as he was about to enter the room, Grady stopped him by placing an arm on his sleeve.

"Before you go in," Grady began, his voice steady but urgent, "remember to not give anything away."

Winston frowned, feeling a twinge of offense at such an insulting remark. "I am a trained barrister. I assure you that won't be a problem."

Grady withdrew his hand. "Would you like me to accompany you?"

"That won't be necessary."

"Then I shall wait outside the door," Grady informed him, his tone leaving no room for argument.

Winston acknowledged Grady's words with a brief nod before he stepped into the study. His eyes sought out Isaac, who stood near the fireplace. Isaac was tall, heavy-set, and had his black hair slicked to one side.

Isaac's eyes flashed with annoyance. "I asked to speak to Lord Dallington, not you, my lord," he grumbled.

"You know who I am?" Winston asked.

"I do," Isaac responded, offering no further details.

Winston straightened his posture, exuding authority. "Then I am at a disadvantage, as I do not believe we have ever been introduced."

Isaac gave him a smug smile. "We haven't, but I am more than aware of who you are," he said.

Winston's expression remained impassive. "That will save us a considerable amount of time, then. What is it that you want?"

With a scoff, Isaac stated, "As if you don't already know. I want my wife."

Winston spread his arms wide. "I don't know where your wife is," he replied.

"I find that hard to believe."

"It is true," Winston said. "In fact, I have never even met my father's younger sister. His family disowned her after she eloped with you."

Isaac took a menacing step closer. "If Sarah isn't here, then where is she?"

Shrugging, Winston responded, "I cannot answer that. I don't even have a wife to lose yet."

"I did not lose my wife," Isaac declared. "She ran away with our son! I want them back home where they belong."

Winston walked over to the drink cart, keeping his movements deliberate. "That is unfortunate, truly. But what does that have to do with me?"

Isaac pointed a finger at him, his frustration palpable. "You know where she is, don't you?"

As he picked up the decanter, Winston replied, "I told you. I do not know where my Aunt Sarah is."

"Do you expect me to believe that?"

"I do, because it is the truth," Winston said, pouring himself a drink. "Now you can depart and leave us be."

Isaac lifted his brow, defiance etched on his face. "I am not going anywhere until I have my wife."

Winston placed down the decanter and picked up his glass. "Then you shall be waiting a long time for nothing," he said. "And I hear that the rooms in the coaching inn are less than stellar. It's the rats, I'm afraid."

Glancing at the door, Isaac's face darkened. "Where is your father? I came to speak to him, not a lowly second son."

Winston met his glare with a calm demeanor. "I'm afraid my father is in a meeting, and he is unable to meet with you," he revealed, bringing the glass to his lips. "I agreed to speak to you out of the goodness of my heart."

Isaac's eyes narrowed. "You think you are so clever, but your vain attempts at bamboozling me won't work."

"I have no idea what you are talking about," Winston remarked. "I am just a lowly second son, as you stated earlier. Why should I know anything of importance?"

"I will bring back the constable and he will demand that you turn over my wife and son to me," Isaac threatened, his voice rising.

Winston lowered the glass to his side. "That would be a waste of your time and the constable's, considering your wife and son are not here."

"But you know where they are!" Isaac exclaimed, his voice edging towards desperation.

Sighing, Winston said, "Now we are just going in circles, and we are not getting anywhere. Perhaps if we try again later."

Isaac took a commanding step towards him. "You will tell me where my wife is or—"

"Or what?" Winston demanded.

Grady stepped into the room, standing guard by the door, his presence a silent warning.

Isaac glanced at Grady, shaking his head in disdain. "You think you are better than me."

"I have never once thought that, partly because I don't know you," Winston said. "Nor do I care to, especially if the rumors about you are to be believed."

Isaac's lips tightened into a white line. "I do not know what you heard, but I love my wife," he spat out.

"Then how exactly did you lose her?" Winston mocked.

His words hit their mark, evidenced by the flare of Isaac's nostrils. "This is not over," he shouted. "I will be back, and you will give me my wife and son."

Winston smirked. "It almost seems like you believe you would be welcomed back into our home a second time."

Isaac's hands balled into tight, white-knuckled fists. "This conversation would have gone much differently if you didn't have your servants here to protect you."

Placing his glass down on the tray, Winston approached Isaac and came to a stop right in front of him. "I do not need my servants to fight my battles for me," he said, his voice firm and unyielding. "Nor do I hit women for pleasure."

"Sarah is my wife, and I will discipline her however I see fit," Isaac retorted.

Winston leaned closer, his eyes boring into Isaac's. "It is a shame, then, that you are no longer in possession of her," he stated. "And if I do ever see my aunt or your son, I promise that I will ensure they go nowhere near you ever again."

Isaac glared at him, his eyes sparking with fury. "I wouldn't be so quick to promise that," he sneered.

They continued to stare at one another, neither one willing to back down. Winston wasn't afraid of Isaac, and he was determined to make that abundantly clear.

His mother's voice came from behind them. "Dear heavens, what is all the yelling about?"

Isaac turned to face his mother, a cruel smile spreading on his lips. "Good afternoon, Lady Dallington—"

Winston cut him off. "You will not speak to my mother," he demanded. "It is time for you to leave."

Grady took a step towards Isaac and gestured towards the door, his expression stern.

Isaac tsked. "I will get my wife back, one way or another," he declared before he departed from the study with a huff. Grady followed him out of the room.

Winston took a moment to collect himself, his thoughts still swirling from the encounter with Isaac. He glanced at his mother, her expression expectant, and sighed inwardly. "That was Isaac—Sarah's husband," he revealed.

His mother's eyes flickered with understanding. "I gathered as much from the raised voices."

"It was unwise of you to intervene," Winston gently chided.

She met his gaze with unwavering resolve. "And what would have happened had I not?" she asked. "After all, it appeared that you two were about to engage in fisticuffs."

Winston walked over and picked up his drink from the tray. "It would have been no less than he deserved."

His mother's disapproval was evident as she shook her head. "I know you box during your time in London, but I do not condone hitting of any kind," she admonished, her voice laced with concern. "I think it is rather barbaric."

Winston remained silent, the weight of her words sinking in. "I understand, Mother," he conceded.

White entered the room and informed him, "Mr. Blythe has departed from the manor."

"Isaac is not welcome in our home. If he returns, deny him entry and send for the constable," Winston said.

"Very good, my lord," White responded.

"And send in Grady," Winston ordered. "I wish to speak to him."

White's brow furrowed in confusion. "Is there something I can assist you with?" he inquired.

"No," Winston responded.

With a nod, White departed from the study to carry out his instructions, leaving Winston alone with his mother once more.

She gave him an expectant look, her eyes searching his for answers. "Will you tell me what is going on?"

"I will, in due time," Winston assured her.

Her expression softened slightly at his reassurance, but the underlying worry remained etched in the lines of her face. "Do not wait too long, Son," she urged. "If you will excuse me, I shall return to the drawing room."

Once he was alone again, Winston released a heavy sigh.

He didn't think he had helped the situation by his confrontation with Isaac, but he sure hadn't made it worse.

Before he could dwell further on the matter, Grady's voice cut through the silence from the doorway. "You wished to see me, my lord."

"Yes," Winston replied, his tone serious. "I want you to follow Isaac. I need to know where he goes and what he is up to."

Grady inclined his head in understanding. "I was hoping you would say that," he acknowledged before turning to leave.

Mattie stepped into the kitchen through the back door of her cottage, a familiar scent of herbs and simmering broth greeting her. She had spent the afternoon with Lady Dallington and her two daughters, where there was never a dull moment.

Mrs. Watson stood at the hearth, her back turned as she stirred a pot. She glanced over her shoulder and smiled warmly. "Welcome home," she greeted. "Your father returned home over an hour ago. I was wondering when you would be back."

"I did not intend to stay with Lady Dallington as long as I did," Mattie admitted, closing the door behind her and stepping into the warmth of the kitchen.

"I am glad that you feel so comfortable there," Mrs. Watson remarked.

Mattie pulled out a chair at the table and sat down with a soft sigh. "I am hoping my father agrees to let Lady Dallington host me for the Season."

Mrs. Watson wiped her hands on her apron and sat beside Mattie. "That is a big ask," she said thoughtfully.

"I know." Mattie sighed again, this time more deeply.

With a knowing look, Mrs. Watson said, "I never said that it was impossible." She reached over and took Mattie's hand. "I wanted to talk to you about me staying behind when you leave for Darlington Abbey."

Mattie frowned. "Well, I do not like it one bit."

Mrs. Watson squeezed her hand tenderly. "This is not about you, my dear. I have always thought of you as a daughter, having watched you grow up. But my son needs me now. His wife is about to have a baby, and they have no one else to help them."

"I understand," Mattie responded, though her voice was filled with sadness.

Mrs. Watson's eyes softened with kindness as she reassured her, "I will still see you, you know. Darlington Abbey is not so far away. I can take the mail coach to visit you."

Mattie blinked back tears. "You would come visit me?"

"Of course," Mrs. Watson said. "I need to ensure that you are taking care of yourself."

"I would like that," Mattie expressed.

Mrs. Watson released her hand and stood up. "Now, you better go speak to your father before you wash up for supper," she said. "He was asking about you."

"What do you think he wants?" Mattie asked, rising.

The housekeeper shrugged. "It could be any number of things. Who am I to say?"

Mattie moved over to the hearth and peered into the pot. "Do you need any help with supper?"

"Absolutely not!" Mrs. Watson declared with mock sternness. "You are the daughter of a viscount now. I can't have you helping in the kitchen."

"But you would let me when I was the daughter of a vicar," Mattie protested.

"That was different, and you know it," Mrs. Watson responded. "You are a lady and should not be concerning yourself with the ins and outs of the kitchen."

Mattie glanced around the familiar room, a place where she had spent so many happy hours. She knew she would miss this place dearly when she left for Darlington Abbey.

Mrs. Watson gave her a knowing look, as if she could read her thoughts. "You will make new memories," she assured her. "It will be different, but that doesn't mean it won't be a good thing."

Mattie nodded, taking comfort in her words. She took a deep breath and turned towards the door, ready to face whatever her father had to discuss with her.

Once she arrived at his study, she knocked gently before pushing the door open. "Father, you wished to speak to me?" she inquired, stepping inside.

Her father rose from his seat and gestured towards a chair. "Yes, please take a seat."

Mattie sat down, giving her father an expectant look. She sensed that this conversation held more significance than a mere inquiry about her day.

He returned to his seat. "Did you enjoy your time with Lady Dallington?"

"I did," Mattie replied.

"Good, good," her father muttered, seeming preoccupied.

Mattie settled back in her seat. "Did you have a productive meeting with Lord Dallington?"

"I did," her father replied. "He is very wise in the ways of land management, despite having only inherited his title a few months ago."

"That is good."

"Yes, it is," her father remarked before abruptly rising. He walked over to the window and looked out for a long moment. "Lord Dallington and I spoke briefly about his wife hosting you for the Season."

"Yes, and?" Mattie asked, her heart hopeful.

Her father turned to face her with a solemn look. "I'm sorry, but I do not think it is a good idea."

Mattie's heart sank. "Whyever not?"

"Franny is not in a good place right now, and Emma…" His voice trailed off. "We both know that Emma can be a handful."

"But it is only for the Season. I shall return and…"

He raised his hand, stilling her words. "I need you at home, Mattie. It is where you belong, for now."

"Father…" she started, her voice trembling with emotion, "I want to participate in a Season. I am one and twenty years old. To many, I am old enough to be considered a spinster."

"God willing, you will have next Season," her father attempted to reassure her.

Mattie bit her lower lip, fighting back the tears. "I have not asked for much over the years, but I am asking for this. Please reconsider."

Her father's face fell, his expression heavy with regret. "I'm sorry. I have made my decision, and I would ask for you to respect it."

"And if I don't?" Mattie's voice quivered with defiance.

"Mattie, be reasonable," her father said sternly. "I don't want you traipsing around London when you are needed at Darlington Abbey."

Mattie felt her anger whirling inside of her and she attempted to bite her tongue. But it didn't work. "No, you are wrong. I am not needed at Darlington Abbey. You just don't want me to go and enjoy myself."

"That is not the case," her father insisted.

"Franny, although she is grieving, will be all right, and Emma will have a governess to tend to her," Mattie said, her voice rising with each word. "I will be doing nothing but twiddling my thumbs or embroidering more handkerchiefs for you."

Her father's eyes flashed with frustration. "Mattie, this is not about depriving you of enjoyment. It is about the family and what we need right now."

"Sometimes I wonder if you even see me as part of the family," Mattie retorted, tears welling in her eyes. "It feels like I am just a convenient piece to move around as you see fit."

"Mattie—" he started.

She spoke over him. "I have done everything you have asked of me without complaint," she said. "Just this once, I want something for myself."

Her father stood silently, his resolve seemingly unwavering yet visibly pained by her distress. "I wish things were different," he said. "But for now, my decision stands."

Mattie stared at him for a long moment, her heart heavy with disappointment. Without another word, she left the study, feeling more trapped than ever in the confines of her family's expectations.

She rushed out the main door and sat down on the bench under the covered porch, the cool evening air doing little to soothe her turmoil. She let the tears flow freely, not caring one whit as they rolled down her cheeks. When had her happiness become less important than the rest of her family's?

A man's voice broke her out of her musings. "Good evening."

Mattie's head came up, startled to see the man who had been watching her from the woodlands standing a short distance away. She jumped up from her seat and rushed over to the door.

"Please, don't go," he called out to her. "I mean you no harm."

She paused, her hand on the door handle. "Who are you?" she demanded.

The man smiled, his expression warm and unthreatening. "I am Mr. Isaac Blythe. I am one of Lord Dallington's new tenants." He pointed towards the horizon. "I am staying at the Stewarts' old place."

Mattie recalled that Mr. Stewart had recently moved, leaving the cottage vacant. She dropped her hand from the door, curiosity mingling with her initial apprehension. "May I ask what you are doing here?"

His eyes crinkled around the edges as he smiled again. "I am becoming better acquainted with my neighbors. You never know when you might need to borrow something." He took a step back, giving her space. "But if I came at an inconvenient time, I understand."

"No, you did not," Mattie responded, wiping her eyes quickly. "I was just…"

"I know it is not my place, but you seem upset," Mr. Blythe said gently. "May I render some assistance?"

"No, that won't be necessary, but thank you." She tried to muster up a reassuring smile.

The door opened and her father stepped out onto the porch, his gaze more curious than anything. "Mattie, who is this?" he asked.

Mattie gestured towards their neighbor. "This is Mr. Blythe. He resides in the Stewarts' old cottage."

Her father tipped his head in acknowledgement. "I am Lord Wythburn. I am the vicar of this parish, at least for the time being."

"It is a pleasure to meet you, my lord," Mr. Blythe responded. "I was just speaking to your lovely daughter. Miss Bawden, is it?"

Mattie dropped into a curtsy. "Yes, it is."

Mr. Blythe bowed. "Well, I should be going," he said. "I do not wish to intrude during suppertime."

Her father cleared his throat, and Mattie knew precisely what he was about to do. "Would you care to join us for supper?"

Putting up his hand in front of him, Mr. Blythe replied, "I could not impose."

"Nonsense," her father said. "It would be no bother, and I insist. It is, after all, the neighborly thing to do."

Mr. Blythe's smile returned. "I am most grateful," he said. "Thank you."

Her father held open the door, indicating that she should go first. After she stepped inside, Mr. Blythe followed behind her as she led him to the kitchen.

When she stepped into the kitchen, Mrs. Watson's eyes widened slightly, but only for a moment. She was used to guests joining them for supper by now. Mrs. Watson quickly went to collect another plate setting for the table, her movements efficient and practiced.

"Excuse me, I need to take a plate to Franny. She has opted to have her dinner in her bedchamber," Mrs. Watson said, addressing Lord Wythburn.

Her father acknowledged Mrs. Watson's words with a nod before he gestured towards a chair at the table. "Please have a seat, Mr. Blythe."

Mr. Blythe waited until Mattie was seated before he did the same.

"What has brought you to this fine village?" her father asked.

"Family," Mr. Blythe said firmly. "I thought it was important that my son grow up around family."

"That is a fine reason," her father praised. "I am familiar with most of the families in this parish. Perhaps I know of your family."

Mr. Blythe's eyes grew pained. "I am afraid it is my wife's family that lives here, but we are estranged. I find that it is rather difficult to talk about, and I do not wish to bother you with my troubles."

Her father bobbed his head. "I understand."

Mr. Blythe leaned forward in his seat, his expression sincere. "From what I have gathered, I must offer my condolences on the loss of your brother, my lord."

"Thank you," her father said, his voice hitching slightly

with emotion. "It has been a rather difficult time for my family."

"I can only imagine," Mr. Blythe remarked. "I, too, am familiar with the loss of family members. It is not for the faint of heart."

Her father grew silent, the weight of shared grief hanging in the air. "No, it is not."

Mr. Blythe clasped his hands together, as if to shift the mood. "But, enough of that. I would like to know more about the village. Do the rats truly outnumber the occupants at the coaching inn?"

Her father laughed. "I'm afraid so."

"That is terrible news, considering I have eaten a meal or two there since I arrived in the village," Mr. Blythe said with a grimace on his face.

"Well, if you are able, avoid the coaching inn at all costs," her father suggested.

Mattie reached for her glass, content to listen to the lively exchange between her father and Mr. Blythe. Being the daughter of a vicar, she was quite used to having unexpected guests join them for supper on any given day. However, she suspected that would change once they moved to Darlington Abbey.

Chapter Eight

Winston leaned back in his chair, his feet propped up on his desk, an opened bottle of whiskey cradled in his hand. He was waiting for the dinner bell to ring, signaling everyone to gather on the main level. Until then, he was just going to wallow in his past.

A soft knock interrupted his thoughts.

"Enter," he commanded.

The door creaked open, and Melody entered the room. Her eyes dropped to the bottle in his hand, her disapproval evident. "Dare I ask what you are doing?"

Winston straightened in his chair, placing the bottle on the desk. "I am reflecting on a past case."

"And you need a bottle of whiskey to do so?" she asked, raising an eyebrow.

He sighed. "What is it that you want, Melody?"

She crossed the room and sat on the edge of his bed, pushing aside his discarded jacket. "I thought we could talk."

Winston looked heavenward. "About what?" he asked dryly.

Melody's eyes softened with concern. "Why are you so terribly unhappy?"

"Why would you think I am unhappy?"

A small, knowing smile played on Melody's lips. "I watch and listen far more than people realize," she replied. "And I have noticed that you are not the same brother that left for London many years ago to become a barrister."

Turning to face her, Winston met her gaze. "That is because I am not." There. Perhaps if he just told her the truth she would leave him be.

But Melody was not deterred. She tilted her head slightly. "Are you unhappy being a barrister?"

"No."

"But you are unhappy?" she pressed.

Winston forced a smile to his lips. "I appreciate what you are trying to do, but I do not wish to discuss it. With you, or anyone."

Melody didn't seem to take offense at his refusal and continued, "Have you tried speaking to Mattie about this?"

He reared back slightly, feeling that particular question to be utterly ludicrous. "And why would I ever do that? Mattie and I are hardly friends."

His sister seemed to consider his words before responding, "My apologies. I see that I assumed incorrectly."

"Yes, you did," Winston said tersely. "It would be far better to speak to a brick wall than talk to Mattie."

"I am glad that you have started calling Mattie by her given name once more," Melody remarked.

"She gave me leave to," he defended.

Melody gave him an innocent look. "I don't doubt that, considering you used to call each other by your given names when you were younger."

"Yes, but that was a different time," Winston said, his voice heavy with the weight of those memories. And he was a different person.

Before his sister could respond, the dinner bell rang, echoing throughout the manor.

"Well, that is our cue," Melody remarked, rising from the bed. "Shall we?"

Winston stood up and reached for his jacket on the bed. He was grateful for the interruption since he found that Melody was far too insightful for his tastes. It had always been this way. She had a quiet strength about her that made her formidable.

After he slipped his jacket on, he walked over to the door and held it open for his sister. "As usual, I have enjoyed our chat."

Melody gave him an amused look. "You are a terrible liar, Brother."

"I pity the line of men that no doubt will be vying for your attention this Season," Winston said. "They have no idea of who they are up against."

"Was that a compliment?" Melody asked.

"It most assuredly was," Winston said as they started walking down the corridor.

Melody glanced over at him. "Do you believe in love?"

Winston's steps faltered for a moment, not knowing how to answer such a question. "Why do you ask?"

"Because I do," she replied. "I want what Mother and Father have. Their love for one another is evident in every smile, every touch and every look."

"I suppose love is possible for some," Winston said, choosing his words carefully.

"But not for you?"

Winston felt his back stiffen under his sister's scrutiny. "I did believe in love once, but my views have become much more jaded since then."

"Fair enough," she said, her tone understanding.

He looked at her with curiosity. "That is it? The interrogation is over?"

She laughed. "This was not an interrogation. I was merely making conversation."

Winston suspected that was not entirely true, especially since Melody was purposeful in what she said and did. But he decided to let it go. After all, he appreciated her concern even if he wasn't ready to confront it.

As they descended the staircase together, he saw that his family was gathered in the entry hall.

"What is this?" he asked.

Elodie glanced up at him. "White informed us dinner was ready to be served so we were just waiting for you and Melody to arrive."

His mother clasped her hands together, a gentle smile on her face. "Shall we adjourn to the dining room?"

"Yes, let us," his father agreed with a nod.

Winston followed his family into the dining room and sat down at the long, rectangular table.

The footmen stepped forward with practiced precision, placing bowls of soup in front of them. Winston reached for his spoon and started eating, hoping to be a silent observer for the time being.

Unfortunately, his mother had other ideas.

She turned her attention towards Winston. "How was your carriage ride with Mattie, my dear?"

"It went well," he said vaguely, hoping to deflect her interest. With any luck, his mother would end her line of questioning, allowing him to continue eating in peace.

"Wonderful," his mother praised, her smile broadening. "I have no doubt that Mattie will create quite a stir amongst the *ton*."

Winston's gaze dropped to his soup. He didn't want to have this conversation, especially not now. Why did he care if Mattie had a line of suitors? He didn't. She was free to do as she pleased, and she could marry whomever she so desired. Yet, despite his attempts to remain indifferent, he felt his jaw clench tightly, a muscle below his ear beginning to pulsate. The reaction was unwanted and confusing.

Fortunately, his mother shifted her focus to Elodie and Melody. "Shall we go around the table and say one thing that we have learned recently?"

As if on cue, Melody groaned. "I do not like this game. I never quite know what to say."

His father spoke up. "Neither do I, but your mother enjoys this particular game. I will start." He paused, a thoughtful expression on his face. "It has been said that Napoleon wrote a romance book."

"That is true," Melody responded eagerly. "It is called *Clisson et* Eugénie. It is about a young soldier and his relationship with a woman."

"You haven't read it, have you?" his father asked.

Melody shrugged. "I have, in fact. It was poorly written, but it wasn't as awful as I thought it would be."

His father did not look pleased. "Where did you find this book?"

"It was in our boarding school's library," Melody replied. "I suppose my interesting fact is that despite being a work of fiction, many accepted that Napoleon's book paralleled his own relationship with Eugénie Désirée Clary."

Elodie shifted her gaze towards her mother. "Is it my turn?"

"I suppose so," she replied.

With animated hands, Elodie shared, "I have been reading up on the Royal Menagerie in the Tower of London and I learned the most fascinating thing. A scientist named John Hunter disproved the rumor that ostriches are able to eat and digest iron."

"Why would someone give ostriches iron?" his father asked, looking puzzled.

"I don't know, but two birds had already died from being fed iron," Elodie responded.

As she finished her words, Grady stormed into the dining

room, his eyes wide with urgency. He met Winston's gaze directly. "My lord, I must speak to you."

White turned towards Grady, and in a stern rebuke, said, "Footmen do not request audiences with anyone."

"Then I quit," Grady announced, not bothering to spare the butler a glance. His voice grew even more determined. "My lord, it is most urgent."

Winston tipped his head. "Very well," he said, assuming this interruption was about Isaac. "We can speak in the corridor."

Once they were alone in the corridor, Winston turned to face Grady. "What is it?"

In a low voice, Grady said, "I was following Isaac, per your request, and he is having supper with Lord Wythburn and Miss Bawden as we speak."

"*What?!*" Winston shouted, his voice echoing down the corridor.

Grady nodded. "Isaac has taken up residency in the Stewarts' old cottage and took it upon himself to visit Lord Wythburn."

Winston ran a hand through his hair, feeling panic well up inside of him. What game was Isaac playing? "I need to go to them," he declared. "They need to know what kind of danger they are in."

"I assumed as much," Grady said. "Our horses are saddled and out front."

His father's voice came from the doorway. "Is everything all right?"

Winston turned towards his father, his expression grim. "No, this is about Isaac," he replied. "I will explain everything when I get back."

Without waiting for his father's reply, Winston hurried towards the main door and stepped out into the cool night air. The chill sent a shiver down his spine, but he barely noticed. His mind was consumed with thoughts of Isaac and

Winston's glare never wavered from Mr. Blythe, who remained seated, a faint, almost mocking smirk on his lips. "Isaac Blythe is not who he claims to be," he declared, his voice firm. "He is a danger to you and your family."

Her father frowned. "Pray tell, what are you talking about?"

Mr. Blythe turned to her father, his demeanor calm and unruffled. "Lord Winston has always been quite the dramatist. I mean you no harm."

"Do not believe him," Winston insisted, stepping closer. "Isaac is not a man to be trusted, by anyone. And I have reason to believe he means you harm."

Mattie's eyes widened in disbelief as she looked between Winston and Mr. Blythe. "Is this true?" she asked.

Mr. Blythe stood slowly, his eyes remaining on her. "Miss Bawden, I assure you, I am here with the best of intentions."

Winston took a step closer to her. "Do not speak to her!" he shouted. "You have no right to even be here."

"No right?" Mr. Blythe scoffed. "You stand here, speaking of what is right? You have stolen my family from me."

Mattie shifted her gaze towards Winston, her confusion growing. "What is he talking about?" she asked.

"I will explain later," Winston replied tersely. "For now, Isaac needs to leave this place at once, or I will have him forcibly removed."

After a long, tense moment, Mr. Blythe said, "Very well, Lord Winston. I will take my leave." He turned towards Mattie, his expression softening. "I apologize for any distress I may have caused. Good evening."

As Mr. Blythe walked past Winston, their eyes locked, and an unspoken challenge passed between them. Mattie watched them, feeling as though she were missing a crucial piece of the puzzle, a piece that could change everything.

A moment later, the main door slammed shut, and Mattie turned her questioning gaze towards Winston. He remained tense as he ran a hand through his hair, looking visibly upset.

"I believe I owe you an explanation," Winston began, his voice strained.

"I think that is only fair, considering you barged into our home and made some rather distasteful accusations against Mr. Blythe," her father stated.

Rather than respond to her father, Winston turned to Mattie, his eyes searching hers. "Are you all right?" he asked, concern evident in his expression. "Did Mr. Blythe say anything or do anything that upset you?"

Mattie shook her head. "No, he did not."

Relief washed over Winston's face. "I am glad that I came in time, then."

Her father cleared his throat. "Lord Winston," he said, his words firm. "Explain yourself."

Winston held her gaze for a moment before taking a step back. "What I am about to share with you must remain between us," he remarked, his voice low and solemn.

"As a vicar, I am familiar with the need for discretion," her father replied.

Shifting in his stance, Winston revealed, "Mr. Blythe is my uncle. He eloped with my father's younger sister, Sarah, many years ago and was cut off from my family. Recently, my aunt escaped my uncle's abusive clutches with her son and came to my father for help." He paused. "We hired a Bow Street Runner to protect my Aunt Sarah and we do not know their location. For their safety, and our own."

Mattie stared at Winston, stunned by the revelation. What a terrible burden he was facing, and she had been completely unaware.

Her father sank into his seat, shaking his head. "Mr. Blythe seemed like a decent bloke. I had no idea he was hiding such a devious past."

"I do not know Mr. Blythe well, mind you, but we spoke

briefly this afternoon, and I have no doubt that his intentions are far from innocent in meeting with you," Winston said. "It would be in your best interests to stay far away from that man."

Mattie clasped her hands in front of her, her mind racing. "How long does he intend to stay?"

"I do not know, but we have no intention of turning over my aunt to him," Winston replied. "My father feels that he would continue to abuse her, and could kill her, given the right circumstances."

"How awful. Your poor aunt," Mattie murmured, her heart aching for the woman she had never met.

Winston sighed deeply. "I did not wish to burden you with my troubles, but Mr. Blythe forced my hand on this. I don't know why he approached your family, but I will find out why."

Mattie met his gaze. "Mr. Blythe was the man that was watching me from the woodlands on our carriage ride."

"He was?" Winston's eyes narrowed.

"Yes, I think it is safe to say now that I know the difference between a tree and a man," Mattie said with a small smile.

Winston's expression softened slightly, but he did not return her smile. "I am sorry for doubting you. I promise that it won't happen again."

"Thank you," she said, holding his gaze. The concern in his eyes was palpable. She didn't quite think he was capable of such an emotion—at least not for her. Winston had a good heart, but he kept it well-guarded.

Her father's next question reminded her that they were not alone. "Do you think we are in danger?"

Winston's eyes shifted to her father. "I cannot say, but I would be wary of Mr. Blythe. I do believe he is a dangerous man, and he won't give up easily. For now, it would be best if you took precautions to ensure your family's safety."

Her father bobbed his head, the gravity of the situation

sinking in. "I will do whatever is necessary to protect my family," he declared.

"I know you will, my lord, but I have also assigned a man to watch over your family, just as an extra precaution," Winston said. "I will not let any harm come to you. You have my word."

Mattie felt a surge of gratitude towards Winston, mingled with a growing sense of unease. As much as she appreciated his protection, she could not help but shake the feeling that their troubles were far from over.

"May I speak to you for a moment, Miss Bawden?" Winston asked.

Mattie glanced at her father for permission, but he seemed lost in his own world. "Very well," she replied. "We can speak on the porch."

Winston gestured towards the doorway, indicating that she should go first. Mattie moved towards the porch, her footsteps echoing in the quiet cottage. Once outside, she paused, the cool night air wrapping around her. She turned to face Winston, her expression expectant.

"Are you well?" Winston asked.

Mattie turned her gaze towards the darkened fields. "I do not know what to feel," she admitted. "I had thought Mr. Blythe was an honorable man until you told me otherwise."

"But you believe me?" he pressed, his voice holding a hint of urgency.

There were a few things that Mattie knew for certain. One of them was that she trusted Winston, wholeheartedly. Never once had he lied to her, despite their many disagreements.

"I do," she replied, meeting his gaze.

A look of incredulity crossed Winston's expression, as if he had expected a different response to his question. "I will keep you safe, Mattie."

Mattie reached out and placed a hand on Winston's sleeve. "I know you will," she responded.

Winston glanced down at her hand on his sleeve with an indiscernible look, and she quickly withdrew it, embarrassed by her brazen actions. What must he think of her? They were hardly friends, and she had no right to touch him in such a familiar fashion.

Instead of the rebuke that she was expecting, she was surprised when he said, "I am touched by your faith in me."

"Why wouldn't I have faith in you?" she asked, genuinely curious.

He took a step closer to her, his eyes burning with an intensity she had never seen before. "Because of that kiss—"

Winston's words came to an abrupt halt when the door opened. Her father stepped onto the porch, his expression unreadable. "It is time for you to go, Lord Winston," he ordered.

Taking a step back, Winston bowed. "Goodnight, my lord. Miss Bawden," he said before approaching his horse.

As Lord Winston rode off into the night, her father asked, "Is something going on between you and Lord Winston?"

She shook her head. "No, we are just friends."

"Interesting," her father said, opening the door wide. "Shall we retire for bed?"

Mattie followed her father into their quiet cottage, but her mind was racing. Winston had brought up their kiss. She wondered if he ever thought about it. Not that she did. But even she knew she couldn't fathom that lie. It was always there, dwelling in her thoughts, a constant reminder of the connection they shared, however fleeting it might have been.

Chapter Nine

Winston stepped into his father's study and saw that he was hunched over his desk, a lone candle burning and providing barely enough light to read the ledgers strewn out in front of him.

His father looked up as Winston walked further into the room, his eyes weary. "Now, pray tell, why did you take off so suddenly during dinner?"

Winston walked over to the drink cart and picked up the decanter. "Isaac was at Lord Wythburn's cottage this evening."

With a baffled look, his father straightened, setting his quill down. "Whatever for?"

"He is playing a game, and I don't like it," Winston replied before taking a sip of his port. "I spoke to Isaac briefly this afternoon and the conversation did not go in his favor."

His father leaned back in his seat. "It is best if you do not antagonize Isaac. He is unpredictable and dangerous."

"He knows we are keeping Sarah and Matthew from him, despite my insistence that we do not know where she is," Winston said.

"We suspected that would be the case," his father

responded with a sigh, "but now we just have to bide our time until he gives up and leaves."

"I do not think he will go quietly," Winston said as he brought the glass to his lips.

His father nodded, a solemn expression on his face. "That is why Sarah is somewhere safe, where Isaac can't get to her."

"But what about Lord Wythburn and Miss Bawden?" Winston asked, his voice filled with worry. "I do not know why, but Isaac has decided to involve them in this."

"I shall speak to Lord Wythburn about this tomorrow when we meet."

Winston lowered the glass to his side and revealed, "I assigned a Bow Street Runner to watch over Lord Wythburn and his family."

"Do you think that is necessary?" his father asked, raising an eyebrow.

"I do," Winston responded firmly.

His father considered him for a moment before asking, "Dare I presume that the footman who interrupted us during dinner was a Bow Street Runner?"

Winston saw no reason to deny it. "He is," he confirmed.

"How many more Bow Street Runners are in our household?" his father asked, his tone holding a hint of amusement.

Winston grinned. "Grady was the only one, and he served his purpose," he replied. "In fact, he has come in handy a few times."

His father closed the ledger in front of him, the sound echoing softly in the quiet room. "I am pleased that you directed White to hire additional footmen to stand guard. The more eyes we have to look out for Isaac, the better."

Walking over to the settee, Winston sat down, the leather creaking under his weight. "We do have a problem."

"Another one?" his father inquired, exasperation creeping into his voice.

Winston clenched his jaw. "Apparently, Isaac claimed that

he is residing at the Stewarts' old cottage," he revealed. "Is there any truth to that?"

"Well, Mr. Stewart did move out, but I did not realize that the cottage had been let out again. I shall have to speak to our man of business about this," his father said, rising from his chair and walking to the window, looking out into the darkness.

"If Isaac is, in fact, renting out one of our cottages, we will need to evict him," Winston stated, his voice steely with resolve.

His father winced. "That is easier said than done," he replied. "If he has a contract—"

"Forget the contract!" Winston shouted.

Coming to sit across from him, his father said in a calm voice, "We have only recently started to rebuild the trust with the villagers. If we evict him, it could spell trouble for us."

"Are you somehow implying we let Isaac stay in the cottage, just a short distance away from Brockhall Manor?" Winston asked incredulously.

"All I am saying is that we need to be careful how we handle this," his father advised. "We must proceed with caution and ensure that whatever action we take does not bring further harm or suspicion upon us."

Winston leaned forward and placed his glass down onto the table. "I understand the legal implications of breaking a contract, but we can't in good conscience let Isaac remain underfoot, not with Aunt Sarah being so close."

His father rubbed his temples. "Perhaps we should revisit me paying Isaac off to leave Sarah alone."

"That won't solve anything," Winston asserted. "He does not strike me as a man who will leave well enough alone."

"What are we to do then?"

Winston turned his attention towards the crackling fire. "We do what you suggested. We bide our time and hope Isaac does not do anything too stupid."

His father huffed, settling back into his seat. "From what Sarah told me, he was constantly doing rather stupid things, especially when he was drunk."

"Even if Isaac went to the constable, it would do him no good since Sarah is not residing with us," Winston said. "I just do not like waiting."

"But you are a barrister," his father pointed out.

Winston smiled wryly. "There are ways to prolong a case if one so desires, but for the most part, we proceed in a timely manner."

"That has not been my experience," his father grumbled. "I do think the judges like to sit around and try to inconvenience everyone around them."

"I assure you that does not happen."

His father grew silent, his gaze thoughtful. "May I ask why you assigned a Bow Street Runner to watch over Lord Wythburn's household?"

Winston's smile dimmed. "Why would I not?" he asked. "They are innocent in all of this, and we do not know what Isaac has planned."

"Yes, but has Isaac implied that he intends to do harm to Lord Wythburn or his daughters?" his father inquired.

"No, but his presence at their cottage was very disconcerting," Winston argued. "It suggests he has an interest in them, and we cannot take any chances. We must be vigilant."

His father bobbed his head. "You are right, of course, but I wonder if this has to do with Miss Bawden more than her father."

Winston frowned. "I do not know what you are inferring…"

Putting his hand up, his father said, "I am not inferring anything. Your mother has mentioned, on multiple occasions, that you and Miss Bawden have grown closer the last few days. Is she mistaken in her assumption?"

Rising abruptly, Winston walked over to the mantel over

the hearth, his mind racing with thoughts and emotions. "Miss Bawden and I have come to an understanding—" he began, choosing his words carefully.

"Oh, is that so?" his father interjected.

"Not that kind of understanding," Winston declared. "We have decided to call a truce of sorts between us."

His father's expression remained skeptical. "Is that all it is, Son?"

"It is," Winston stated firmly, hoping to end this line of uncomfortable questioning. His father had no right to pry into his personal affairs.

"I will take you at your word, but your mother," his father hesitated, "she will be a different story. You know how she is."

"I can handle Mother," Winston responded.

His father's eyes twinkled with amusement. "I used to think that as well, but I have since learned otherwise," he said. "But enough of that. How is your sheep farm going?"

Winston winced inwardly, not sure if this topic was any better than the last. "It could be better," he admitted. "Fortunately, I have a steward that is tending to the sheep farm's day-to-day activities."

"That is good. The right employee can make a big difference in any business."

"I bought the land that the sheep graze on, and there is a small cottage there where I plan to reside when I am overseeing things," Winston shared. "I have been told the roof leaks, but I can fix that with some work."

His father lifted his brow. "You do not intend to do the work yourself, do you?"

"Surely it cannot be too hard," Winston replied.

"You are a barrister. What do you know about fixing roofs?"

Winston shrugged. "I don't, but the coffers are not exactly full, considering I am living on a barrister's income," he responded. "I have discovered being a barrister is not as lucrative as I thought it would be."

Rising, his father walked over to his desk. "How much do you need to repair the cottage?" he asked, pulling out a drawer.

"Father, I do not need your money," Winston protested.

"This is not the time to be prideful. I have the funds to help you."

Winston gave his father a knowing look. "I thought Mr. Stanley embezzled a large sum of your money."

His father pulled out another ledger. "He did, but we are not destitute, and I do not want to see my son fixing a roof like a common laborer."

With a shake of his head, Winston responded, "If it helps, fixing the roof wasn't even my first priority. I have other things that will take up my time and money."

"No, that does not help," his father said flatly, closing the ledger.

Winston reached down for his glass and tossed it back. "Let me worry about my sheep farm and you worry about your estate."

"My father helped me establish my household and I saw no shame in that."

"We are vastly different people, Father," Winston said. "I want to prove that I can do it all on my own."

His father returned the ledger to the drawer. "You are stubborn, just like your Uncle Richard, but he was a good man."

"As are you," Winston said.

"Now I wonder if your head is bottle-weary," his father joked.

Winston smiled as he walked the glass over to the drink cart and placed it down. "I am tired, and I think it is best if I retire for bed."

"Before you go, you might want to stay far away from the drawing room," his father advised. "Your mother and sisters are engaged in an intense game of whist."

"Duly noted," Winston said as he headed towards his bedchamber, being mindful to avoid the drawing room. The last thing he wanted was to be pulled in to play games this evening. He just wanted to be alone.

With the morning sun streaming through the window in her bedchamber, Mattie stared up at the ceiling. She'd had a restless night of sleep, her thoughts constantly drifting back to the moment Winston had brought up their kiss. What did that mean? Did it mean anything? Or was she just overthinking it, as she always did?

Even if Winston thought about the kiss as much as she did, it didn't necessarily indicate any affection on his part. They had only recently declared a truce in their constant bantering. Surely, if he held any feelings for her, he wouldn't have insulted her so harshly just the day before.

The sound of the door slamming could be heard echoing throughout the cottage, followed by her sister shouting, "I'm home!"

Mattie sat up in her bed and let out a sigh. She should be happy that her sister was home, but Emma always made everything about herself. It had been that way since she was little. Mattie couldn't recall meeting anyone as self-absorbed. Hopefully, her time away at boarding school had done her some good.

Rising, Mattie slipped her wrapper on and headed down the stairs. She stepped into the drawing room just as her sister was instructing the driver as to where to place her trunks.

"Emma," Mattie greeted.

Her blonde-haired, blue-eyed sister turned towards her with a bright smile. "Mattie!" she exclaimed, rushing over to her. "You didn't have to come down so disheveled on my account."

Mattie smoothed back the red hair that had fallen out from her cap. "I wanted to be the first to greet you."

"And you succeeded, but aren't you worried to be seen in such a state?" Emma asked, taking a long look at her.

"It is good to see you, too," Mattie muttered, her enthusiasm waning.

Emma's eyes roamed over the drawing room. "This place has not changed one bit," she said.

"Why would it?" Mattie asked. "You know how particular Father is."

"Yes, but Father is a viscount now. He can't live in such squalor anymore," Emma remarked dismissively. "I heard that Franny is here."

"She is, but I do believe she is still sleeping," Mattie confirmed.

Emma glanced over at the stairs. "Shall we go wake her? I have no doubt she wishes to see me."

Mattie mustered up a smile, hoping to distract her sister. "Have you had breakfast yet?"

"No," Emma said, placing a hand to her stomach. "I have not. The companion Father sent to accompany me refused to wait a moment longer at the boarding house this morning. She claimed an insufferable headache."

"Well, why don't we have Mrs. Watson prepare something for you to eat?" Mattie suggested. "That is far preferable to waking up our cousin at such an early hour."

Emma's eyes lit up at the prospect of food. "I suppose you are right," she said, walking towards the kitchen. "Is Father not awake?"

"I heard him leave for a meeting with Lord Dallington a short time ago," she informed her sister.

Perking up, Emma said, "I would have liked to accompany him. I think very highly of Lady Dallington and her daughters. I read in the Society pages that Lord Dunsby was recently married. What of his brother, Lord Winston?"

Mattie entered the kitchen behind her sister and shared, "Lord Winston is not married and is residing at Brockhall Manor for the time being."

Emma smiled. "Lord Winston has always been very kind to me."

"Yes, he has that effect on most women," Mattie remarked as she looked around the empty kitchen. "I am not sure where Mrs. Watson has gone—"

Her words stopped when Mrs. Watson stepped through the back door with a basket of food in her hands.

"Mrs. Watson!" Emma shouted. "I am home."

The housekeeper smiled warmly at her. "Yes, I can see that. How was your journey?"

"Finally, someone asked me about that," Emma said, casting a frustrated glance at Mattie. "It was dreadfully boring, and I did not like the way the men stared at me at the coaching inns. It made me rather uncomfortable."

"Don't concern yourself with that. The men at coaching inns are notorious for admiring beautiful young women," Mrs. Watson said.

"It is true," Emma responded. "I suppose I did them a service since many of them have such pathetic lives."

Mattie resisted the urge to roll her eyes. "Mrs. Watson, would you mind making something for Emma to eat?"

"I would be happy to," Mrs. Watson said, placing the basket down. "Just give me one moment to start the fire."

Emma turned back towards Mattie. "I think we should wake up Franny so we can all eat breakfast together."

"And I think that is a terrible idea," Mattie countered.

Walking towards the corridor, Emma asked, "Is she staying in your bedchamber?"

"No, we put Franny in your bedchamber since your room is larger than mine," Mattie replied.

Emma looked put out. "I cannot wait until we reside at Darlington Abbey and I have a bedchamber befitting my new status," she said. "Then I won't have to share a room with anyone."

"Franny is having a hard go of it right now. We should try to be as compassionate as possible," Mattie encouraged.

"Why?"

Mattie frowned. "Her parents just died."

"Was that not weeks ago?" Emma asked with a furrowed brow. "Surely she is over it by now.

"Her parents did die weeks ago, but she didn't receive word until recently when the letter arrived from India," Mattie explained.

Emma pulled out a chair and sat down. "Is she upset because her father died before our grandfather, meaning she won't inherit a title?"

Mattie's mouth dropped. "Emma, why would you say such a thing?" she chided.

"Is it not true?"

Taking a deep breath, Mattie said, "I think that is the least of Franny's worries right now. Perhaps you should work on saying something nice when you see her."

Emma shrugged one shoulder. "It is not that I can't say something kind, but don't you think she would prefer the truth?"

"Sometimes, people need kindness more than they need the truth," Mattie responded.

Emma sighed dramatically. "Very well. I shall try to be more considerate since Franny is an orphan now. But it is so difficult when everyone around me seems so... delicate."

Mattie turned towards Mrs. Watson and mouthed, "Help."

Mrs. Watson gave her an amused look. "Emma, would you care for some bread?"

"I would," Emma replied. "The bread at the boarding school was terrible. By the time I arrived for breakfast each morning, only the burnt pieces remained for me."

"Why didn't you come down earlier?" Mattie asked.

Emma blinked, her expression incredulous. "Why on earth would I ever wake up that early?" she asked in disbelief. "It is not as if I had to collect the eggs for our breakfast. No offense, Mrs. Watson."

"None taken, Miss Emma," Mrs. Watson responded kindly. "Speaking of which, would you care for an egg with your breakfast?"

"I would," Emma said.

As Mrs. Watson went about preparing breakfast, Mattie's father stepped into the room with the newssheets under his arm.

"Good morning, my dears," he greeted, coming to kiss Emma on the top of her head. "I am happy that both of my daughters are home, where they belong."

Emma beamed. "I understand you went to speak to Lord Dallington this morning."

"I did," her father confirmed. "Lord Dallington is helping me with estate management since I will be running Darlington Abbey for the foreseeable future."

"I understand that Grandfather is on his deathbed," Emma remarked.

Her father shook his head. "We have since received word that he is doing much better. With any luck, he will be home soon."

A look of disappointment flashed in Emma's eyes, but it disappeared as quickly as it had come. "Wonderful news," she said, her words lacking any emotions.

Mattie never quite understood her sister and how she cared so little for other people's misfortunes. She watched as her father sat down next to Emma at the table, unfolding the newssheets.

"What do you ladies have planned for today?" he asked, looking from Emma to Mattie.

Emma's hands grew animated. "Well, I wish to take a bath and get this layer of dirt off of me," she said. "Then I was hoping to go to the village and purchase some new ribbons for my hair."

"We are in mourning," Mattie reminded her sister. "The dressmaker should be bringing by a black woolen gown for each one of us today."

"I look terrible in black," Emma remarked, pouting slightly. "What if we forgo mourning, just this once?"

Mattie couldn't help herself and finally rolled her eyes in exasperation. "That would be a great insult to Father, and especially Franny."

Emma reached for her father's hand. "You wouldn't mind, would you?"

Her father tenderly encompassed his daughter's hand. "I know mourning is not exciting for anyone, but we do not wish to tarnish my brother and his wife's memory by dishonoring them."

"What if I wore my mourning gown and went to the village?" Emma asked hopefully.

Mattie opened up her mouth to reply, but her father spoke first. "I suppose that would be all right, assuming Mattie goes with you."

"But, Father—" Mattie started.

With a wink at Emma, her father said, "Just one time will not be an issue. Will it, Mattie?" He turned his attention towards her, a smile on his face.

Her jaw grew tight. "No," she said through clenched teeth.

Her father's smile grew. "Perhaps Franny would like to

accompany you," he suggested. "Every young woman enjoys looking at ribbons."

"I doubt Franny will accompany us since she refuses to leave the cottage for now," Mattie stated.

His smile disappeared. "You make a good point. It might be best if you brought her back some ribbons. Something pretty."

Emma bobbed her head. "I will find her something that she will like."

Mattie turned her back towards her sister and father and took a deep breath. How had Emma so easily manipulated Father to do her will? They were supposed to be in mourning, not traipsing around the village without a care in the world.

Mrs. Watson approached her with a cup of tea, her eyes holding compassion. "I thought you could use this," she said in a hushed voice. "I made it extra strong, just for you."

"Thank you," Mattie whispered as she accepted the cup and saucer.

After she took a sip, letting the warm drink calm her, she heard Emma telling Father all about her journey home and how it was utterly unbearable for a myriad of reasons.

Mattie was tired of being around her sister, and she had only just arrived. She put the teacup down on the table and said, "Excuse me. I feel like I need to go on a walk."

Emma looked at her with wide eyes. "You aren't going out looking like that, are you?"

Mattie ran a hand down her wrapper. "No, I shall change first."

"And do your hair," Emma advised. "It looks as if a mouse made a nest in it."

Not bothering to respond to her sister, Mattie departed from the kitchen and headed up the stairs. She had just turned the corner when she saw Franny sticking her head out of the door.

"Did I hear Emma?" Franny asked.

Mattie nodded, trying to be positive. "You did."

Franny acknowledged her words with a brief smile before she closed the door. It would appear that Mattie was not the only one who was less than excited about her sister returning home.

Chapter Ten

Winston sat atop his horse, his eyes wandering over the expansive fields that stretched out before him. The light rain had dusted his clothes, but the dampness did little to deter him from lingering. He needed this moment of reprieve from his relentless thoughts, a temporary escape from the burdens that weighed heavily on his heart.

Why couldn't he find an ounce of peace? His past had hardened him, and he questioned whether he was worthy of happiness anymore. Was he destined to be miserable for the remainder of his days?

The last time he had been happy—truly happy—was when he had kissed Mattie. That unexpected moment had made his heart come alive, as if he had been waiting for Mattie all along. But she had not felt the same.

Movement in the woodlands caught his eye, and he turned his head to see a shadowy figure heading down a path. He couldn't ignore it, especially with Isaac lurking around, no doubt waiting for an opportunity to cause trouble.

Winston urged his horse towards the path and stepped under the canopy of trees. The smell of rain mingled with the scent of the earth and leaves, reminding him of his carefree childhood days.

He dismounted swiftly, leading his horse further into the woodlands. Approaching the stream, he spotted Mattie sitting on the rock, a pensive expression on her face. Her eyes held a sadness in them, and he wished he had the power to wipe away her troubles.

In a gentle voice, he said, "Mattie."

She turned to him and offered him a weak smile. "Good morning, Winston," she greeted.

Winston secured his horse and noticed Grady was a short distance away, keeping watch over Mattie. He tipped his head in acknowledgment, and the Bow Street Runner did the same. At least Mattie was safe.

He approached her and asked, "Dare I ask what has you so troubled this morning?"

Mattie pressed her lips together, a clear sign that she was upset. It was just one of the many things he had noticed about her over the years. "It is my sister," she replied. "She returned home this morning and I do not think she has changed one bit."

"Did you expect her to?"

"Yes… no… I don't know," Mattie sighed. "I suppose I hoped that as she grew older that she would gain some perspective."

Winston sat down next to Mattie on the rock but was mindful to keep a proper distance. Although nothing about this situation was proper. "She is still young," he attempted to reassure her.

"She is, but she only thinks of herself," Mattie shared. "It is maddening, considering my father indulges her every whim."

"Have you spoken to your father about this?"

Mattie turned her gaze to the stream. "There is no point since he sees nothing wrong with Emma's behavior."

"But you do?"

She let out a slight huff. "She is far more concerned about her elevation in status than Franny's grief. I even suspect she is disappointed our grandfather managed to recover from the fever."

Winston lifted his brow. "That is awful," he murmured.

"Emma has only been home for a few hours and I already needed a moment away from her," Mattie said. "I can't help but think it is my fault for the way that she turned out, considering I helped raise her after my mother died."

"You mustn't blame yourself," Winston stated. "Every person is responsible for their own actions."

"But I indulged her far too often when she was younger," Mattie responded.

Winston nodded. "My mother has spent her life indulging Elodie and Melody, but they both have kind hearts. Elodie may say outlandish things, but she truly cares about others. Melody is the same, but she stops and observes before she takes her next step. Both of my sisters are very different, yet I count them as friends."

Mattie's smile returned. "I adore Elodie and Melody."

"I know you do, and they, for some reason unbeknownst to me, feel the same way about you," Winston said, softening his words with a smile.

She laughed, just as he had intended. "Gentlemen are supposed to be charming, my lord."

"I'm afraid I missed that course at Oxford," he joked.

Mattie's smile faded as she asked, "What should I do about my sister?"

"You are asking me?" he inquired. "You must be desperate."

With a shake of her head, Mattie responded, "I am at a loss as to what I should do."

Winston thought for a moment. "Did you do the best you could, knowing what you knew then?"

"I did."

"Then you did enough," he said. "You must recognize that Emma is forging her own path and may not want your help."

"And if that path is wrong?" Mattie questioned, her voice tinged with worry.

Winston gave her a knowing look. "Who says it is the wrong path for her?"

Mattie leaned over and nudged his shoulder with hers. "When did you get so wise?"

"I have always been wise, but you never stopped and listened before," Winston teased. "I am, after all, a highly sought-after barrister."

"I don't doubt that," Mattie said. The way she spoke her words sounded sincere and Winston felt his chest swell with pride. Why was it that her praise meant so much to him?

As a comfortable silence descended over them, Winston chose his next words carefully, unsure of how Mattie would respond. "I want to do more with my life than be a barrister."

"What is wrong with being a barrister?"

"Nothing," he replied quickly. "But the things I have seen and heard…" His words trailed off. "I don't know how much longer I can go on as I have been."

Mattie's eyes held compassion. "Then you must do as your heart dictates."

"Only a foolish man listens to his heart. A wise man uses logic when making an important decision," Winston argued.

"All right, wise man, what does your logic tell you?" Mattie said with amusement in her voice.

"I want to become one of the largest landowners in England," Winston replied.

Mattie bobbed her head. "That is rather ambitious."

He felt a stab of disappointment at her words. "I know it seems impossible—"

She interrupted him. "No, you misunderstood me," she said. "It is ambitious, but if anyone can do it, you can."

"Do you mean that?"

Her face softened. "We have known each other most of our lives, and although we have spent most of it fighting, I know the type of person you are. Stubborn. Infuriating. Pig-headed."

"Is there a point in all of that?" he asked.

She grinned. "Despite all your many flaws, you are also one of the smartest people I know. And when you set your mind to something, you can do anything."

Winston felt a warmth spread through him at her words. "Thank you, Mattie. That means a great deal to me."

They stared at one another for a moment, and Winston couldn't help but think how easy it would be to lean in and kiss her. But would she welcome the kiss?

The sound of wood snapping in the distance broke the tension, reminding him of the precariousness of their situation.

Mattie looked up at the trees and let out a long, drawn-out groan. "I should be heading back," she said. "The dressmaker is arriving soon with our mourning gowns, and then I am accompanying Emma to the village."

Before Winston could stop himself, he said, "I will join you."

She eyed him curiously. "We are going into the village to shop for some ribbons. I daresay that you might be bored with such an endeavor."

"It would be my pleasure," he said. Drats. Why couldn't he just stop speaking? But he already knew the answer. He found that he wanted to spend more time with Mattie, even if it meant going ribbon shopping.

"Very well," Mattie responded. "To be honest, I am pleased that you will be accompanying us. Perhaps you can fix my sister."

He chuckled. "I doubt I can do anything in such a short time."

"One can always hope," Mattie said lightly.

Winston rose and held his hand out to assist her in rising. Mattie slipped her gloved hand into his and stood up. He didn't release her hand right away, and she made no attempt to remove it.

"Mattie," he said.

"Yes?" she breathed, her eyes searching his.

What did he want from Mattie? Nothing. But all of his thoughts had disappeared, and he found himself struggling to come up with something to say.

Isaac's mocking voice came from behind them. "Have the rules of polite Society changed since I was young?"

Winston dropped Mattie's hand and turned to face Isaac, shielding her from his view. "What are you doing here?" he demanded.

"I was merely out for a walk and I stumbled across you and Miss Bawden," Isaac replied.

"Need I remind you that you are trespassing?" Winston growled.

Isaac shrugged. "I didn't think you would mind since we are family and all," he stated with a smirk.

Winston narrowed his eyes. "We are not family."

Placing a hand over his heart, Isaac said, "But I am your uncle."

"You need to go. Now!" Winston ordered.

Isaac dropped his hand to his side and took a step back. "I will leave you to it, then. Whatever it was that you were doing," he said before he started down the path.

Winston kept his eyes on Isaac's retreating figure until he was out of view. He turned back around to Mattie. "I am sorry about Isaac."

"You have no reason to apologize."

"But I do," Winston said. "He is here because of my family."

Mattie's eyes flickered towards the trees where Grady was

standing. "I am sure the man you assigned to watch over us will keep us safe."

"It is the least that I can do," Winston replied, a note of frustration in his voice. "Isaac is making a nuisance of himself."

Mattie placed a reassuring hand on his arm. "It is all right," she said. "Now that we know about Isaac's true intentions, we will be better prepared to deal with him."

"I just wish I could do more," Winston sighed, feeling discouraged. "I don't want anything to happen to you or your family because of Isaac."

She offered him a reassuring smile. "You are doing more than enough. We will be careful, and we can handle whatever comes our way together."

Together.

Had she truly meant that or was it just a slip of the tongue?

Mattie withdrew her hand. "I should go."

"Would you care for me to escort you home?" he asked, not wanting the time with Mattie to come to an end.

She smiled. "No, because then I would have to explain where our paths met, and I do not wish to share that."

"Point taken." Winston turned his attention towards Grady. "Keep Miss Bawden safe," he ordered.

Grady stepped out from amongst the trees and nodded. "Yes, my lord."

Winston watched as Mattie walked down the path that would lead her home, and he found himself wondering how different their lives would have been if she had responded to his letter. The one he wrote after their kiss.

As Mattie walked towards her cottage, she noticed Emma

was sitting under the covered porch. "What now?" she muttered under her breath.

Emma's face lit up when she saw her. "Mattie, you are home," she exclaimed. "I was thinking about something."

Mattie closed her eyes, a sense of dread washing over her. No good ever came from her sister when she was "thinking."

Jumping up from her seat, Emma continued, oblivious to Mattie's apprehension. "Father told me that he doesn't want you to have a Season this year because we are in mourning," she said. "But that poses a problem for me."

"It does?" she asked, wondering where this was going.

"Yes, as you know, I am almost seven and ten years old, and I was hoping to debut next Season," Emma said. "But Father won't let me debut with you. He says that wouldn't be fair of me to do so."

Mattie stepped into the cottage, with Emma following closely behind. "I fail to see what the issue is."

"Surely you must see the problem for me," Emma remarked. "I was hoping you would forgo your debut since you will be two and twenty years old. That way I can be presented in Court."

Spinning around, Mattie said, "But if I did such a thing, I would be considered a spinster amongst high Society."

Emma nodded. "Well, you will be two and twenty years old. What kind of match do you truly expect anyways?"

Mattie stared at her sister, a feeling of disbelief washing over her. Her sister wanted her to throw away her future for the sake of hers. "No," she said firmly. "I am sorry you won't be able to debut next year but I have earned the right to do so."

Her sister's face fell. "Why are you being so unreasonable about this?" she asked. "With your red hair, you hardly can expect a good match."

"What is wrong with my red hair?" Mattie asked.

"It is hardly desirable amongst the *ton*," her sister

responded. "I was most fortunate that I was spared that burden."

Mattie reached up and smoothed back her hair. "My red hair is not a burden. It is the same color as Mother's hair."

"It makes you stand out, and not in a good way," Emma declared.

Mattie pursed her lips as she tried to control the anger that was whirling inside of her. When she was younger, she had been self-conscious about her hair color, but now that she was older, she was grateful that she shared that trait with her mother.

Emma dropped down on the settee in a huff. "I do believe you would make a good match with a widower," she said. "And to do so, you don't need to debut. I am sure that Father could arrange such a thing for you."

Mattie blinked, taken aback by the callous thing her sister had just said to her without a hint of remorse. "You cannot be in earnest."

As her sister was about to respond, a knock came at the door, interrupting their conversation.

Not bothering to wait for Mrs. Watson, Mattie walked over to the door and opened it. A tall, lanky man stood there, holding black gowns in his arms.

"Miss Bawden?" the man asked.

She nodded. "That is me," she replied.

He extended the gowns to her. "The dressmaker asked me to drop these three gowns off for you," he revealed. "She said she would have the rest of the dresses you commissioned in a week or so."

Mattie accepted the gowns, draping them over her arm. "Thank you," she replied before closing the door.

A groan came from behind her. "Do I truly have to wear a black gown?" Emma protested. "It will make me look so drab."

Turning around, Mattie responded, "Yes, you have to wear the gown. We are in mourning for our aunt and uncle."

Emma held her hand out wide. "The things I do for my family," she declared. "At least I can go to the village soon."

"By the way, Lord Winston will be accompanying us," Mattie shared, extending Emma a gown.

Her sister's eyes grew wide. "Lord Winston?" she asked. "When did you speak to him?"

"I spoke to him briefly when I was on my walk," Mattie responded, keeping her response vague. She didn't want to divulge that she had been alone with Winston in the woodlands.

"Perhaps I shall go on a walk with you tomorrow," Emma said. "I hadn't realized Lord Winston was such an early riser."

The thought of Emma going on a walk with her was laughable. Her sister was not one for nature, waking up early or walking, for that matter. Frankly, everything about a morning walk went against her sister's core beliefs

Rather than respond to Emma's ridiculous remark, Mattie suggested, "Why don't you change before Lord Winston arrives?"

"I think I shall," Emma said eagerly.

After Emma hurried up the stairs, Mattie followed at a much more sedate pace. She entered her sister's bedchamber and saw Franny sitting on her bed, staring vacantly at the wall.

"Franny," Mattie said gently, "the dressmaker dropped off our mourning gowns. Would you like me to help you change?"

Franny met her gaze and nodded. "I would like that," she responded in a weak voice.

Mattie stepped forward and helped Franny into her gown. Once dressed, her cousin resumed her seat on the bed, looking lost in thought.

Hoping to break Franny out of her pensive mood, she shared, "We are going to the village today. Would you care to join us?"

Franny opened her mouth to reply, but Emma interrupted. "You don't want to go with us, do you?" she asked. "It will be boring for you."

Mattie shot her sister a frustrated look. "Franny is welcome to come with us."

"But the carriage will be crowded if she comes, especially since Lord Winston is accompanying us," Emma pointed out.

"Regardless, we can make it work," Mattie said, turning her attention back towards her cousin. "It is your decision."

Franny offered her a weak smile. "I think I would like to stay here."

Mattie sat on the edge of the bed. "What if we went on a walk later today?" she suggested. "There is a charming spot in the woodlands where I like to sit on a rock and listen to the stream."

"I think I would like that," Franny said softly.

"Wonderful," Mattie responded.

Emma spoke up. "I will join you, as well," she said. "You never know when you might run into a rich, eligible gentleman."

Mattie rolled her eyes. "I assure you, we will not encounter any eligible gentlemen on our walk."

"Then why go at all?" Emma asked.

Ignoring her sister's question, Mattie smiled at her cousin. "Have you had breakfast yet?"

"Mrs. Watson brought me up a tray," Franny replied, gesturing towards the discarded tray on the dressing table.

Mattie rose. "Well, I should change, but if you decide to accompany us to the village, you are more than welcome."

Franny shook her head. "I won't, but I do thank you."

Emma, who was pulling her hair into a stylish coiffure, said, "We will bring you back some ribbons."

"That is not necessary," Franny responded.

"We insist," Emma declared. "We need to keep your mind off your parents' deaths so you will stop moping around."

Mattie frowned. "Emma, you are being rude," she chided.

"Am I?" Emma asked innocently. "I do not think I am. I am merely stating a fact."

"Well, do try to keep your facts to yourself," Mattie said, her frustration evident.

Franny adjusted the sleeves of her black gown as tears filled her eyes. "I am sorry for moping around."

"You have nothing to apologize for," Mattie rushed to reassure her. "You have the right to grieve your parents as you see fit."

Emma walked over to the dressing table, admiring her reflection in the mirror. "I do think Franny is making a big ado out of nothing. When Mother died, I hardly grieved at all."

Mattie was growing increasingly frustrated by her sister's insensitive remarks. Did she not hear herself speak? "That is because you were five," she stated. "And Father and I protected you the best we could."

"Yes, but grief is a choice, and I chose not to be sad," Emma remarked.

Bringing a hand up to her forehead, Mattie couldn't quite believe that she and Emma were related. They were both so different in every way. Emma was so self-absorbed that she failed to feel any empathy towards others.

In a strained voice, Mattie asked, "Could you not at least show some sympathy towards Franny?"

Emma grew thoughtful, and for the briefest of moments, Mattie thought she might have gotten through to her sister.

"I suppose I can," Emma said as she walked over to Franny and patted her shoulder. "There. There. I'm sorry." Her words were bland, lacking any genuine emotion. It was evident that her sister wasn't putting in much effort.

As Mattie contemplated sending Emma away to a convent, Mrs. Watson appeared at the door. "Lord Winston and his sister, Lady Elodie, have arrived," she announced.

Emma perked up. "Please inform them we will be right down."

Mrs. Watson tipped her head before she left to do Emma's bidding.

Turning back towards Mattie, her sister instructed, "You need to change, and quickly. We do not want to keep Lord Winston waiting."

For once, Mattie and Emma were in agreement. She made quick work of changing into the black gown.

Her sister shot her a concerned look. "We still have time for you to fix your hair."

Mattie reached up to adjust the neat chignon at the base of her neck. "What is wrong with my hair?"

"Nothing," her sister started hesitantly, "but it is rather plain. You should try harder when in the presence of the Lockwood family. They are known for their sophistication, and your current coiffure may give the impression that you are not."

Mattie frowned. "I think I will take my chances," she said as she headed towards the door.

As they headed down the stairs, Emma brushed past Mattie and entered the drawing room first.

Winston and Elodie were standing in the center of the room, engaged in a conversation of their own.

Emma gracefully dropped down into a low curtsy. "Lord Winston. Lady Elodie. Welcome to our humble home," she greeted.

Mattie couldn't help but think that her sister could have a career in the theatre, if she so desired. She curtsied as well, addressing her friends with equal politeness. "My lord. My lady," she said.

Elodie raised an eyebrow. "Why are you being so formal?" she asked. "Is the Prince Regent in attendance?"

Mattie laughed. "I'm sorry, Elodie."

"That is much better," Elodie declared before turning her

attention to Emma. "Miss Emma, I hardly recognized you. It has been too long since we have last met."

Emma's eyes flickered to Lord Winston before settling on Elodie. "Thank you for noticing, my lady. I hope to debut soon, although the exact date is still undecided."

Winston bowed slightly. "It is a pleasure to see you again, Miss Emma. And thank you for allowing me to accompany you and your lovely sister to the village today."

"No, it is *our* pleasure, I assure you," Emma stated as she batted her eyelashes at him.

As Winston's gaze fell upon Mattie, his eyes seemed to search hers, but for what, she could not say. "Miss Bawden," he spoke in his deep baritone voice.

"Lord Winston," she replied.

Elodie approached Mattie and looped arms with her. "The carriage is waiting out front," she informed them. "I wanted to take the coach but Winston was insistent that we take the open carriage."

"The open carriage allows for better views of the countryside," Winston said.

"Yes, but there is a greater chance of swallowing a bug," Elodie declared.

Winston chuckled. "Then I suggest keeping your mouth closed, dear sister."

As they made their way outside, Mattie caught Winston staring at her. But instead of looking away, he winked at her. In that moment, she realized that the feelings she had tried so hard to rid herself of were still there. She cared for Winston, more so than she should.

Chapter Eleven

Winston sat in the open carriage as it traveled towards the village. He gazed out at the passing countryside, feigning interest in the rolling hills and lush green fields, but his true focus was on Mattie. She seemed troubled, her usually bright eyes holding a sorrow that tugged at his heartstrings.

He wanted to say or do something that would offer her some form of comfort. But what could he possibly say to ease her pain?

Winston cleared his throat, drawing Mattie's attention. "I have failed to ask how you are faring." There. That was safe.

Mattie offered him a weak smile. "I am well. Thank you for asking."

"You mentioned your cousin was struggling," he continued. "How is she handling the passing of her parents?"

Before Mattie could answer, her sister, Miss Emma, interjected, "Franny is moping about, making everything about her."

Winston lifted his brow, taken aback by Miss Emma's insensitivity. "Surely she has every right to mourn their loss," he pointed out gently.

Miss Emma blinked, as if the thought hadn't occurred to

her. "Well, yes, of course. I just meant that I don't know how to help her. And I want to," she rushed out. "I even suggested going on a walk later today to help ease her pain."

Mattie turned towards her sister. "You did?"

"Yes, and Franny was receptive to the idea," Miss Emma said. "You are welcome to join us, my lord." She batted her eyelashes at him.

Winston was many things, but he was not a fool. He could see through Miss Emma's façade, knowing she cared more for herself than others. It was a common theme amongst women in high Society. It was one of the reasons why he avoided social events in London.

But Mattie was not like that. He could see it in her expressions, hear it in her voice, how deeply she cared about others. She was not like any young woman he had ever met. Even when they were at odds, she couldn't hide her caring nature.

Knowing that Miss Emma was still waiting for a response, he replied, "You are most kind to invite me along, but I'm afraid I have work that I must see to this afternoon."

Miss Emma's disappointment was evident in the frown that appeared on her lips. "Perhaps some other time then," she muttered.

Taking a moment to observe Miss Emma, Winston noted that he had little doubt she would stand out in the marriage mart when she debuted. With her blonde hair, blue eyes, and fair complexion, she fit the mold of what was considered beautiful by the *ton*. Yet, he was more partial to red hair.

Sitting next to him in the carriage, Elodie started swatting in the air. "Good heavens, did you see that?" she asked. "A bug nearly attacked me."

He chuckled at his sister's exaggeration. "I did not see such a thing."

"The bug was huge, probably the biggest I have ever seen, and it was going straight for my mouth," his sister declared with a shiver of disgust.

"And why would it do that?" he asked.

Elodie shrugged. "Perhaps the bug had a death wish," she retorted. "I cannot explain the thoughts of an enormous bug."

"Or maybe it was looking for some shade from this relentless sun?" Winston teased.

"In my mouth?!" Elodie asked. "If that is the case, it is not the smartest bug and most likely won't last much longer."

Winston smirked. "I do not think bugs are particularly intelligent. Not like you, Sister."

Elodie shook her head. "You may jest, but wait until you swallow a bug," she said. "Then you will change your tune."

"Some people consider eating bugs a delicacy," Winston pointed out.

Miss Emma spoke up. "That is rather a disgusting thought," she stated. "I would never eat a bug. Frankly, I would rather die first."

Winston exchanged a glance with Mattie and he could see the amusement in her eyes. "That is a shame because our cook was going to prepare a plate full of bugs for supper tonight," Mattie joked.

"That is hardly funny," Miss Emma declared, her chin jutting in the air.

If Winston needed further proof that Miss Emma would fit well into high Society, her pretentious attitude confirmed it.

Elodie swatted at the air again. "Good heavens, the bugs are everywhere," she exclaimed. "This wouldn't have been an issue if we had taken the coach, as I suggested."

Winston nudged her shoulder playfully. "Yes, but then we wouldn't have been able to admire the beautiful countryside."

"It is beautiful," Mattie remarked as she turned her gaze back to the rolling green hills. The sound of sheep bleating could be heard in the distance, adding to the picturesque scene. "May I ask where your sheep farm is located?"

He pointed towards the horizon, a smile spreading across

his face. "In the next county over," he replied. "It isn't too far away from Brockhall Manor by coach."

"When do I get to see your sheep farm?" Elodie asked eagerly.

"Whenever you would like," Winston replied. "I should note that there is a small cottage on the property, but it leaks when it rains."

Elodie smiled. "Sounds charming."

Winston's chest swelled with pride. "But the land where the cottage sits and the sheep graze all belongs to me," he shared. "I love nothing more than sitting on the porch and watching the sunrise."

"That sounds rather perfect to me," Mattie said wistfully, meeting his gaze.

"It is," he replied softly.

Hearing the sound of approval in Mattie's voice made him realize how much he longed to share that moment with her. Alone. With no one else.

Winston turned his head towards the countryside as he tried to quell his wayward thoughts. Why was he even thinking about such things? He and Mattie were just friends. Which was rather impressive, considering their tumultuous past. And he didn't want to do anything to jeopardize what they had.

As the village came into view, Miss Emma perked up. "I have not been to the village in ages," she declared. "I do hope the shops will have an array of ribbons for me to look at."

"You can look, but I think it would be best if you only selected dark colors," Mattie suggested. "We are, after all, in mourning."

Miss Emma glanced down at her black gown with disdain. "Do not remind me," she muttered. "I look awful in black."

"Mourning is not for our sake, but to keep the memory alive of the deceased," Elodie remarked.

"But no one here knew my aunt and uncle," Miss Emma protested.

"Your cousin did," Winston pointed out.

Miss Emma pursed her lips together, clearly not pleased with this reminder. "Yes, well, there is that," she said flatly. "And I suppose my father is grieving the loss of his brother."

Silence descended over the group as they rolled into the village. The carriage glided to a stop in front of a shop and Winston stepped down onto the cobblestone pavement. He reached his hand back to assist the ladies out of the carriage.

As Miss Emma exited the coach, she gripped his hand tightly, flashing him a coy smile. "Thank you, my lord."

Winston worked to keep the emotions off his face. Miss Emma was far too young and naive to understand how inappropriate her behavior was. She wasn't even out of the schoolroom yet. Did she truly not understand how inappropriate it was for her to flirt when she was in mourning? He was beginning to see what Mattie had been dealing with all along.

But as he assisted Mattie out of the coach, her hand slipped into his and she thanked him with genuine gratitude. Her touch was gentle and demure, a stark contrast to Miss Emma's brazen advances. And in that moment, Winston felt more drawn to Mattie than ever before. He pushed aside his thoughts and released her hand, pretending that her touch had no effect on him. Or his heart.

Botheration.

This would not do. He had been down this path before and it only led to heartache.

Elodie's voice cut through his musings. "The cobblestone pattern is rather interesting, is it not?" she asked, a hint of amusement in her voice.

Winston lifted his gaze. "My apologies. I was lost in thought."

"About the cobblestones?" she asked. "Because, if so, your thoughts must be incredibly dull."

He grinned. "No, I was not thinking about the cobblestone."

"Good," Elodie replied. "Because we do not want you getting trampled by a horse while admiring the ones in the street."

"You are a delight, Sister," he remarked.

Elodie beamed. "I know."

Offering his arm, Winston asked, "May I escort you inside the shop?"

"Thank you," Elodie replied, taking his arm. "I think I shall purchase a fan to keep the bugs away from me on the journey home."

"You seem to be the only one bothered by bugs," he commented.

Elodie shrugged. "Perhaps, or maybe you were too distracted by Mattie to notice them."

Winston stiffened at the mention of Mattie's name. "I do not know what you are referring to."

His sister simply patted his sleeve. "It is all right, but I would refrain from staring at her too much. But that is just me. You can do as you please."

Not liking where this conversation was headed, Winston dropped his arm and reached for the door to the shop. He held it open for Elodie and followed her inside, feeling out of place among the hats, ribbons and fans on display.

As he glanced towards the door, considering making a quick exit, Mattie caught his eyes from near the ribbons and smiled. And just like that, he decided to stay.

Winston approached her and saw that she was fingering some black ribbons. "Those are some fine-looking ribbons," he remarked.

Mattie gave him an amused look. "Do you know much about different types of ribbons?"

"I'm afraid not, and quite frankly, I do not care," Winston replied.

The Gentleman's Miscalculation

"Then I won't bore you with the details, my lord." Mattie lowered her voice as she turned towards him. "We shouldn't be here. We are in mourning."

Winston resisted the urge to reach out and offer a comforting touch. This was not the place to do so. "But you are here, and you might as well make the most of it."

Mattie turned her attention towards her sister, who was browsing through brightly colored ribbons, despite being in mourning attire. "I do not know what to do with my sister. She is balking at mourning and has been rather insensitive towards Franny."

"Miss Emma is young," he attempted.

"That is no excuse for her callous actions," Mattie sighed. "I should try to speak to my father about this."

Winston grew thoughtful. "Do you think that will improve the situation?"

Mattie winced. "It can't hurt to try."

Miss Emma approached them with a bright pink ribbon in her hand. "This would be perfect for my hair," she declared.

"Emma…" Mattie started.

Lowering the ribbon to the table, Miss Emma responded defensively, "I won't be in mourning forever, Mattie." She lifted her chin and walked away in a huff.

Mattie pressed her lips together before asking, "Would you like another sister?"

Winston couldn't help but chuckle at the suggestion. "I can barely handle the two sisters that I have," he joked.

"Pity," Mattie murmured.

Hoping to make Mattie smile, Winston reached for a dark gray ribbon that was lying on a nearby table. He held it up and inspected it closely. "Now this," he said with exaggerated seriousness, "is truly a magnificent piece of ribbon. It is straight and the color is superb."

Mattie's lips twitched. "Well, then, I simply must have it," she declared.

"Allow me the honor of purchasing it for you, Mattie," Winston replied with a flourish of his hand.

His efforts were rewarded when she smiled, lighting up her entire face. He would daresay that he had never seen anything so beautiful before.

With a deep breath, Mattie stood outside of her father's study. She had been rehearsing in her head what she intended to say, knowing it would be a difficult conversation with no guarantee of how her father would react. Would he be supportive of her or take Emma's side—just as he always did?

The door swung open, interrupting her thoughts, and her father stood there with a furrowed brow. "Mattie? Why are you standing outside of my study?" he asked.

"I needed to speak to you," Mattie responded.

Her father took a step back and motioned for her to take a seat in one of the worn leather chairs. "Please come in," he said. "I was planning on visiting the Wilcox family, but it can wait a few moments."

Mattie sat rigidly in her seat, trying to calm her nerves. This was ridiculous. Why should she be nervous about speaking the truth? She would just say what needed to be said and be done with it.

"I want to speak to you about Emma," Mattie began.

Her father frowned before he closed the door. "I expected as much," he said, settling into his chair. "What is it that you wish to discuss?"

There were so many things she wanted to address, but she decided to start with the most pressing matter. "Emma is being rather vocal about going into mourning," Mattie explained. "And she isn't being very compassionate towards Franny."

"This does not surprise me in the least," her father remarked. "Emma has never been as tender-hearted as you."

Mattie sank back into her chair. "Furthermore, I caught her flirting shamelessly with Lord Winston on our outing to the village."

Her father's expression turned disapproving at this revelation. "I do believe that Emma is determined to grow up far too quickly."

"What should we do?" Mattie asked, feeling at a loss.

To her dismay, her father only shrugged. "This is precisely why I did not want you to have a Season this year. You are needed at home to tend to Emma."

"Emma doesn't need a nursemaid," Mattie insisted. "And I do believe she will balk at hiring a governess for her."

"Then what can we do to help her?" her father asked.

Mattie let out a deep breath. "I was hoping you would know," she replied. "But I do believe that we have both coddled her for far too long. She has become rather self-absorbed."

Her father rubbed his temples wearily. "If only Emma could be more like you. You have grown into such a fine young woman."

"Thank you," Mattie said, brushing the compliment aside. "Emma even had the audacity to suggest that I forgo next Season in favor of her debuting."

Dropping his hand to his side, her father responded, "She said something similar to me. I tried to talk her out of it."

"Well, it didn't work, because she thinks it is a solution to all of her problems," Mattie muttered as she tried to keep the anger out of her voice. Emma had been so rude to her, and insulted her, left and right. But the worst part was that Emma had no idea—or she did not care—about the pain she inflicted on other people.

Her father turned his attention towards the open window.

"What would your mother have done?" he asked, almost to himself.

"I was considering sending Emma off to a convent," Mattie joked half-heartedly.

A soft chuckle escaped from her father's lips. "I do not think that would solve anything."

Mattie grew serious. "I was thinking we could move Franny into my bedchamber," she said.

"But your room is the smallest."

"I doubt that Emma will switch rooms with me, making it a moot point," Mattie remarked. "But I grow tired of the jabs she makes at Franny about how she should be over her grief."

Her father's gaze met hers and his eyes looked tired. Defeated. "Your mother would have known how to help Emma," he said with a wistful tone.

"Mother is not here, but you are," Mattie stated firmly. "Emma needs a stern reminder of how to behave."

"I have never been one to issue a stern rebuke, at least to my daughters," her father admitted with a sigh. "But I do not share the same reservations for my congregation."

There was a moment of strained silence as Mattie mustered up the courage to voice her next thought. "I was hoping you might reconsider Lady Dallington hosting me for a Season."

Her father huffed. "Surely you cannot be serious?" he asked, sounding exasperated. "With everything we have discussed, you are needed more at home than ever."

"No," she said adamantly, shaking her head. "I do not think I can change Emma's behavior. And I need to live my own life."

"You will have your chance next Season," her father asserted.

"Father…" Mattie started to protest.

Her father raised his hand, silencing her words. "I thought we had agreed that this was what was best for you."

Mattie's jaw dropped in disbelief. "You are wrong! This is what is best for *you*," she declared, her voice rising in frustration.

"Mattie, you are being unreasonable," her father scolded.

"I am one and twenty years old and I want to have a Season before the *ton* declares me a spinster," Mattie argued, her frustration bubbling over.

"You are hardly a spinster," her father countered.

Mattie stood up from her seat, unable to contain her emotions any longer. "Young women are presented at Court as young as seven and ten years old. I am competing against people that are four years younger than me," she exclaimed.

Her father leaned back in his seat and looked up at her. "There are plenty of widowers or older gentlemen that are looking for a mature young woman, such as yourself."

Her eyes grew wide in shock. "Pardon?" How could her father have said something so insulting to her? Did he even know how hurtful it was to her?

He must have had some inkling that he had hurt her because his next words were much gentler. "Let us not argue about this," he said calmly. "I am in no rush for you to wed, and you shouldn't be either."

A thought occurred to her, one that she hoped wasn't true. "You don't want me to get married, do you?"

Her father lifted his brow. "Of course I want you to marry, but in due time. I need your help with Emma."

"This has always been about Emma, not me," Mattie said sadly, the weight of realization pressing heavily on her shoulders. "Her needs—and her wants—will always come before mine."

"Mattie…"

She walked over to the door and opened it. "You have been wrong to do so, Father," she remarked before leaving the study, feeling both frustrated and resigned.

As she walked away, she heard her father let out a deep

sigh. The sound was heavy and filled with disappointment, causing Mattie's heart to ache. She hoped he realized how unfair of a position he had placed her in. She was not her sister's keeper, yet she was being forced to bear the responsibility. Yes, she had helped raise Emma, but that didn't give her father the right to cast her aside.

Mattie headed out the cottage door and found herself walking towards Brockhall Manor. Her mind was in turmoil and she found herself needing a friend more than anything right now. Someone who would sympathize with her and offer comfort.

Brockhall Manor loomed in the distance when Isaac stepped out from behind a cluster of trees. Mattie glanced over her shoulder and saw Grady a short distance away, keeping a watchful eye over her. She felt grateful for his presence, and she felt safe from Isaac.

Isaac approached her but stopped short. "Your father was wrong to treat you in such a fashion," he said, his words gentle and understanding.

"How exactly did you overhear my conversation?" she demanded.

"If you wanted the conversation to remain private, you should have closed the window," Isaac chided.

Mattie rolled her eyes and continued walking towards Brockhall Manor. Isaac stayed behind her but continued to follow her across the field.

"Your father does not do you justice," Isaac said. "You are far too beautiful to be forced into a marriage with a widower."

"That is none of your concern," Mattie replied sharply, speaking over her shoulder. She wasn't about to have this conversation with Isaac, especially knowing what she knew about him.

Isaac didn't seem deterred by her dismissive remarks. "If you were my daughter, I would have shown you off to everyone."

"That is disturbing, and I would prefer it if you did not speak to me," Mattie asserted.

Isaac came to a stop and shouted, "I have a proposition for you."

"I am not interested in hearing what you have to say," Mattie exclaimed as Brockhall Manor stood before her.

Mattie hurried towards the main door and knocked. The door was promptly opened and White greeted her. "Good afternoon, Miss Bawden," he said, standing to the side. "Please come in."

"Thank you," Mattie acknowledged as she stepped into the grand entry hall. "I was hoping to speak to Lady Dallington."

That was not entirely true, but she didn't dare admit that she actually wished to talk to Winston. It was not proper for ladies to call upon gentlemen, no matter the reason.

However, it appeared that luck was on her side. Winston's voice echoed through the corridor as he approached her. "What a pleasant surprise," he said with a smile.

She offered him a brief smile in return. "I am here to call upon your mother."

Again, with a lie. But she didn't dare tell him the truth.

He eyed her curiously. "Is something wrong?" he asked with genuine concern in his voice.

Mattie pressed her lips together, struggling to hold back tears. "My father said some terrible things and then Isaac propositioned me…"

"*What?!*" he exclaimed, his voice filled with shock and anger. "He propositioned you?"

Realizing how her words could be misconstrued, Mattie quickly put her hand up in a calming gesture. "No, I misspoke," she corrected herself. "Isaac said he had a proposition for me."

"I'm not sure if that is any better," Winston stated, his expression darkening.

"I walked away from him and I didn't hear him out," Mattie informed him.

Winston bobbed his head in approval. "That pleases me since no good will come out of associating with Isaac. I can promise you that." He pursed his lips, and there was a terseness in his next words. "I do not like the fact that Isaac was able to approach you so easily. Where in the blazes was Grady when this conversation took place?"

"Grady was watching over me from a short distance away," she explained.

"Not well enough, if you ask me," Winston asserted. "His job is to keep you safe, not allow you to make chit-chat with the enemy."

Mattie offered him a reassuring smile. "I was never in any true danger. Isaac was just making a nuisance of himself, and I had no doubt that Grady would have interceded if necessary."

Her words seemed to appease Winston and his eyes filled with compassion, making Mattie feel at ease. "Now, dare I ask what terrible things your father said to you?"

In a tentative voice, Mattie revealed, "He seems to believe that if I marry, it will be to a widower or an older gentleman that wishes for a more mature woman. And it is not just my father who believes that. Emma also said something similar."

With a disbelieving expression, Winston declared, "What utter nonsense! You are a beautiful young woman and I have no doubt you will have countless suitors vying for your hand this Season."

"You are kind, but we both know that is unlikely," Mattie said with a sad smile.

"Why do you think that way?"

Mattie hesitated, not wanting to admit her insecurities. But with a deep breath, she mustered the courage to speak her truth. "Emma is the undeniable beauty in our family, and I have come to accept that."

Winston took a step closer to her, causing her to tilt her head back to meet his gaze. "We may have been adversaries over the years, but never once did I see you as anything less than beautiful."

She stared up at him, her heart beating faster in her chest at his close proximity. Could he truly mean what he was saying?

He reached out and gently brushed a stray lock of hair behind her ear, his touch sending shivers down her spine. "You are, and always have been, the most intriguing young woman in any room," he said in a hoarse voice. "That is why I will take you as you are—a friend and a worthy opponent."

Mattie managed to piece together the only words she could muster up. "Thank you." At least she hoped she said those words. But he was looking at her in such a way that made her question everything.

Lady Dallington's voice interrupted them from behind. "Mattie," she exclaimed in a loud voice, far louder than what was necessary.

Winston took a step back and bowed. "Miss Bawden, as always, it has been a pleasure," he said before turning and walking away.

"Shall we adjourn to the drawing room for some tea?" Lady Dallington asked.

Mattie forced a smile, her mind still reeling from Winston's words and touch. "Tea would be lovely," she replied. But as she followed Lady Dallington into the drawing room, all she could think about was Winston and how his touch still lingered on her skin.

Chapter Twelve

Winston stepped out onto the veranda and started muttering curse words under his breath. He couldn't believe he had let down his guard and shown vulnerability to Mattie. She was undeniably the most beautiful young woman he had ever known, but now he regretted exposing his feelings to her.

For a man that prided himself on staying composed under pressure, he sure had made a muck of things. What if Mattie expected something from him in return? He had no desire to pursue her. He had already laid his heart bare to her and she had trampled on it. No, he would not go down that path again… for any reason.

When he had touched her, his heart reminded him that a part of Mattie still lingered there.

"Botheration!" he muttered in frustration. He needed to regain control of his thoughts and actions before it was too late. This was a game that he couldn't afford to lose.

The sound of Melody's amused voice broke through his thoughts. "Is everything all right, Brother?" she asked.

Winston turned to see Melody sitting on a nearby bench, stroking Matilda with gentle motions.

"Everything is fine," Winston said, keeping his face expressionless.

But Melody didn't seem convinced. "So it is a common occurrence for you to be muttering under your breath in the gardens?" she asked.

He should have known that Melody would see through that lie. It wasn't even a good one. "I was just merely thinking things through," he attempted to explain.

"Anything you'd wish to share?" Melody inquired with a playful smile. "Matilda and I are excellent listeners."

Winston frowned, not wanting to admit his inner turmoil to anyone, let alone a goat. "I do not understand why everyone indulges that blasted animal," he grumbled. "Matilda has no right to claim a bench as her own."

Melody quickly covered Matilda's ears. "Don't let her hear you say that," she joked.

He made his way over to his sister and asked, "May I sit?"

"I don't know why you are asking me," Melody teased. "This is Matilda's bench and she is kindly allowing me to sit here."

Winston gently moved Matilda aside before taking a seat on the bench. "I hate goats," he mumbled.

"I know, and cats," Melody responded. "But you do like sheep."

"That I do," Winston said. "Sheep are far more docile than goats, especially Matilda."

Melody laughed. "Matilda is a special kind of goat."

In response, Matilda let out a loud bleat, almost as if she understood the conversation they were having.

"Now what has you so troubled?" Melody inquired with genuine concern etched onto her features.

Winston turned away from her, his jaw clenched. "I do not wish to talk about it."

Melody shrugged. "I must assume it is about our mutual redheaded friend, then."

Winston shook his head. "Why must you assume such a thing?" he asked. "There are many things that could be troubling me at this precise moment."

"Very well," Melody said. "Forget I asked."

"I will," Winston grumbled through gritted teeth.

"Good," Melody declared with finality.

As they sat in uncomfortable silence, Winston couldn't help but notice the gentle breeze ruffling through his hair. He glanced back at the manor and wondered how Mattie was faring after the terrible words her father had spoken to her. Did he not see how beguiling his own daughter was?

Melody followed his gaze and suggested, "You could always go inside and speak to her."

Winston knew precisely who Melody was speaking about, but he didn't dare reveal that he had been thinking of Mattie this whole time. "Who?"

"You know, the tall, redheaded young woman who can beat you soundly at pall-mall," Melody stated matter-of-factly.

"I know who Mattie is," he muttered.

"Do you?" Melody challenged, raising an eyebrow. "Because I suspect she is inside the manor, which is why you are out here in the gardens with me and Matilda."

Winston met his sister's gaze. "I came to spend time with you."

"Liar," Melody retorted, her voice laced with amusement. "For someone who is such a successful barrister, I would think that you could lie better."

"I don't lie. I outwit my opponent," Winston defended.

Melody regarded him thoughtfully for a moment before finally asking, "Can we please skip this game and you just tell me what is truly bothering you?"

Winston had a choice. He could walk away and ignore his sister's question. Or he could tell her the truth and hope she could provide some additional insight on the matter. Coming to his decision, he shared, "Mattie's father implied that she would likely marry a man that wants a mature woman, such as a widower."

"And you disagree because you wish to marry her?" Melody pressed.

He reared back. "Of course not!" he protested. "I have no designs on Mattie."

Melody's lips twitched. "My apologies," she said with a mischievous glint in her eyes. "I spoke out of turn."

"You did," Winston declared. "It baffles me how Lord Wythburn is so oblivious where Mattie is concerned."

"Does it now?" Melody asked coyly.

Winston looked heavenward. "I don't know why I try to talk to you," he said. "You seem to have concocted an entirely false scenario in your head about Mattie and me."

Melody laughed. "It is fascinating to me that you cannot see what is right in front of you."

He shifted uncomfortably in his seat, feeling exposed under Melody's scrutiny. He decided it was best if they changed subjects and steered the conversation away from himself. "I would much rather speak about you."

"Why?" Melody asked, tilting her head slightly. "I assure you that I am not that interesting."

"I disagree," he countered.

Melody glanced down at Matilda, running her hand through the goat's fur as she spoke. "I suppose I have been reading a lot as of late, resigning myself to the fact that I will inevitably have to get married."

Winston could hear an undeniable sadness in her voice and it concerned him. "Do you not wish to marry?" he asked gently.

"Oh, I do," Melody rushed to respond. "But when I do get married, I will have to give up a part of myself."

"Not if you find the right one," Winston argued.

Melody offered him a weak smile. "It is not that simple,

I'm afraid," she said with a hint of resignation in her voice. "What I do, how I occupy my time, will fall under scrutiny."

Winston lifted his brow. "Now I am curious as what you do to occupy your time."

"The usual pursuits, I suppose," Melody remarked dismissively. The way she spoke her words made him think there was so much more to it. It caused Winston to wonder what she was truly passionate about. But was it fair of him to press her when she clearly did not want to talk about such things?

Their conversation was interrupted by a footman coming to a stop in front of them and bowing. "My lord, your father wishes to speak to you in his study," he announced.

Winston tipped his head in acknowledgement before he stood up. "I shouldn't keep Father waiting."

Melody placed a hand on her forehead, shielding her eyes from the sun. "Will you promise me one thing?"

"Depends on what it is," Winston replied cautiously.

"There are cracks in everything, but you mustn't let it distract you from the beauty of it all," Melody remarked. "But I want you to promise me that you will chase after the happiness that you truly deserve."

Winston didn't deserve to be happy, but he didn't want to tell his sister that. She wouldn't understand what he had been through, what he had done. No, he couldn't burden her with his troubles. "All I can promise is that I will try… for now," he said.

"Very well," Melody responded, lowering her hand. "It is time for me to return to the library. I have a book waiting for me."

"Anything of note?" he asked in an attempt to lighten the mood.

Melody gently moved Matilda from her lap before she rose. "Not particularly," she replied. "It is just one of the many Russian novels I have been reading."

Winston's brows knitted. "You speak Russian?"

"It is just one of the many things you do not know about me, Brother," Melody said playfully.

As they walked towards the manor, Winston couldn't seem to let the matter drop. "Russian? Truly?" he asked incredulously.

"Elodie speaks a little Russian as well," Melody revealed. "Perhaps if you came out of your room more often you would have learned that about us."

"Does Father know?"

Melody shook her head. "Good heavens, no!" she exclaimed. "He would lecture us about how it isn't proper to know such an uncouth language."

"It is not an uncouth language," Winston said.

"Not according to Father," Melody pointed out.

A footman opened the door and they stepped inside. Once they reached the study, Winston said, "Enjoy reading."

"I always do," Melody replied before she continued down the corridor.

Winston stepped into the study and saw his father was hunched over his desk, reviewing a ledger. "You wished to see me, Father?"

His father looked up and adjusted the spectacles on his nose. "Yes, do come in," he encouraged, gesturing to a chair in front of the desk. "I spoke to Mr. Halverson about Isaac."

Now his father had his attention. "What did he say?" he asked, walking closer to the desk.

"Isaac is indeed one of our tenants," his father began, tapping a finger on the open page of the ledger, "and it is within our rights to evict him."

"How did he manage such a feat?"

His father leaned back in his seat, his expression grim. "Isaac approached Mr. Halverson about renting the Stewarts' old cottage and he drew up a contract. It was all aboveboard," he replied. He paused and let out a heavy sigh. "Which is why

Mr. Halverson does not recommend evicting Isaac just yet, citing the same issues that I had brought up previously."

Winston felt frustration whirling within him. "So that's it?" he asked, clenching his fists at his sides. "We just sit back and let Isaac remain underfoot."

"It is only a matter of time until Isaac gives up and goes home," his father replied calmly.

"But he is harassing Miss Bawden," Winston shouted, his voice cracking with emotion.

His father removed his spectacles off his nose and looked at Winston with a steely gaze. "Isaac is making a nuisance of himself, but that is all he is. A nuisance. He holds no power over us. It is a game that he will lose, especially since I have no intention of handing my sister or her son over to him."

Winston's frustration turned to worry as he paced back and forth in front of the desk. "And what if he gets desperate?" he asked, his voice strained.

"What is Isaac going to do?" his father asked, his voice laced with confidence. "He can't get to us, not with all of our servants here, and you have a Bow Street Runner watching over Miss Bawden and her family."

Despite his father's reassurances, Winston couldn't shake off a feeling of unease that had settled deep within him. Something about Isaac's relentless pursuit of Miss Bawden unnerved him, and as a barrister, he knew all too well the lengths people would go for wealth and power.

"It will be all right, Son," his father said.

Winston stopped pacing and turned to face his father. "I do not share the same confidences as you do."

With that, Winston left the study, determined to do whatever it would take to keep Mattie safe from Isaac. But at that precise moment, he was unsure of what exactly that would entail.

Mattie sat in the drawing room as she listened to Lady Dallington's words of comfort. She knew her ladyship meant well, but her thoughts kept drifting towards her last conversation with Winston. He had called her beautiful, which was something no one else had ever said to her before.

And she had believed him.

Good heavens, what was she thinking? She couldn't be fooled by him again. He was the one who had kissed her and then treated her with only contempt afterwards. It was evident that he had regretted their kiss.

But she hadn't.

Interrupting her thoughts, Lady Dallington's gentle voice brought her back to the present. "Are you even listening to me, Dear?" she asked.

Mattie lowered the teacup and saucer to her lap. "I apologize but I was woolgathering."

Lady Dallington gave her a small smile. "A terrible habit for a lady of genteel breeding, but I do understand given your circumstances. I was simply suggesting that I could always speak to your father on your behalf."

Mattie shook her head firmly. "No, my father is stubborn and I doubt he would appreciate me seeking your help."

With compassion in her eyes, Lady Dallington replied, "Your father is a good man, but perhaps he is just overwhelmed with his responsibilities."

"But he is jeopardizing my future," Mattie stated with frustration.

"I don't think he sees it that way," Lady Dallington argued. "And as for you marrying an older man, that is rubbish. One and twenty years is hardly considered a spinster."

Mattie leaned forward and placed her cup onto the table.

"What am I to do?" she asked. "I cannot bear the thought of waiting another Season to make my debut."

"Would it be so awful if you waited?" Lady Dallington questioned.

Frowning, Mattie asked, "You are siding with my father?"

Lady Dallington quickly waved her hand in front of her. "Goodness, no. I am just merely attempting to play devil's advocate."

"I just feel so alone at home," Mattie admitted. "My father has always been far too busy to even notice me, and as for Emma…" She struggled to find the right words. "Emma is just Emma."

"There is no need to explain yourself," Lady Dallington reassured her. "But I hope you can find solace here with us."

Mattie nodded. "I do, which is why I come so often."

"And you are always welcome," Lady Dallington said kindly. "You are family to us, and as much a part of Brockhall Manor as anyone else."

"Thank you," Mattie murmured, touched by the genuine warmth and acceptance of Lady Dallington.

Just then, Melody entered the room with a bright smile. "Mattie, what a pleasant surprise," she greeted, taking a seat next to her mother on the settee. "What brings you by today?"

Mattie let out a sigh, her shoulders slumping in defeat. "My father is refusing to let your mother host me for this Season. He wants me at home so I can tend to Emma," she explained, her tone heavy with disappointment.

"That seems like an utter waste of time to me," Melody remarked. "After all, isn't Emma nearly seven and ten years old now?"

"She is," Mattie confirmed. "Her birthday is next month."

Melody reached for the teapot and poured herself a cup of tea. "You could always hand Emma a mirror and she wouldn't even notice you were gone," she joked.

Lady Dallington gave her daughter a reproachful look. "Melody, that was not very kind of you to say."

But Melody shrugged it off. "I was merely speaking the truth," she said, sipping her tea.

Mattie chimed in, "Melody isn't wrong."

Lady Dallington shook her head disapprovingly at both of them. "Regardless, we do not speak ill of others."

Melody smirked. "Very well, but I couldn't help but notice that you didn't disagree with me either, Mother."

"Emma is young and we need to show her compassion," Lady Dallington said. "Can we discuss something else now?"

A sly grin came to Melody's face. "I had a thought. What if we smuggled Mattie in our trunks when we travel to Town for the Season? No one would be the wiser."

Mattie laughed. "That plan is positively ingenious!"

Lady Dallington looked heavenward, but her words were light. "Why do my children insist on coming up with ludicrous ideas?"

"It is far easier than thinking up something practical," Melody quipped.

"Lord Wythburn is a rational man, and I have no doubt that he will come around to our way of thinking soon enough," Lady Dallington said.

Mattie did not share the same hopeful outlook as Lady Dallington. "I do not think that is the case."

Lady Dallington's smile only seemed to widen at Mattie's skepticism. "Oh, ye of little faith," she said. "What if Winston speaks to your father? If anyone can convince him to give you a Season, it is him."

Melody nodded in agreement. "Winston is relentless when it comes to debating. He will surely persuade your father."

Mattie bit her lower lip. "Do you think Winston will agree to such a thing?"

"You leave Winston to me," Lady Dallington responded,

amusement in her voice. "Who do you think taught Winston the art of debate?"

A deep chuckle came from the doorway, causing Mattie to turn her head. She knew immediately who it belonged to—Winston. His laugh was so familiar to her.

Winston walked further into the room. "I would be happy to speak to Lord Wythburn." He turned to face her, his gaze piercing. "Assuming Miss Bawden is in agreement."

Mattie hesitated, unsure of how to respond. On one hand, she wanted Winston's help in convincing her father to let her have a Season this year rather than wait. But on the other hand, she feared that her stubborn father might buckle down even more.

But, then again, what did she have to lose?

Taking a deep breath, she found the courage to speak. "Yes, I would like you to speak to my father."

"Then it is settled," Winston said.

Mattie had a thought. "Perhaps," she started slowly, "you could join my family for dinner and speak to my father afterwards over a glass of port."

Winston considered her proposal before nodding once more. "Shall we do so tonight?"

Rising, Mattie replied, "Yes, that would work nicely. I should go and inform our cook at once."

Winston put his hand up. "Wait," he urged. "Allow me to call a carriage for you."

"That won't be necessary. I do not mind walking," Mattie responded.

"I insist," Winston said firmly.

Mattie cocked her head. "I do not understand your insistence, my lord, considering I walked here earlier."

Winston's expression grew solemn. "I have decided it would be best for you to err on the side of caution, especially with Isaac lurking about."

"But Grady is already ensuring my safety," Mattie argued.

"This is not up for debate," Winston declared.

Mattie's brow shot up. "I beg your pardon?" she asked. "You are not my keeper, my lord."

In a soft voice, Lady Dallington whispered, "Oh, dear."

Winston took a step towards her. "No, I am not your keeper, Miss Bawden. But I have made it my duty to keep you safe, and if that means you are inconvenienced for a short time, then so be it."

Despite her annoyance at being told what to do by him, a small part of Mattie appreciated his concern for her wellbeing. However, a much larger part of her resented being ordered around.

Turning to face Lady Dallington and Melody, Mattie forced her voice to remain calm. "Thank you both for the lovely chat," she said, curtsying before them. "But I must take my leave before I lose control of my sharp tongue."

Mattie shifted her gaze to Winston and continued, "Thank you for your concern, but I believe I shall walk home now."

"Miss Bawden…" Winston started.

Not wanting to hear whatever excuse or argument he had prepared, Mattie headed towards the entry hall. Just as she was about to walk out the door, Winston gently grabbed her arm and turned her around to face him.

His eyes were sparking with fury. "Did you not hear me, Mattie?" he asked. "It is not safe for you to be wandering around these fields by yourself."

Mattie stood her ground, meeting his gaze with unwavering determination. "I am not 'by myself.' Grady is watching over me," she argued, her voice laced with defiance.

"That isn't enough!" Winston shouted, dropping his arm to his side. "Not any longer. Isaac is playing a game and is dangerous." He turned towards the butler. "Bring a coach around for Miss Bawden, at once."

White tipped his head in understanding before promptly departing from the entry hall.

Mattie placed a hand on her hip as she tried to keep her voice steady. "I am not yours to control," she said. "If I wish to walk home, then so be it."

"Why are you being so obstinate about this?" Winston demanded, his voice rising in exasperation.

"Perhaps it has something to do with you *telling* me what to do," Mattie countered. "You have no right to dictate my actions."

Winston took a step closer to her, causing her to tilt her head to meet his gaze. "I am only trying to keep you safe," he explained.

Mattie huffed. "By ordering me about?" she retorted.

"That was not my intention," Winston assured her. "I simply cannot bear the thought of you getting hurt, especially through no fault of your own."

Some of the fight drained out of Mattie as she listened to Winston's heartfelt words. But that still didn't excuse his behavior. She was so tired of people deciding what was best for her. Her father did it. And now Winston.

"You could have at least talked to me about it first," Mattie said.

Winston bobbed his head in agreement. "You are right," he admitted. "I was wrong to act so brashly, and I apologize."

A small smile tugged at the corners of Mattie's lips. "Is this the first time you have ever apologized to me?" she asked, unable to resist teasing him.

"Do not make this into a big deal, I beg of you," Winston pleaded, his dark brows furrowing in mock irritation.

"Oh, but I think it is a rather significant moment," Mattie said, her smile widening. "I have been waiting for an apology from you since you knocked me into the river all those years ago."

Winston looked heavenward. "That was nearly ten years ago. You really need to let that go."

Mattie couldn't help but laugh at his words. "I should go

home and write about this in my journal," she said. "My posterity deserves to know about this exact moment."

"You are rather impossible to be friends with," Winston muttered, but there was a hint of playfulness in his voice.

White appeared once again in the entry hall and announced, "The coach is ready and waiting outside, my lord."

"Thank you," Winston acknowledged before turning back to Mattie with a faint smile on his face. "May I escort you to the coach?"

Mattie accepted his proffered arm. "This seems so unnecessary," she said. "My cottage is only a short distance away."

"Yes, but it will ease my conscience greatly," Winston responded as he led her towards the waiting coach. "I shall see you tonight for dinner."

With a glance at Brockhall Manor, Mattie remarked, "I should warn you that dinner is not as extravagant an affair at my cottage as it is here."

"I assure you that our dinners can get quite lawless when we don't have any guests," Winston said. "Elodie has been known to throw rolls at us."

Mattie giggled. "That does not surprise me in the least."

Winston assisted her into the coach. "Good day, Mattie," he said before stepping back. "I shall see you soon."

The coach rolled forward, and Mattie realized that she was still smiling.

Chapter Thirteen

Winston stood back as the coach carried Mattie away, his heart heavy with conflicting emotions. Every moment spent with Mattie chipped away at his defenses, leaving him vulnerable. And that was a problem. He didn't dare start feeling things for her again. He needed to move on, and that meant a life without Mattie.

From the corner of his eye, Winston noticed Isaac watching the coach, a smirk playing on his lips. It would have been wiser to ignore Isaac, but Winston found himself unable to do so. Acting on impulse, he closed the distance between them.

"You are trespassing," Winston growled, his voice low and threatening.

Isaac feigned innocence, a mocking gleam in his eyes. "Am I? I suppose I just came in for a closer look at Miss Bawden. She is a beautiful young woman, is she not?"

Winston took a commanding step closer to Isaac. "You leave Miss Bawden out of this," he ordered.

"I'm afraid I cannot," Isaac responded. "You have made her a part of this. But if you return my wife and son to me, I will be able to depart, leaving you and Miss Bawden alone."

"I don't have your wife," Winston stated.

Isaac narrowed his eyes. "We both know that is a lie," he spat out. "I was able to confirm that Sarah is not residing at Brockhall Manor."

"And how did you discover that?" Winston demanded.

Isaac grinned, a smug satisfaction radiating from him. "Your servants are not as loyal to you as you believe. A few coins can make any servant talk."

Winston pursed his lips together, his temper barely in check. "I don't know what you intend to do, but you will lose. My advice to you is to leave before it is too late."

Isaac put his hands out wide. "And miss these pleasant chats? Besides, I am not leaving here without my wife and son."

"Then you shall be sorely disappointed," Winston replied, his voice firm and unyielding.

Isaac's expression turned almost gleeful. "I read the most interesting article in the newssheets this morning. A traveler from London gave me his paper at the boarding house when I was dining."

"I do not care…" Winston began, his patience fraying.

Isaac spoke over him. "It was about a boy named Johnny that died in a workhouse. A tragic ending, considering his mother was hung right in front of him."

Winston clenched his jaw. "What do you know about that?"

"Only that you were the reason why Johnny's mother was killed and why he was sent to that workhouse. Alone. Without anyone to care for him," Isaac said. "Can you imagine how lonely he must have felt?"

"You are lying," Winston shot back. "Johnny was sent to live with his aunt."

Isaac's eyes turned cold. "His aunt couldn't care for him and sent him to the workhouse. It is all in the article. I would be happy to show you."

Winston's hands balled into fists, his struggle to control his anger evident in every taut muscle.

"You are upset," Isaac remarked, his smile growing. "I am not quite sure why you care so much, especially since you represented the lord that brought the charges against Johnny's mother. If it wasn't for you, Johnny might still have a mother."

With a steely gaze, Winston said, "You know not what you are talking about."

"I know only what has been reported in the newssheets," Isaac responded. "You have quite the reputation for winning. How fortunate for you."

Winston knew that Isaac was trying to goad him, and the worst part was that it was working. How did Isaac know exactly what to say or do to provoke such a reaction? Winston's mind whirled, trying to process the information and control his mounting anger. It would be best to walk away and take a moment to clear his head.

Without another word, Winston turned on his heel and started to walk away, his shoulders tense with suppressed rage.

"Enjoy your evening, my lord," Isaac called out jovially.

Winston's steps faltered. He should keep walking and put distance between him and Isaac. But his anger boiled over, clouding his judgment. Spinning around, he strode back to Isaac, his movements purposeful and commanding. "I want you to leave and never come back."

Isaac stood his ground, looking thoroughly amused. "Give me my family back and I will be able to."

"I will never give you what you want," Winston stated.

"Then we are at a stalemate, my lord," Isaac said. "And I have all the time in the world. Unlike Johnny or his mother."

The taunt was too much. Unable to control his anger any longer, Winston reared back and punched Isaac square in the jaw, sending him sprawling to the ground.

Isaac touched his reddened jaw, a twisted smile forming.

"That was an impressive hit. I wouldn't have expected that from you."

Grady appeared by Winston's side, placing a steadying hand on his shoulder. "Do not let him get to you, my lord," he advised. "Isaac is trying to get a rise out of you."

He had succeeded.

Winston flexed his throbbing hand, the pain a stark reminder of his loss of control. "Get off my property, Isaac, or else I will have you forcibly removed."

Isaac rose slowly, dusting off his trousers with deliberate movement. "I will go, for now. After all, I would not want you to go through all that trouble just for me," he said, his tone dripping with sarcasm. "I do hope you have an enjoyable meal with Miss Bawden. I would hate for anything bad to happen to her."

Winston lunged forward, fury propelling him, but Grady held him back, stepping between him and Isaac. "Do not let him goad you, my lord," he insisted. "He isn't worth it."

Isaac's lips twitched. "I would listen to your guard," he said before walking away.

Grady didn't release him right away but kept a firm grip on him. "You cannot lower yourself to Isaac's level."

"He threatened Miss Bawden," Winston said through clenched teeth. "What other choice did I have?"

"You always have a choice," Grady replied, finally letting go. "Reacting with violence only gives him what he wants."

Winston watched Isaac's retreating figure, his mind racing with thoughts of Mattie's safety. "I won't let him harm Miss Bawden."

Grady nodded. "You are doing everything you can to ensure her protection."

A thought occurred to him. "Why are you here and not at Miss Bawden's cottage?"

"I thought my presence here was more important, considering you couldn't help but engage in fisticuffs with

The Gentleman's Miscalculation

Isaac," Grady responded, his tone a mix of concern and reproach.

"I hate that man," Winston said, his voice low.

Grady gave him a thoughtful look. "Besides threatening Miss Bawden, did he say something else to upset you?"

"Does it matter?"

"No, I suppose not," Grady said. "But do not underestimate Isaac. He has a lot to gain by getting Lady Sarah back in his life."

Winston bobbed his head, his mind still replaying Isaac's words. The mention of Johnny and his mother had struck a nerve. Guilt and sorrow welled up inside of him, and he desperately needed to be alone to process everything. The realization that he was responsible for the deaths of two people was almost too much to bear.

"Go keep Miss Bawden safe. I will be fine," Winston ordered before he headed towards Brockhall Manor.

But he knew that was far from the truth. How could he be all right, knowing that Johnny was dead? He would need to confirm what Isaac told him, but it could take days until the newssheets arrived from London.

As he stepped into the entry hall of the manor, he was met by his mother and sisters, their faces etched with concern.

"What is wrong?" Winston asked. He worked hard to mask his inner turmoil.

His mother frowned. "Why did you hit Isaac?" she inquired, her tone holding censure.

Seeing no reason to hide the truth, Winston replied, "I assure you that it was warranted. I want everyone to stay far away from him."

"What was he doing here?" Elodie asked.

Winston sighed heavily. "He was threatening Mattie," he revealed, the weight of the admission pressing down on him. "He can't get to us so he is trying to go after her."

Melody spoke up, her eyes full of understanding. "That is

why you were so insistent that she ride in a coach from now on."

"It is," Winston said, his patience wearing thin. He wanted to be alone, and he was tired of answering these questions. "If you will excuse me…"

He was about to retreat to his bedchamber when Elodie approached him, wrapping her arms around him in a comforting embrace. After a moment, she stepped back and said, "You looked as if you needed a hug."

"Thank you," he responded, genuinely touched by her gesture, though his mind was still a storm of conflicting emotions.

Once he retreated to his bedchamber, Winston closed the heavy door behind him, shutting out the world. He sank into the leather armchair by the fireplace, the flickering flames casting shadows that mirrored his troubled thoughts. He needed the quiet, the isolation, to sift through the chaos in his mind.

Isaac's taunting words echoed endlessly, stirring up memories he had tried to bury. Johnny's tragic fate and his mother's death weighed heavily on his conscience. Winston clenched his fists, the pain of his earlier punch throbbing in his knuckles, which was a small penance for the guilt gnawing at him.

He stared into the fire, trying to find solace in its warmth, but the flames only reminded him of the hell he felt trapped in. How was he to seek any form of redemption? He had been sending money to Johnny's aunt to provide for him, but that had been in vain. Johnny had been sent away, and he hadn't known.

In the flickering light, he resolved to find out everything about Johnny's fate. He would contact his sources in London and insist on an investigation. Until then, he would protect Mattie with every ounce of his being.

Winston reached for the bottle of whiskey that sat on the table next to him. He shouldn't drink, but he wanted to forget, even if it was just for a moment. The familiar image of Johnny staring up at his mother as she hung right in front of him, the tears of anguish that flowed down his cheeks as he was led away, haunted him. The scene replayed in his mind, relentless and unforgiving.

He needed a drink.

The clock on the mantel chimed, alerting him to the time. He was supposed to depart for Mattie's cottage for dinner soon.

But he couldn't go.

Not now.

Removing the top of the whiskey bottle, Winston took a long drink, hoping that for tonight, he could forget.

The sun had long since dipped below the horizon, casting deep shadows across the room as Mattie gazed out the window. Her thoughts were consumed with worry for Winston. They had planned for him to dine with her family this evening, with the hope that he would speak to her father afterwards.

She wondered what could have detained him, her mind racing with possibilities. Winston was many things, but he was not one to disregard others so easily.

Emma let out a loud, dramatic sigh, breaking the tense silence. "I am starving," she declared, rising from the settee with an exaggerated stretch. "Can we please go eat?"

Her father, seated comfortably in his high-backed chair, looked up from his book and glanced at the long clock ticking softly in the corner. "I must agree with Emma. It is late, and I do not believe Lord Winston is coming."

Even Franny glanced her way with a hopeful expression, her eyes reflecting the warm glow of the candles.

Mattie reluctantly rose, her heart heavy with disappointment. "Very well," she said, forcing a smile. "I would hate for our food to grow cold."

"Perhaps he misunderstood your invitation to join us this evening?" her father asked, placing the book down.

With a weak smile, Mattie responded, "Perhaps."

Emma ran a hand down the pink gown that she had insisted on wearing this evening, despite being in mourning. "If I had extended the invitation to Lord Winston, I promise you that he wouldn't have misunderstood," she declared confidently.

They walked towards the dining table and sat down. The table was elegantly set, with polished silverware and delicate china gleaming under the chandelier's light. Mattie couldn't help but notice the extra plate setting, a glaring reminder that Winston had broken his promise to come.

Her father took his seat at the head of the table, his expression thoughtful. "Lord Winston is a busy man, and I am sure that something came up," he said, trying to reassure her.

"More important than dining with us?" Emma asked skeptically as she took her seat. "No, I do think the problem lies with Mattie."

"Thank you for the vote of confidence," Mattie muttered under her breath.

Franny claimed the seat next to Emma and reached for her cup. "I am glad that Lord Winston didn't come. I am not up to visiting with a stranger."

Emma waved her hand dismissively. "Lord Winston is not a stranger, at least to us. He is tall, handsome and very intelligent. He is a barrister in London," she shared with a hint of admiration. "And I have read about many of his cases in the newssheets."

Her father gave Emma a look of mild displeasure. "You read the newssheets?" he asked.

"Just the parts that interest me," Emma declared unapologetically. "I do not care much about most of the drivel that is reported on."

"I would prefer it if you didn't read the newssheets," her father said. "It is uncouth of you to do so."

Emma shrugged, brushing aside his criticism. "Can I at least read the Society page?" she asked.

"Yes, that is perfectly acceptable," her father replied.

Mrs. Watson stepped into the room, carefully balancing the bowls of soup in her hands. "I take it that Lord Winston is not joining us for supper this evening," she observed.

"No, but we have decided that Mattie is to blame for the misunderstanding," Emma responded.

Mattie rolled her eyes. "Can we please move on and talk about something else?" she asked, trying to keep the exasperation out of her voice.

Emma leaned to the side as Mrs. Watson placed the bowl down in front of her. "I do not know why you are upset since you made us wait hours to eat dinner. I thought I might die from hunger," she said dramatically.

Her father cleared his throat. "You made your point, Emma," he remarked. "Now let us eat our soup that Mrs. Watson graciously prepared for us."

Reaching for her spoon, Emma remarked, "I hope I do not soil this gown since I wore it especially for Lord Winston."

"You shouldn't have changed out of your mourning gown," Mattie admonished.

"I look terrible in black," Emma declared defiantly. "Can I not go into half-mourning and wear dark colors?"

Mattie frowned, her frustration growing. "You haven't even mourned for one full day."

"Because it is so difficult to do so," Emma said. "My skin is far too fair to be paired with a black gown."

Mattie was done with this ridiculous conversation. She turned her attention towards Franny and asked, "Did you enjoy going outside for our brief walk?"

Franny placed her spoon down onto the table. "It was nice to step outside, even for a moment."

Emma chimed in, "If you don't go outside, you are going to become far too pale. You must think of your complexion."

"I am sure that Franny has other things on her mind right now," Mattie stated, giving Emma a stern look.

Shifting her gaze towards her uncle, Franny asked, "When are we departing for Darlington Abbey?"

"Soon," he promised. "The vicar is traveling to our village now."

"I admit that I am anxious to return home," Franny said.

He smiled warmly at her. "I know, Dear, but I do not wish to leave this village without a vicar. It would be terribly unfair of me to do so."

Franny nodded slowly. "I understand," she murmured.

Emma pushed the bowl of soup away from her, her expression thoughtful. "I have been thinking of the bedchamber that I want at Darlington Abbey, and I think I want the room that has green-papered walls. It is the largest of the guest rooms, and I think it would be perfect for me."

"We shall see," her father said, his tone measured. "We will discuss such things with the housekeeper at Darlington Abbey."

"Why would we discuss such things?" Emma asked, looking perplexed. "Shouldn't we tell Mrs. Devan what we want, and she accommodates us?"

Her father pursed his lips together. "That is rather a high-handed thing of you to say. I would think we would work together as a team."

"But they are servants, Father," Emma protested. "Our servants."

Mattie lifted her brow. "You seem to forget that just a few days ago, we lived in humble circumstances."

Emma raised her hands. "We still do!" she said, her voice

rising. "But everything has changed now that Father is a viscount. We need not live in squalor any longer."

"We hardly live in squalor," Mattie claimed, her tone edged with irritation.

Lifting her chin, Emma responded, "We shall have to agree to disagree, Sister," she said. "You may have been content as a vicar's daughter but I never was. I knew I was destined for great things and I am grateful for the chance to prove it."

Franny pushed back her chair and rose. "Excuse me, I am no longer hungry," she said before fleeing from the room.

Mattie shook her head at Emma. "Why can't you show an ounce of compassion for Franny and her circumstances?"

"I am not entirely sure why she is so sensitive," Emma argued. "People die all the time. You can cry for a day or two, but then you must move on."

Rising, Mattie said, "I should go speak to Franny."

"Why?" Emma asked.

Mattie didn't understand what was wrong with her sister. "You upset her, and she hardly ate her soup. I am hoping that I can convince her to come back down for supper."

Emma looked uninterested. "Suit yourself."

Mattie had had just about enough with Emma. How could someone be so utterly self-absorbed and rarely show an ounce of compassion for anyone? She knew there was no point in arguing with Emma, but she found herself at her wit's end. "What is wrong with you?" she demanded.

"What is wrong with me?" Emma repeated in surprise. "I have done nothing wrong except tell the truth."

Mattie tossed up her hands. "No, you only tell *your* truth. Which is always wrong. You can't even muster up enough compassion for what our cousin is going through."

Emma tilted her chin. "How long must we cater to Franny's whims?"

With a disbelieving huff, Mattie turned her attention

towards her father. "Will you please try to talk some sense into Emma?" she asked.

Her father tipped his head, his expression solemn as he went to address Emma. "Mattie is right—"

Emma cut him off. "Why are you taking her side?"

Mattie pressed her fingers to the bridge of her nose. "Because, dear sister, you run roughshod over everyone. You are being intolerably rude to Franny and are balking at tradition by wearing pink when we are supposed to be in mourning. Do you care about anyone but yourself?"

"You are just upset that Lord Winston didn't show up this evening, and now you are taking out your frustrations on me," Emma stated.

Mattie knew there was no point in continuing this argument with Emma. Her sister would never see reason so why bother trying? With a sigh, she turned and headed towards the stairs. Reaching Emma's bedchamber, she knocked gently.

No response.

She opened the door and stuck her head in. "Can I come in, Franny?" she asked. "Just for a moment?"

Franny sat on her bed, wiping away tears. "Is Emma with you?" she inquired warily.

"No," Mattie assured her, stepping inside and closing the door behind her. "I figured that she had upset you enough this evening."

Swiping at the tears that continued to fall down her cheeks, Franny asked, "Are you glad that my parents are dead, too?"

Mattie's heart dropped at that question. "I do not share Emma's sentiments. I wish your parents were still alive. I truly do."

Franny huffed. "Why is Emma so insensitive?"

"That is an excellent question. How long do you have?" she asked, trying to lighten the mood. "I suppose we should have suspected Emma's callous behavior at a young age when she kicked some dolls out of her collection for not being pretty enough."

"I miss my parents," Franny murmured, her voice breaking.

Mattie sat down next to Franny and slipped her arm around the girl's shoulders. "I know you do, and there is nothing wrong with that," she said. "But you must know that my father and I are here to support you the best way we know how."

"I don't want Emma to have the bedchamber with green-papered walls," Franny revealed. "That was the room that my mother promised me before they left for India."

"Then it should be yours," Mattie responded.

Franny looked unconvinced. "What about Emma?"

Mattie tightened her hold on Franny. "I am sure she will complain and pout, but she will come around."

Leaning into her, Franny asked, "Can I start sleeping in your bedchamber? Emma says my breathing keeps her up at night."

"I would greatly enjoy having you as a roommate," Mattie said with a smile. "I will have Mrs. Watson help us move your mattress after dinner."

Franny sighed. "I miss my bed at Darlington Abbey."

Mattie offered her cousin a wistful look. "Do you want to know what I miss most about your father?" she asked. "Whenever we would visit Darlington Abbey, he would send up chocolate to my bedchamber, knowing how much I adored it. It was an expense that my father could hardly afford."

"My father loved having chocolate for breakfast, more so than my mother," Franny shared, a small smile playing on her lips.

"I also remember how kind he was to me when my mother died," Mattie remarked. "He gave the best hugs."

Franny bobbed her head, tears welling up again. "That he did."

Mattie kissed the top of Franny's head. "You will get through it, but you must give yourself the grace to do so," she said gently. "And you have to eat."

As if on cue, Franny's stomach growled.

Removing her arm, Mattie leaned back to meet her cousin's gaze. "Come back down for dinner."

"What if Emma says something ridiculously offensive?" Franny asked.

Mattie laughed. "She probably will." She rose and offered her hand. "But I will be there. As will my father."

Franny hesitated as she looked at Mattie's proffered hand. "I suppose I am hungry," she said as she accepted Mattie's hand in rising.

They walked over to the door and Mattie opened it. "Perhaps we can play a card game this evening."

"I would like that," Franny responded.

As they descended the stairs together, Mattie felt a great relief that she had gotten Franny to return to dinner. However, a part of her couldn't help but wonder what had kept Winston from coming this evening.

Not that she missed him. Heavens, no! She was merely worried about him.

Chapter Fourteen

Winston heard a faint knocking in the distance, but all he could seem to focus on was the throbbing in his head. What time was it? He managed to open his eyes wide enough to see the sun streaming through the windows. How long had he slept? And why had he been sleeping on the ground?

The knocking grew more insistent, forcing him to lift himself onto the settee.

"*What?!*" he shouted, immediately regretting it as his head throbbed even more. Blazes. How much did he drink last night?

The door opened and Melody stepped into the room. Judging by the tight set of her lips, she was not pleased with him. "You missed breakfast," she remarked.

"Well, thank you for informing me of something so utterly unimportant," he muttered dryly.

Melody glanced down at the empty bottle of whiskey, her frown deepening. "Did you enjoy yourself?"

Winston looked up at her through half-lidded eyes. "Leave me alone, Woman."

Melody's hand went to her hip. "I beg your pardon?" she asked, her words holding a warning.

Knowing he was going to fight a losing battle, he decided it was best to apologize. "I'm sorry. I am rather bottle-wearied," he said.

Walking over to the bottle, Melody held it up. "Is this what you did last night?"

"It was," he admitted.

Melody went and placed it on the table. "And what of your plans with Mattie and her family? Did you intend to miss dinner with them?"

Winston groaned. He had every intention of going until he started drinking. Then the rest of the night was more of a blur.

"Did you at least send word to them?" Melody pressed.

"No."

Melody sighed, clearly disappointed in him. "What are you doing, Winston?" she asked. "This is not you."

"It is who I have become," Winston stated.

"Says who?"

Winston brought his hands up to his head, hoping this blasted headache would go away. "Just leave, Melody."

"No."

He turned his head towards her. "No?" he asked. "But I don't want you here."

"I care not what you want," Melody replied.

"I do not want you to see me like this."

Melody shrugged. "Then you shouldn't have drunken yourself into oblivion last night," she said. "I have no doubt that Mattie will be upset, as well she should be, but you can fix this."

"For what purpose?" he demanded.

Leaning towards him, Melody replied, "Let's start with it is the right thing to do."

He scoffed. "What do you know about right and wrong?"

"Apparently, more than you do," Melody retorted before she cocked her head. "What is troubling you?"

Rising, Winston removed the cravat that hung around his neck and tossed it onto the floor. "Leave it," he stated firmly, turning away from her.

Melody appeared unbothered by the sharpness of his words. "You can shut me out, you can shut everyone out, but that is only hurting yourself."

Spinning around, Winston demanded, "And what do you know about pain? You live in a gilded cage, and do not have a care in the world."

Melody stood there, taking a moment to consider his words, her expression thoughtful. When she finally spoke, her voice was steady and calm, a stark contrast to his. "It appears that we both know very little about one another." She walked over to the door. "But the difference is, I am not actively trying to ruin my future."

Winston felt a stab of guilt at how he was treating his sister. He had no right to talk to her in such a fashion, especially since she was only trying to help him. "Melody… wait," Winston said. "I'm sorry."

His sister placed a hand on the door handle. "When you are ready to talk, I am here to listen. But I am not going to force you. That isn't fair to you, or me."

After his sister left his bedchamber, Winston hung his head. What was wrong with him? The worst part was that he knew Melody was right. He was trying to ruin his future because he didn't think he was worthy of one.

He had wanted to forget, but his actions last night were inexcusable. He had been a terrible friend to Mattie, especially since she had been counting on him. And he had let her down. For what? A chance to forget his past?

It didn't work. His memories were still there, haunting him every time he closed his eyes.

Winston walked over to the bed and sat down. What was he to do? He couldn't keep going on as he had been. But what choice did he have? He felt trapped in his own despair, unsure of the way forward.

His dark-haired valet, Brown, entered the room, offering a polite but knowing smile. "Good morning, my lord," he greeted. "I took the liberty of calling for a bath for you."

"I do not require a bath," Winston grumbled, rubbing his temples.

"That is not what Lady Melody said," Brown responded with a touch of humor. "I believe her exact words were 'Lord Winston stinks and requires a bath at once.'"

Winston lifted his arm and smelled his armpit, grimacing at the offensive odor. His sister wasn't wrong.

Brown went about tidying up the room. "Lady Melody also requested you be sent up a tray of food."

"Since when did you start taking orders from my sister?" Winston asked.

Holding a cravat in his hand, Brown responded, "Your sister can be rather frightening."

"Melody?" Winston asked, raising an eyebrow.

Brown tipped his head in acknowledgement. "She may be very soft-spoken, but I do not dare defy her. Her words have authority."

Winston let out a soft chuckle. "Melody is harmless."

"I am not so sure that is true," Brown said, continuing his task. "Have you seen her shoot a pistol? She has remarkable aim."

His brow furrowed. "Melody can shoot a pistol?"

"Yes, my lord," Brown replied. "She practices nearly every day in the gardens. Have you not seen her?"

With a glance at the window, he replied, "I suppose I haven't."

Brown placed the discarded clothing onto the dressing table. "Lady Melody also can speak many languages. It is rather unnerving."

"Every genteel woman speaks a few languages," Winston

defended. "But I will admit it is odd that she can speak a little Russian."

"A little?" Brown asked. "I daresay she is fluent, at least that is what Lady Melody's lady's maid informed me of."

Winston gave his valet a look of disbelief. "I doubt that to be true."

Brown shrugged. "Regardless, she also asked for me to order some flowers for Miss Mattie Bawden, Miss Emma and their cousin, Miss Francesca Bawden."

"That is not an awful idea," Winston said. "Do you have time to go into the village?"

"I can make the time, my lord," Brown assured him.

Winston bobbed his head. "Good," he stated. "Women like flowers, and that might make the upcoming conversation with Miss Bawden much more tolerable."

A knock interrupted their conversation.

Brown walked over and opened the door, revealing a footman with a metal basin. He brought it in and placed it down by the fireplace. Additional footmen walked into the room and filled the basin full of water.

Winston walked over to the basin and dipped his fingers into the water. It was cold. "Did you not instruct the cook to boil the water?"

"Your sister was insistent that you needed a bath as quickly as possible," Brown responded, turning away from him.

"Need I remind you that you work for me?" Winston remarked as he removed his white shirt.

In a jovial voice, Brown said, "I am well aware, but I do not wish to upset Lady Melody. For any reason."

Winston just shook his head, more amused than anything by his valet's irrational fear of Melody. He quickly undressed and stepped into the bath. The cold water was uncomfortable, but he had no intention of lingering. He had far more pressing matters to attend to.

A short time later, he stepped out of the bath and Brown

extended him a towel. He dried off and walked over to the bed where his clothing had been meticulously laid out. Once he was dressed, he approached the mirror and began adjusting his cravat.

"You are married, are you not?" Winston asked, his gaze still fixed on the mirror as he smoothed the fabric into place.

"Yes, my lord," Brown replied. "I have been for some time now."

Turning slightly, Winston met Brown's gaze in the mirror. "Are you happy?"

Brown eyed him curiously. "Why do you ask, my lord?"

Winston dropped his hands to his sides. "Does a wife make you happy?"

"She does make me happy, but that is not why I am happy," Brown replied. "Unless one is truly happy within one's own heart, one cannot be happy no matter the circumstances."

With a sigh, Winston said, "I was afraid you were going to say that." He walked over to the door, pausing for a moment. "Good day, Brown."

Once Winston was alone in the corridor, he felt a deep sense of emptiness. He was never going to be happy. Not even taking a wife would change that. Which was a relief since he didn't want one. Especially now. Perhaps he should just retire to the cottage on his sheep farm and live out the remainder of his days. Alone.

Winston started down the stairs and he saw Elodie was speaking to White. She turned towards him. "Good morning, Brother."

"Good morning," he greeted.

Elodie observed him for a moment before saying, "You don't look as awful as I thought you would."

"You must have been talking to Melody," Winston remarked.

"I was, and I saw the metal basin being brought up the

stairs for you," Elodie said. "How bad was your night last night?"

Winston winced. "It wasn't the best."

"Do you want to talk about it?" Elodie asked.

"No."

Elodie smiled. "Well, don't say that I didn't try," she said. "Besides, Melody told me that you weren't in a chatty mood."

Winston ran a hand through his hair. "It would appear that Melody is the chatty one this morning."

"Well, the coach is out front, waiting to take you to Mattie's cottage," Elodie said, her smile growing.

"I thought I would wait until Brown ordered flowers to be delivered to their cottage," Winston shared.

Elodie bobbed her head in approval. "That is a fine idea. What shall we do while we wait?" She glanced towards the drawing room, her eyes twinkling. "We could always practice our embroidery."

"I don't embroider."

Placing a hand to the side of her mouth, Elodie whispered, "I am not very good at it. But Mother is insistent I work on it. Like a performing monkey."

Winston chuckled. "You are not a performing monkey."

"I am not complaining," Elodie responded with a slight shrug. "I saw monkeys perform tricks at the traveling circus and I thought they were adorable."

"Well, as informative as this conversation is, I think I shall go eat something," Winston said. "Melody requested a tray be sent to my room, but I finished dressing before it arrived."

Elodie took a step towards him. "I'll join you."

Winston sighed inwardly. He wanted to be alone, knowing he was in rather a foul mood. "That wasn't an invitation."

"I know, but I think you could use the company," Elodie insisted. "Follow me. If we hurry, there might be some plum cake left over from breakfast."

Winston knew he had no choice but to follow after his sister. At least he would get some plum cake out of it.

Mattie sat in the drawing room of her cottage, diligently working on her needlework. Her cousin, Franny, was sitting next to her, quietly reading a book. Across the room, Emma lounged in their father's armchair, a look of utter boredom plastered on her face.

"Can we go into the village?" Emma asked, her voice dripping with whiny impatience.

Mattie lowered her needlework to her lap and looked up. "Whatever for?" she asked. "We do not need anything."

"It might save me from dying from boredom," Emma responded dramatically.

"We are in mourning," Mattie reminded her, trying to keep her voice patient. She had lost count of how many times she had had to say this.

Emma sighed heavily. "Mourning is so boring," she claimed. "Why can't we mourn people by doing fun things?"

"We could go for a walk," Mattie suggested.

"No, I do not want to soil my boots and have to clean them," Emma said, inspecting her perfectly clean boots. "I will enjoy having a lady's maid to do that tedious task for me."

Mattie tried to hide her annoyance but was failing miserably. Emma seemed determined to ruin this quiet afternoon by her incessant complaining. "What if we ask Mrs. Watson to make us biscuits?"

Emma adjusted the sleeves on her black gown, her expression uninterested. "No, I need to fit into all the gowns that I will be commissioning when we arrive at Darlington Abbey."

"For what purpose?" Mattie asked. "What is wrong with the dresses that you own?"

Her sister looked at her like she was a simpleton. "My dresses were acceptable before, but now that Father is a viscount, we must look the part."

"Father is not one to waste money when your gowns are sufficient," Mattie said. "Furthermore, you do not need a new wardrobe until you have a Season."

"Which will be next year," Emma stated confidently.

Mattie pressed her lips together, feeling her patience wear thin. Not this again. "No, I am debuting next Season," she reminded her sister firmly.

Emma waved her hand dismissively. "No one will care about you debuting, but I will be the diamond of the first water."

"You are remarkably humble," Mattie muttered under her breath.

A sudden pounding came from the door and Mrs. Watson emerged from the kitchen to answer it. A moment later, she stepped into the drawing room with three bouquets of flowers set in ornate vases.

Emma jumped up and approached Mrs. Watson eagerly. "Who are the flowers from?" she asked.

"Lord Winston," Mrs. Watson replied as she carefully placed the vases on the table. "He sent flowers to each of the ladies in the house."

Emma spun in a circle, her face lighting up. "This is the first time a gentleman has sent me flowers," she gushed. "This is all so exciting."

Mattie stood up and went to admire the flowers. "They are exquisite. Was there no card?"

"I was not given one," Mrs. Watson replied.

Another knock came at the door, and Mrs. Watson went to answer it. She returned to the drawing room and she was followed by Winston.

Winston's eyes landed on Mattie, and there was something in his gaze—an apology, perhaps, or a plea for understanding.

Before she could address Winston, Emma approached him with a graceful curtsy. "Thank you for the most beautiful flowers, my lord," she said. "How did you know that roses were my favorite flower?"

Winston shifted uncomfortably. "I was not aware of that fact, but I am pleased you are happy with the flowers."

"I am very happy," Emma said. "It almost makes up for you not coming last night. Almost." She flashed him a coy smile.

Winston winced. "I do apologize for not coming last night as planned, but something came up."

"Oh, is everything all right?" Emma asked.

Winston nodded. "It is." He shifted his gaze towards Mattie. "Would you care to take a walk with me?"

Mattie was about to refuse him since she was still upset about his absence the night before. But it was his eyes that were causing her pause. They were trying to tell her a story, one that she could not quite decipher. She took a step forward, her curiosity and concern intertwining. "Yes, I would like that."

Winston offered his arm and Mattie accepted it. He led her outside, and they started walking through the open fields that surrounded her cottage. The fresh air was a welcome change, and for a moment, they walked in silence.

He broke the silence, his voice tinged with regret. "I want to apologize for not joining your family for dinner last night. I should have sent word."

"Did something happen?" Mattie asked.

Winston grew silent, his face shadowed by thought. Finally, he spoke. "I had a conversation with Isaac after you departed from Brockhall Manor."

"I take it that it did not go well," Mattie said.

He shook his head. "No, it did not," he responded. "He threatened you, and I'm afraid my temper got the best of me. I hit him squarely in the jaw."

Mattie smiled despite herself. "Is it unchristian of me to be pleased by that?"

"I should not have lost control, considering I was playing into Isaac's hands," Winston replied, his voice heavy with self-reproach.

"There is no shame in expressing one's emotions," Mattie said gently.

Winston frowned. "You seem to forget that I am a barrister. I am trained to mask my emotions so as not to give anything away."

She glanced at him. "Does that apply to when you are in the courtroom or to your everyday life?"

He looked displeased by her question and turned his gaze towards the horizon. "Do you accept my apology or not?" he asked curtly.

"I do," Mattie replied, sensing his inner turmoil. "But I feel as if you are wearing your mask with me now. Why is that?"

Winston came to a stop and dropped his hand. "Mattie… I appreciate what you are trying to do, but I do not wish to burden you with my troubles. You have your own to contend with at the moment."

"I am not really good at this truce thing, but I think we are becoming friends," Mattie said. "But if I am wrong, then tell me and I will walk away."

"You aren't wrong," Winston admitted quietly.

"Then friends confide in one another," Mattie said. "I may not be able to offer advice, but I would be happy to listen."

Winston considered her for a moment before saying, "You don't know what you are asking of me."

Mattie took a step closer to him. "I think I do," she replied. "I'm asking you to remove the mask for me and let me in."

"And what if you don't like what I have to say?" Winston asked, his words holding an edge to them.

"I am a daughter of a vicar so nothing you say will surprise me," Mattie responded.

Winston ran a hand through his dark hair, frustration evident on his face. "You think you know me, but you know nothing about me," he declared.

In a steady voice, Mattie said, "You and I have been at odds since we were young, but during that time, I have seen glimpses of who you truly are. I have always, much to my great annoyance, admired you."

"There is no reason to admire me," Winston stated, turning away from her.

Placing her hand out to still him, she said, "I see how you treat your sisters and mother with kindness. I see how you treat your father's tenants—people that are far beneath you. And lastly, I have seen the way you treat my family. Me, especially. Despite our differences, you have shown me kindness."

Winston glanced down at her hand on his sleeve and she quickly withdrew it, silently chiding herself on her brazen behavior. "You flatter me, but I am not a good man," he said.

"I don't believe that to be true," Mattie insisted.

"It is true, and I cannot—I will not—let you say otherwise," Winston argued. "You don't know me, Mattie. I only let you see what I want you to see, what I want the world to see."

Mattie lifted her brow, a hint of a challenge in her eyes. "You are not that good of an actor, my lord."

Winston huffed. "Why do I bother speaking to you?" he asked. "You are an obstinate young woman who is truly unsufferable."

"And yet, here we are, speaking nonetheless," Mattie responded.

With pursed lips, Winston said, "Allow me to escort you home."

"No."

"No?" His tone was incredulous.

Mattie stood her ground, her resolve unwavering. "Not until you tell me what is troubling you," she insisted.

Winston took a commanding step towards her. "You have no right to dictate my actions," he said, his voice rising. "I do not have to tell you anything."

"That is true," Mattie responded calmly. "We can walk back to my cottage in silence, and you don't have to tell me one thing. But you would be wrong to do so."

"And why is that, Miss Bawden?" Winston growled.

Mattie ignored the formality, pressing on despite knowing she was provoking his anger. "Because I believe I can help you."

"Help me with what?" he retorted.

She had a choice. She could say a response that would pacify him so they would return to the way they were before. Or she could tell him the truth, hoping he was ready to hear it.

Taking a deep breath, Mattie met his gaze and said, "I see the pain in your eyes. It is very familiar to me. You have lost something, and I want to help you get it back."

"And what do you think I have lost?" Winston's voice was a mix of skepticism and bitterness.

"Joy," Mattie simply replied.

Winston reared back, his expression hardening. "You are too presumptuous, Woman. I do not need—or want—your help."

Mattie stepped forward, her hand trembling slightly as she placed it on his chest. "I know that look of pain because I saw it in myself. It was when my mother died and I thought all was lost. But it wasn't. Joy can be misplaced, but it never completely disappears. Not in our hearts."

His eyes flickered with an emotion she couldn't quite decipher. Anger? Surprise? When Winston did finally speak, his words were much softer. "Miss Bawden... Mattie... I'm sorry for your loss, but you and I are not the same."

"I respectfully disagree," Mattie said.

As she went to withdraw her hand, Winston placed his hand over hers, keeping it in place. "I am a broken man," he admitted softly.

"No one is too broken to be put back together," Mattie said.

Winston tightened his hold on her hand. "The pieces may fit, but there will always be cracks in it."

Mattie offered him an encouraging smile. "The cracks are what make us special."

Winston's face fell, a look of despair overtaking him. "What if you are wrong?"

"I rarely am, so why would this be any different?" she asked, attempting to infuse humor into this conversation.

His eyes met hers with an intensity she had never seen before. It wasn't anger, but more of resignation. "What I am about to share with you could alter the way you look at me," he said. "You may even be disgusted with me."

"Why are you so certain of such a thing?"

"Because it is the way I look at myself," Winston responded, his voice thick with emotion. "What I have done..." His voice trailed off.

Mattie held his gaze, knowing that nothing he could tell her would change how she thought of him. "Trust me, Winston."

Winston closed his eyes tightly but not before she saw them glisten with unshed tears. A stirring in her heart caused her to reach her other hand up and cup his cheek. "Let me in, and I promise never to betray your confidences," she said.

His eyes opened and he leaned slightly into her hand, as if he needed her touch to strengthen him. "I'm afraid if I let you in, I will never let you go," he admitted, his voice barely more than a whisper.

Mattie felt her heart pound in her chest, and she was fearful that Winston could hear it. "I don't want to be let go."

Winston stared at her for a long moment as emotions flickered across his face. "You might not feel that way when I tell you that I am responsible for the deaths of two innocent people."

Chapter Fifteen

Winston watched Mattie closely, looking for any signs of disgust. To his surprise, her face softened, and her eyes filled with compassion.

Remaining close, Mattie said, "I know you, Winston, and I trust that there is more to the story. Perhaps you should start at the beginning."

He closed his eyes, grappling with whether he had the strength to share something so vulnerable, so raw. What if Mattie hated him for what he was about to reveal? Could he handle such a thing? A part of him wanted to flee, but a larger part of him wanted to stay. With Mattie.

Mattie dropped her hands from his person, and he immediately missed the loss of contact. But then, she held his hand, intertwining her fingers with his.

Winston opened his eyes and stared at Mattie through unshed tears. "Why are you still here?"

She offered him a weak smile. "There is no other place that I would want to be than right here. With you."

"You say that now…"

She interrupted him. "I will say that always," Mattie

insisted. "Regardless of what has transpired between us, I care about you, Winston. I always have, and I always will."

Winston hoped that was true. He truly did. He was starting to care far too much about what Mattie thought of him. It was rather inconvenient. He almost preferred it when he was indifferent towards her.

Drawing in a shaky breath, Winston began, his voice low and unsteady. "It was one of my first cases. Lord Hallsands came to me and told me that one of his maids had stolen a diamond necklace from his wife. During the course of the investigation, we discovered one of their maids, Clara, was in possession of a pair of Lady Hallsands's earrings."

Winston winced, recalling the details. "Clara was adamant that she was just cleaning the earrings, but Lord Hallsands demanded she be taken to trial as a thief. The case seemed straightforward enough. However, I didn't realize that Clara had been a pickpocket when she was young, nor that she had a child."

He swallowed, unsure if he had the strength to go on.

"Is that all?" Mattie prodded gently.

"No, it gets far worse," he admitted.

Mattie tightened her hold on his hand. "Then I shall wait until you are ready to share," she said in an encouraging voice.

Winston could do this. He needed to tell someone about what he had done. And he hoped his trust wasn't misplaced in Mattie. But heaven help him, he did trust her. That thought both terrified and excited him.

In a voice that was filled with his conflicting emotions, Winston revealed, "We went to trial, and based upon Clara's past and the gravity of her crime, the judge decided she should be put to death. I tried to argue the punishment did not fit the crime, but the judge wanted to make an example out of Clara."

Winston hesitated before sharing, "I normally avoid public

hangings, but I decided to go. I saw a boy that was no more than ten years old, standing in front of the platform that had been erected for the hangings that day. I later learned that he was Johnny, Clara's son. He watched his own mother hang before being led away."

Mattie gasped but she remained quiet, allowing him the freedom to continue. Or not.

Glancing down at their entwined hands, Winston felt strength that he didn't know he had. He had already come so far. "I… um… felt responsible for Clara's death, so I was paying Johnny's aunt ten pounds a month to care for him. I thought it was penance for what I had done."

"That was most kind of you," Mattie said.

Winston shook his head, the weight of guilt heavy on his shoulders. "It wasn't enough. Johnny deserved his mother, not ten pounds a month. But it didn't matter in the end. Isaac informed me that Johnny died in a workhouse. His aunt had sent him away and was pocketing the money I was sending for Johnny's care."

Mattie's eyes widened. "That is awful."

"It is, but that isn't even the worst part," Winston admitted, his voice cracking on the last word. "After Clara was hung, I saw Lady Hallsands at a soiree and she was wearing the diamond necklace that she claimed had been stolen. When I confronted Lord Hallsands about it, he explained that they found it behind the dressing table. It had fallen in the crack and no one had noticed it until later."

"Oh, dear," Mattie murmured.

Winston's eyes filled with tears. "There was no crime. No reason for Clara to die," he said. "I was responsible for her and Johnny's deaths. I wish I had never taken the case."

He waited for Mattie's judgment. Her words that would confirm it was indeed his fault and he was an awful person. But none came.

Instead, in the next moment, he found himself enveloped

in her arms, drawn into a comforting embrace. It happened so suddenly that he was momentarily stunned. But within moments, he wrapped his arms around her, holding her close, her head resting on his chest.

Tears streamed down his face as he felt an overwhelming sense of safety in Mattie's embrace. She didn't say anything, but her silence spoke volumes. The warmth of her presence, the steady rhythm of her breathing, conveyed more compassion and understanding than any words could.

He tightened his hold on her. In that moment, he realized he wasn't alone in his pain. Mattie was there, sharing it with him, willing to help him carry the burden.

Slowly, Mattie pulled back just enough to look into his eyes. "I'm sorry," she whispered.

"For what?"

"That you have been forced to carry around these burdens alone, especially since you did nothing wrong."

Winston dropped his arms and took a step back, his voice rising in frustration. "Nothing wrong? Did you not hear anything that I said?"

"I heard every word."

"Then you would know it was entirely my fault," Winston said. The familiar feeling of anger surged within him. Why had he let his guard down around Mattie? She clearly hadn't been listening to him.

Mattie's eyes held unwavering compassion. "The justice system failed Clara and her son. Not you."

"But I was the barrister that argued the case," Winston countered.

"Did you sentence her to die?" Mattie asked pointedly.

"No, but…"

Mattie spoke over him. "Did you know that the diamond necklace hadn't truly been stolen?" she pressed.

"No, but…"

She took a step closer to him, her gaze steady and warm. "The only thing you are guilty of is doing your job."

Winston ran a hand through his hair. "It is not that simple," he stated.

"You are right," Mattie said. "It is very complicated and messy, but my opinion of you has not changed. You are an honorable man who tried to right a wrong."

"A wrong that I committed!" he shouted.

Mattie's expression remained resolute. "I do not see it that way. You are the only one in your story that showed an ounce of compassion for a woman and her son."

Winston scoffed. "I know you mean well, but you are wrong."

"I think it is *you* who wants to believe that."

He looked at her incredulously. "And why is that?"

Mattie held his gaze, her voice gentle. "You do not want Clara's death to be in vain."

"But it was in vain!" he exclaimed, tossing up his hands in despair. "She never should have died, and neither should have Johnny."

Mattie reached for his hand, her touch warm and steady. "I agree. They should not have died, but you are not the villain in this story. You must believe me, because in my heart, I know the type of man you are. And I wish I could take the pain away from you."

Winston looked at her, truly looked at her, his eyes searching hers for the truth in her words. "You truly believe that?"

"I do," Mattie said firmly. "And I believe that you can find a way to forgive yourself."

Winston tightened his hold on her hand. "You are too kind to me, Mattie."

"It is not kindness," she replied. "It is the truth. You have to forgive yourself. Only then can you find the joy you have lost."

Winston sighed deeply, as if a heavy burden had been lifted, albeit slightly. "I don't know if I can," he admitted.

Mattie gave him a reassuring smile. "You don't have to do it alone. I am here with you."

He stared at her, his heart pounding. The sincerity in her eyes gave him a sliver of hope he had not felt in years. "Why do you care so much about me?" he asked, his voice barely above a whisper.

"Because you are someone worth caring about," Mattie said.

Winston's eyes grew moist, and he blinked back the tears that threatened to fall. For the first time in a long while, he felt the possibility of redemption, of finding peace. He gave Mattie's hand a gentle squeeze. "Thank you, for everything," he whispered, his voice thick with emotion.

As they stood there, hand in hand, Winston realized that he was in trouble. He had made the terrible mistake of letting Mattie in once again. Now he didn't want to let her ever go. The feelings that he had buried deep down had now resurfaced with a vengeance, and he knew he was helpless against them.

Winston dropped her hand and took a step back. "I… um… should walk you home now," he said, his voice far too formal for the conversation they had just shared.

A line between Mattie's brow appeared. "Is something wrong, Winston?"

Yes.

Everything was wrong.

He loved her.

Glancing up at the sky, Winston said, "It is growing late in the day and I do not wish to keep you."

"I do not mind—"

"But I do," Winston responded, gesturing towards the direction of her cottage. "I have work that I need to see to."

Mattie tipped her head, but not before he saw the look of

confusion on her features. He didn't fault her for such a reaction. He was rather confused himself. He had fought so hard to not love Mattie. But he couldn't deny it any longer. Loving her was like breathing. And that is what scared him the most.

As Mattie started walking towards her cottage, Winston felt like such a fool. She had given him the greatest gift: the promise of redemption. Yet he thanked her by dismissing her. But what was he supposed to do? It wasn't as if he could confess his love for her and hope she felt the same way.

No.

He had tried that before and failed. He should just be grateful that Mattie was in his life... as a friend.

Mattie glanced over at him with uncertainty in her eyes. "Did I say or do something to upset you?"

Now Winston felt like a jackanapes. "You did nothing wrong." There. That was the truth.

"Very well," Mattie said, turning her gaze straight ahead.

As they stepped onto Mattie's covered porch, Winston stopped and took a deep breath, the words he needed to say caught in his throat. "Mattie, I..." he began, struggling to find the right words. "I appreciate your kindness today. More than you could ever know."

Mattie gave him a small, sad smile. "You don't have to thank me, Winston. I meant every word."

He nodded, feeling a lump in his throat. "I know you did. And that means the world to me."

She reached out and touched his sleeve gently. "We all have our burdens to bear. You don't have to carry yours alone."

Winston felt his resolve weakening, the urge to pull her into his arms nearly overwhelming. But he couldn't. Not now.

"Good day, Mattie," he said, his voice strained.

She let go of his arm, her touch lingering in his memory. "Good day, Winston," she responded, turning to leave.

"Wait," he said. "May I call upon you tomorrow?"

Her brow lifted in question.

He cleared his throat, suddenly feeling very nervous. "I... um... thought it would be a good time to speak to your father," he rushed out.

"Yes, that would be wonderful," she said before she disappeared into the cottage.

Winston's heart started to ache with unspoken words and unrealized dreams. He had to find a way to live with his feelings, to accept that Mattie could only ever be his friend. Yet deep down, he knew that would never be enough. Not for him.

But for now, he would have to be content with her friendship, even if it meant hiding the depth of his love. It was a small price to pay to keep Mattie in his life, and he would bear it, no matter how much it hurt.

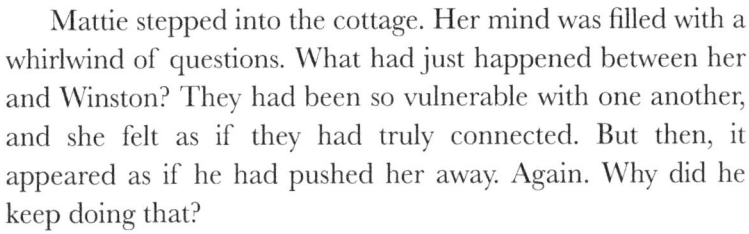

Mattie stepped into the cottage. Her mind was filled with a whirlwind of questions. What had just happened between her and Winston? They had been so vulnerable with one another, and she felt as if they had truly connected. But then, it appeared as if he had pushed her away. Again. Why did he keep doing that?

She couldn't help but care for him deeply, even though she knew it was not reciprocated in the same way. They were nothing more than friends, and she tried to be content with that. She refused to spend her days pining after a man who would never fully let her in.

As she entered the drawing room, Emma jumped up from the settee to greet her. "Where have you been?"

"I went for a walk with Lord Winston," Mattie responded, knowing she didn't owe Emma an explanation.

"You were gone for quite some time," Emma observed. "What did you two discuss?"

Mattie raised an eyebrow, having no intention of betraying Winston's confidences to anyone, much less her sister. "Why do you ask?"

"Did Lord Winston happen to mention me?" Emma asked eagerly.

With a perplexed look, Mattie inquired, "Why would Lord Winston mention you?"

Emma shrugged her shoulder. "No particular reason," she replied.

Mattie turned her attention towards Franny, who was engrossed in a book on the settee. "Would you like to go for a walk with me before supper?"

Franny looked up from her book. "That sounds lovely."

"What of me?" Emma interjected. "Can I not come along?"

Suppressing a sigh, Mattie replied, "If you wish."

Emma lifted her chin. "I think I shall," she declared. "I am dreadfully bored, and Father won't allow me to go into the village to shop for more ribbons."

"Do I need to remind you, yet again, that we are in mourning?" Mattie remarked.

"That doesn't mean I can't wear pretty things," Emma retorted as she turned to show off the pink ribbon in her hair.

Mattie rolled her eyes. "You aren't supposed to wear such bright colors in mourning."

"Who is going to notice, Mattie?" Emma drawled. "The woodland creatures?"

Rising from her seat, Franny said, "Let me go grab my shawl."

As Franny walked up the stairs, Mattie gave her sister a disapproving look. "You should at least make an effort to mourn properly."

"I think this is a good compromise," Emma argued as she reached back and touched the pink ribbon in her hair.

Mattie saw no point in continuing this argument, so she was relieved when her father stepped into the drawing room. "May I speak with you for a moment in the study, Mattie?"

"Of course, Father," Mattie responded before she followed him into the study.

Her father closed the door behind him. "I was hoping to keep this conversation private," he said.

"Is everything all right?"

He went to sit down behind his desk. "Emma has been rather relentless about her debut," he began. "What if you both debuted together?"

Mattie's eyes went wide in disbelief. "Surely, you cannot be in earnest?"

Her father raised a hand to silence her objections. "Hear me out," he responded. "You and Emma are very different, and it is not as if you are competing for the same type of suitors."

"Pardon?" she asked, confused by his words.

"I am merely saying that you do not have the same lofty aspirations as Emma does and you would be satisfied with a simpler life," her father explained.

Mattie rose from her seat, feeling insulted. "What do you mean, Father?"

Her father leaned forward in his seat, trying to reassure her. "We have discussed this before," he said. "You have a sensible head on your shoulders and any gentleman would be lucky to have you as his wife."

"Assuming he is looking for a more mature wife," Mattie said, repeating her father's words from a previous conversation.

"That is not a bad thing," her father insisted, clearly taken aback by her response. "I meant it as a compliment."

Mattie's mouth dropped. "How is that a compliment, Father?"

Her father shook his head, his expression somber. "Emma is much more—"

"Selfish. Inconsiderate," Mattie said, interrupting him with a tone of defiance.

His lips pressed into a thin line as he gave her a chiding look. "I was going to say determined," her father replied. "She doesn't want to wait until she is eight and ten years to debut."

Mattie walked over to the window as the weight of her father's words sank in. "You don't think I will make as good of a match as Emma, do you?" she asked quietly, her voice tinged with disappointment and hurt.

Her father let out a heavy sigh, rubbing his temple wearily. "Emma has her cap set on marrying a lord, and now that I am a viscount, it is in the realm of possibilities for her."

Her shoulders slumped slightly at the confirmation of her fears. "But not for me?" she said, feeling tears prick at the corners of her eyes.

"Mattie…"

She cut him off. "You can stop, Father," she stated. "This could be solved if you would allow Lady Dallington to host me for this upcoming Season. Then Emma can debut next Season without me."

Her father frowned. "I need you at home to tend to Emma and Franny."

"Why?"

"I have explained my reasonings," her father said, his tone growing curt.

Mattie let out a frustrated huff, crossing her arms over her chest. "So you bow to Emma's incessant complaining, but you won't yield on what I want? Why is that?"

Her father rose, his voice becoming more forceful. "This conversation is over," he declared, clearly not wanting to continue the argument. But she was not willing to let it go so easily.

Taking a step towards the desk, Mattie demanded, "I deserve to know why, Father. You owe me that much."

"Fine," her father said, tossing up his arms. "I need you! You have been a constant support to me since your mother died and I don't want you to go away." He paused, his expression softening. "I don't know how to handle Emma and her incessant complaining. Or even Franny. What do I know about having a ward?"

Mattie felt some of her anger dissipate at the vulnerable admission from her father. "You want me to put my life on hold to help you?"

"I don't know what I want," her father admitted, sinking into his chair. "Now that I have said it out loud it seems very selfish of me."

She couldn't help but agree with him as she returned to the seat across from him. "Because it is," she said. "You need to let me lead my own life. Maybe I wish to marry a lord."

Her father gave her a knowing look. "Do you?"

Mattie shrugged as an image of Winston came to her mind. But she dismissed it as quickly as it came. "No, I do not care much about being titled."

"You don't, but Emma does," her father said, a hint of resignation in his voice. "She always has."

In a soft voice, Mattie responded, "All I want is a love match. I want what you and Mother had."

Her father went quiet at the mention of his late wife. "I miss her every single day," he said, his voice thick with emotion. "You look so much like she did at this age; it is almost uncanny."

"I miss Mother, too," Mattie said.

"I know you do."

Mattie held her Father's gaze for a long moment before summoning up all of her courage and determination once again. "Mother would have wanted me to have a Season without Emma being underfoot," she said firmly.

Her father's face fell before he turned his head towards the window. After a long pause, he asked, "The only question is: what am I going to do without you?"

A spark of hope ignited in Mattie's heart at the uncertainty in her father's voice, making her believe he was weakening. "I will not be gone forever," she assured him.

He brought his gaze back to meet hers, studying her intently. "Once the *ton* sees you for who you truly are, I have no doubt that you will have many suitors vying for your hand."

"Is that a bad thing?"

"No, I suppose not," her father replied. "You have my permission to attend the Season with Lady Dallington and her family."

Mattie clasped her hands together in excitement. "Do you truly mean it?" she asked earnestly.

"I do," her father said, his eyes growing moist. "But that means you need to start preparing now. I assume you will need a whole new wardrobe and accessories."

"I will."

"Then I shall see those funds are available to you," her father stated. "Will there be anything else?" The lines on his face tightened with emotion as he spoke.

Mattie rose from her seat. "Thank you, Father."

"I have no doubt that you will make me proud," her father said.

As she approached the door, she spun back around and hurried over to her father. She threw her arms around him in a warm embrace, saying, "I love you."

"I love you, too," he responded, returning the hug.

She dropped her arms and departed from the room. When she entered the drawing room, Emma was waiting for her with an expectant look on her face. "Well?"

"Well, what?" Mattie asked.

Emma let out a dramatic sigh. "What did you and Father talk about?" she asked, as if it were her right to know.

Mattie decided it was best just to tell her the truth. "Father said Lady Dallington can host me for the Season," she said, feeling a sense of excitement building within her.

"And what of me?" Emma asked.

A small smile came to Mattie's lips. "Which means that you can debut next year," she replied, watching as Emma's face lit up with joy.

Emma spun around in a circle. "What wonderful news," she exclaimed. "Now I do not have to worry about outshining you."

Mattie chose to ignore Emma's remark and turned her attention towards Franny. "Shall we go for that walk now?"

"Yes, please," Franny said.

Just as she uttered her words, Mrs. Watson's voice came from the kitchen. "Do not dally for too long because supper is almost ready."

"Maybe we should go on our walk after dinner?" Mattie suggested. "That way we will have more time."

Franny bobbed her head in agreement. "That is probably for the best."

Emma walked over to the settee and gracefully lowered herself onto it. "I wonder what we are having for dinner."

"Mutton!" Mrs. Watson's voice echoed through the cottage.

Mattie smiled. "I will miss this cottage when we are at Darlington Abbey," she said wistfully.

"Why?" Emma asked, genuinely puzzled.

"This is where we both grew up," Mattie replied. "Won't you at least miss a small part of it?"

Emma considered her words for a moment before answering with a dismissive shrug. "No, I won't miss it."

Mattie wondered what it would take to get through to her sister, because she was clearly failing to do so.

Franny spoke up. "I will miss this cottage," she said. "On the rare occasions we came to visit, it was always filled with love and warmth."

Mrs. Watson stepped into the room, wiping her hands on the apron that hung around her neck. "Shall we eat?" she asked cheerfully.

"Yes!" Emma exclaimed, rising.

"Before we adjourn to the table, I wanted to let Mattie know that I cut out the fabric of the gown you suggested," Mrs. Watson said. "I think it will look splendid as a lining in your bonnet."

Emma turned towards Mattie. "What fabric?"

"We brought some of Mother's old dresses down from the attic and we are trying to find a way to reuse the fabric," Mattie explained. "Would you care for us to save you some?"

"No, I shall buy new bonnets when we arrive in London," Emma replied. "There is no reason to keep my old ones."

"I thought it would be nice to use some of Mother's fabric as a way to remember her," Mattie said.

Emma did not look impressed by that idea. "But I doubt Mother's old fabric is even fashionable anymore."

As Mattie went to respond, Emma cut her off abruptly. "Can we go eat now? I am famished, and I do not care about such things."

"Very well," Mattie said. "Let us eat."

Chapter Sixteen

Winston sat in the library, staring at the fire, a drink long forgotten in his hand. The warmth of the flames danced on his face, but his thoughts were far away. He found that he didn't want to forget his afternoon with Mattie. He had been vulnerable with her, more so than he had ever before been with anyone, and he didn't regret it. Those were the memories he wanted to hold on to.

When he had shared his story about Johnny and his mother, Clara, he had expected judgment. But there was none from her. She had listened and accepted him for who he was, making him feel less alone. The weight of his burdens felt lighter, as if he wasn't entirely to blame for their deaths.

But now he faced a greater problem. Revealing so much of himself to Mattie made him confront things that he had long since buried. He loved her. That blasted kiss had changed everything between them. He was content abhorring her, but once his lips met hers, he saw a future with her.

Even when he hated her, a part of him had always loved her.

Botheration.

What was he to do? What *could* he do? He had to continue

playing the part and hope no one could see how he truly felt about Mattie.

Melody entered the room, holding a paper in her hand. She looked at him curiously. "What are you doing up so late?"

"I could ask you the same question," he said.

She glanced down at his nearly full glass. "I see that you heeded my stern reprimand this morning."

Winston leaned forward and placed his glass down. "I do listen to you… on occasion," he said, softening his words with a smile.

"That is good," Melody responded, sitting across from him.

Winston smirked. "You should know that my valet is rather afraid of you."

Melody looked baffled. "Why?"

"I do not know, but he said you could be 'frightening' at times," Winston said. "Those are his words, not mine."

"Then I shall have to strive to appear less frightening," Melody remarked. "How did it go when you called on Mattie? Did she forgive you?"

"She did," Winston confirmed. But she had done far more than forgive him. She had made him feel understood.

Melody bobbed her head in approval. "I am pleased that you two are getting on rather nicely."

"I wouldn't read too much into it."

"How can I not?" Melody asked.

Now he needed a drink.

Winston leaned forward and picked up his glass. As he brought it to his lips, he couldn't help but smile at the thought of Mattie.

"You are smiling," Melody pointed out.

He wiped it away quickly.

Melody gave him a knowing look. "I suspect I know who brought that smile to your face. Could it be that you have finally come to recognize that love and hate are separated by a fine line?"

And now he needed another sip of his drink.

"You can say nothing, but your silence just confirms what I already know to be true," Melody said.

Knowing that he needed to change topics, Winston glanced down at Melody's hands and saw that she had ink on her fingertips. "Who did you write?"

"My friend, Josephine," Melody replied.

"You write to her quite often," Winston said.

Melody nodded. "I do."

He lifted his brow. "Dare I ask what you find to write about?"

"We always find a wide array of things to write about," Melody responded, her face lighting up. "It is rather enjoyable to send letters and receive them in return."

Winston returned the glass to the table. "How is your Russian coming along?"

"It is good," Melody responded.

The long clock in the corner chimed, alerting them to the time. "It is late. We should retire to bed," he said as he stood up.

Melody didn't make an effort to rise. "I think I shall stay here and work on my letter to Josephine."

The way Melody said Josephine's name made Winston pause. He had a hunch, but he hoped he was wrong. There was only one way to find out. "Does Mother know Josephine is actually a gentleman?"

Melody's eyes went wide. "How did you know?"

"I suspected it only because your face lit up when you spoke about what you wrote about," Winston explained.

"Are you going to tell Mother?" Melody asked.

Winston returned to his seat, regarding his sister with the sternest expression he could muster up. "It depends," he began. "Do you have an understanding with this gentleman?"

Melody hesitated, her eyes shifting away. "We have an arrangement of sorts."

"What does that mean?" Winston pressed.

"We exchange letters only because we value one another's friendship," Melody replied, her tone measured. "I assure you that there is nothing romantic in nature."

Winston frowned. "Your reputation is at risk if anyone discovers the truth. After all, a woman should only write to a gentleman once they are betrothed."

Melody looked amused. "You are lecturing me on propriety now?"

"Will you at least tell me the name of the man you are writing?"

The amusement slipped from Melody's face, replaced by a solemn expression. "I trust that you will keep this between us, for now."

"I give you my word."

Appearing satisfied with his response, she replied, "It is Lord Emberly."

Winston was well acquainted with Lord Emberly, having spent time with him at Eton. He considered him to be an honorable person, but that didn't mean he liked knowing his sister was exchanging letters with no formal understanding between them.

"I would proceed very cautiously," he advised. "I would hate for you to be trapped in a marriage that neither of you want."

Melody huffed, a touch of indignation in her voice. "I would never marry Lord Emberly. Just that mere thought of a union between us is ludicrous."

"Yet you write to him, constantly," Winston pointed out.

She waved her hand dismissively. "Yes, but it is purely innocent."

"Are you sure that Lord Emberly feels the same?"

"Quite sure," Melody responded quickly. Too quickly.

What was his sister up to? His sister always followed the rules, almost to a fault. So why was she risking her reputation to write to a man that she claimed she would never marry?

Melody smiled, no doubt in an attempt to reassure him. "You can stop worrying, Brother. I know what I am doing."

"How do you know I was worrying?"

"Because I know you," she simply replied. "Do you intend to call upon Mattie tomorrow?"

Winston knew what Melody was truly asking but wasn't saying. "I am, but only so I can speak to Lord Wythburn about the upcoming Season."

"If that is the only reason…" Melody's voice trailed off, leaving the implication hanging in the air.

He let out a sigh. "Just as you and Lord Emberly do not have an understanding, neither do Mattie and I."

"Yes, but you and Mattie belong with one another," Melody pressed, her voice filled with conviction.

Winston was done with this ridiculous conversation. It was late, and he wanted to retire to bed. Perhaps if he slept long enough, he would forget that he desperately loved Mattie. But he doubted that.

"Goodnight, Melody," he said, standing up and heading for the door, hoping to escape the turmoil in his heart, if only for a few hours.

After he departed from the library, Winston headed towards his bedchamber but remembered he had left the ledger for his sheep farm in the study. He decided to retrieve it before retiring for the night. Changing course, he descended the stairs.

As he approached the study door, he noticed a shadow moving from under the door. Was his father up at this late hour?

Winston slowly opened the door and was taken aback to find Isaac rummaging through the drawers of his father's desk. A lone candle flickered on the desk, casting eerie shadows on Isaac's face.

"What in the blazes are you doing here?" Winston shouted, his voice echoing through the corridor.

Isaac looked up from the desk, unfazed. "I would think it was clearly obvious," he said. "I came to find what is rightfully mine."

Winston turned and shouted, "White! Get in here now!"

Isaac slammed the drawers shut. "Just tell me where Sarah is and this will all be over," he growled. "I hate this godforsaken village. I want to go home."

"No one is stopping you," Winston said.

"I won't go home without my wife and son," Isaac responded.

White appeared beside him. "Yes, my lord?"

"Send for the constable," Winston ordered. "It would appear that I have caught a thief."

Isaac's eyes narrowed. "I'm the thief?" he asked incredulously. "You are the one who stole my wife and son from me."

White tipped his head and went to do his bidding, but not before Winston noticed two footmen had come to stand behind him.

"We stole nothing," Winston said. "It is merely your fault that you misplaced your wife and son."

Isaac walked over to the open window. "This isn't over, my lord," he mocked.

"I think it is, considering stealing is a serious offense," Winston said, his tone unyielding.

Raising his hands in mock surrender, Isaac responded, "I stole nothing."

"The constable might think differently," Winston remarked. "There is no place for you to hide now."

Isaac grinned, a dangerous glint in his eyes. "You underestimate me, and that is going to be your undoing."

"I truly doubt that," Winston said. "Your words are just the words of a desperate man."

His grin dimmed but didn't disappear entirely. "I will show you desperate." With that, he leapt out the window.

Winston hurried over to the window and saw Isaac's retreating figure, his boots slapping against the wet lawn.

A footman spoke up from behind. "Shall we go after him, my lord?"

"There is no need," Winston replied. "We know where he is residing. I will direct the constable to his cottage."

Melody stepped into the study, her face etched with concern. "I heard shouting. Is everything all right?"

Winston turned to face his sister. "Isaac was here, searching through Father's desk. No doubt he was trying to learn of Aunt Sarah's location."

"Was he successful?"

"No, considering we don't know where Aunt Sarah even is," Winston replied, approaching his sister. "But White is sending for the constable. I will ensure Isaac pays for breaking into our home."

Melody glanced at the open window, her unease palpable. "I do not like knowing that Isaac was here. I do believe I will sleep with a pistol under my pillow for the time being."

"That hardly seems safe," Winston remarked, frowning at the thought.

"Perhaps not, but it would greatly ease my mind," Melody said.

Winston placed his hands on his sister's shoulders. "I will keep you safe," he promised.

Something flickered in Melody's eyes—determination, perhaps, or maybe a flash of anger. It was hard for Winston to decipher.

Melody took a step back and Winston's arms dropped to his sides. "It is late, and I think it is best if we both retire to bed," she said.

Winston knew he wouldn't be able to sleep. Not now. "I will remain here until the constable arrives."

"All right," Melody responded. "Goodnight, Brother."

After his sister left the room, Winston went to retrieve the sheep farm ledger from the desk and tucked it under his arm. It was going to be a long night.

Mattie exited the coach and approached Brockhall Manor with a bubbling sense of excitement. The early morning sun cast a golden hue over the grand estate, making it look even more magnificent than usual. She hoped it wasn't too early to call, but she could barely contain her eagerness. She had wonderful news to share.

The door opened and White greeted her with his usual stoic expression. "Good morning, Miss Bawden," he said, standing to the side to grant her entry. "Do come in."

Mattie stepped into the entry hall, her eyes wide with admiration for the sheer elegance that surrounded her. The opulence of Brockhall Manor mirrored the grandeur of Darlington Abbey, where she would soon be spending much of her time. Her grandfather had spared no expense in renovating the estate after inheriting his title. And now, as a viscount's daughter, she felt the weight of her new responsibilities. She was determined to rise to the challenge.

A movement caught her eyes, and she turned her attention towards Winston descending the grand staircase. She took a moment to admire him, acknowledging that she would never meet another man more dashing than him. In her imagination, whenever she read books, the hero always looked like Winston—a tall, dark and handsome man who used his cleverness to solve problems.

Winston's eyes landed on her, and he smiled, causing her

breath to hitch. "Good morning," he greeted, approaching her. "What a pleasant surprise to see you at such an early hour."

"I hope it is not too early," she said, her excitement barely contained. "I have the most wonderful news to share."

His eyes seemed to twinkle with merriment. "Then you must share it with me at once," he said.

Mattie could barely contain herself as she shared, "My father agreed to let your mother host me for the upcoming Season."

His smile broadened, spilling into his eyes. "That is wonderful news! How did you convince him to do so?"

With a slight shrug, Mattie said, "I am very convincing when I want to be."

"That you are, considering I have seen it firsthand," Winston responded.

Mattie clasped her hands together. "I suppose I have my sister to thank. She was insistent about having a Season next year and my father suggested we both debut together."

"That would have been a terrible idea."

"I thought so as well, so I pushed back, and he relented," Mattie said. "Although, truth be told, my father did say some hurtful things to me."

Winston's smile faded. "What did he say?"

Mattie pressed her lips together, wondering why she had brought this up with Winston. "He doesn't think I am capable of making as good of a match as Emma."

"Whyever not?"

She sighed. "Emma is precisely what the *ton* deems as beautiful, and I—"

Winston took a step closer to her. "You are beautiful, Mattie," he said. "And I will not have you think otherwise."

"Even my father believes I pale in comparison to Emma," Mattie stated, trying to keep the hurt out of her voice.

Reaching for her hand, Winston said, "Beauty is not just

about having a pretty face. It requires intelligence, kindness, loyalty and, most importantly, a beautiful soul. And you, my dear, are in possession of all those things."

Mattie glanced down at their joined hands. "Do you truly mean it?"

"I do, and I cannot stand by and let you talk bad about yourself," Winston replied. "Not when I can see the real you."

"I see the real you, as well," Mattie admitted. "Even the parts you don't want me to see."

Winston's eyes crinkled around the edges with a warm smile. "I should have known I wouldn't have been able to hide from you for too long."

Lady Dallington's voice echoed from the corridor. "Mattie, what a wonderful surprise," she said loudly.

Winston quickly slipped his hand out of hers and took a step back. She hadn't realized how close she was to him until that moment.

Coming to a stop in front of Mattie, Lady Dallington said, "I was just about to break my fast. Would you care to join us for breakfast?"

"I do not wish to be a bother," Mattie attempted.

"Nonsense!" Lady Dallington exclaimed. "You are more than welcome, and I am sure Winston feels the same."

Winston cleared his throat. "She is more than welcome to join us, but be wary of Elodie when she is buttering her bread."

Mattie gave him an odd look. "Why?" she couldn't help but ask.

"That is when Elodie has a knife, and she is not afraid to wield it," Winston said with a wink.

"Come along, Child," Lady Dallington encouraged.

As Mattie walked with Lady Dallington, she noticed Winston trailed closely behind. "I just came to tell you the most wonderful news."

"Which is?" Lady Dallington asked.

Mattie beamed. "My father has granted permission for you to host me this Season."

Lady Dallington returned her smile. "What wonderful news!" she exclaimed. "We have so much that we must do to prepare."

They entered the dining room and Winston pulled out a chair for Mattie. Once she was situated, she murmured her thanks, secretly pleased when Winston sat down next to her.

"I shall need to create a list of everything we must do in anticipation of this upcoming Season," Lady Dallington declared. "We must get you a whole new wardrobe, accessories..." She paused thoughtfully. "How are you on dancing?"

Mattie winced slightly. "I dance well enough."

"That will not do," Lady Dallington said firmly. "We shall need to get you lessons with the dancing master. Dancing in the countryside is much different than dancing in Town. Winston can help with that."

"I am but your humble servant, Mother," Winston replied with a hint of amusement.

Lady Dallington leaned to the side as a footman placed a plate of food in front of her. "I could use less sarcasm from you. But, if you have no objections, you shall be Mattie's dance partner when the dancing master arrives."

"I would be happy to," Winston responded.

Mattie snuck a glance at Winston, surprised by how easily he agreed to such a thing. He almost seemed pleased by the prospect of dancing with her.

A footman placed a plate in front of Mattie and she reached for her fork and knife, realizing she hadn't eaten breakfast in her rush to share her news.

Elodie stepped into the dining room and smiled. "Good morning, Mattie," she said.

"Good morning," Mattie responded, smiling back.

Coming to sit across from her at the table, Elodie gave her

a questioning look. "Not that I am complaining, but I am curious as to what brings you by at such an early hour."

Mattie put her fork and knife down, eager to share her news. "I came to inform Lady Dallington that I will be joining you for this Season."

Elodie bobbed her head in approval, her eyes sparkling. "That is wonderful news," she exclaimed. "Just think of all the gentlemen that will be vying for your attention."

"I doubt that," Mattie said, glancing at Winston. She noticed that his jaw was clenched.

Reaching for her teacup, Elodie continued, "Oh yes, it will be such fun to see gentlemen falling over themselves to make a good impression on you."

Mattie hadn't considered that. But she should have. The point of having a Season was to find a match. "You flatter me, Elodie, but I do not know…"

Elodie spoke over her. "Do not worry. Winston will be with us to ensure only the gentlemen with the most noble intentions will dance with us." She turned her attention towards her brother. "Isn't that right, Winston?"

A muscle pulsated just below Winston's ear and Mattie wondered what she had said—or done—that could have upset him.

"Yes, I will remain by your sides," Winston said through clenched teeth.

Elodie looked satisfied by his response. "We are going to have such fun this Season. We will go on carriage rides, visit the Royal Menagerie and eat ices from Gunter's."

Melody entered the room and Elodie immediately announced, "Mattie is here because her father has agreed to let her have a Season."

"Thank you for that, Elodie," Lady Dallington interjected with a hint of reproach. "But it was not your news to share."

Mattie laughed. "I do not mind, my lady."

Elodie picked up a knife and carefully began buttering her

toast, ensuring the butter reached all corners. "Having Mattie there will make the Season that much more exciting," she said, glancing at her brother. "Isn't that right, Winston?"

Winston frowned, clearly annoyed. "Why do you insist on injecting me into this conversation?"

"I was hoping to get your opinion on it," Elodie said, placing the knife down and taking a bite of her toast.

"I have no doubt that Mattie will have an enjoyable Season," Winston said, his words flat and emotionless.

Mattie couldn't help but wonder what had come over Winston. They had had a pleasant conversation in the entry hall, just a few moments ago. Now, he seemed distant, almost as if he were anxious to be away from her.

Melody, who had taken a seat next to her sister, haphazardly plopped some butter onto her toast and took a large bite.

Elodie scrunched up her nose. "Why do you insist on eating toast that way?"

"What way?" Melody asked, feigning innocence.

"The butter should be spread evenly throughout so every bite is just as scrumptious as the last," Elodie said with a touch of exasperation.

Melody grinned mischievously, making Mattie think that she was doing it on purpose to goad her sister. "I am satisfied with my bite of toast."

Turning her attention towards Mattie, Elodie asked, "How do you butter your toast?"

"I have never given it much thought before," Mattie admitted.

Winston chuckled, breaking his aloof demeanor. "Leave Mattie alone," he encouraged. "I am sure the way she butters her toast is perfectly acceptable."

Elodie looked disappointed. "I am surrounded by savages," she said, her voice light and teasing.

Leaning forward, Winston reached over and took a piece of toast off Elodie's plate. "Allow me to see if your way is better," he said before taking an exaggerated bite. "It is... sufficient. But I have had better toast."

Picking up her knife, Elodie held it up. "Give me back my toast or face the consequences, Brother."

Lady Dallington sighed deeply. "Do you two have to do this now?" she asked. "We have a guest."

"Mattie isn't truly a guest," Melody said with a smile. "She is like family."

"Yes, but she is probably not used to people stabbing one another with knives during the course of a meal," Lady Dallington pointed out.

Winston returned the toast to Elodie's plate. "You are welcome."

"For what?" Elodie asked, raising an eyebrow.

"I confirmed that your bread was not poisonous," he said with a mock serious expression. "You may now eat it without worry."

Elodie rolled her eyes dramatically. "It is no surprise that you are not married."

"Elodie!" Lady Dallington chided. "Be nice to your brother."

"Yes, Mother," Elodie muttered, a playful grin tugging at her lips.

Shifting her gaze towards Mattie, Lady Dallington said, "I am sorry you had to witness that. They are normally on better behavior when we have guests."

"I find it rather amusing," Mattie admitted, her smile genuine. The banter and warmth of the Lockwood family was refreshing, and she felt a sense of belonging that she cherished deeply.

Lady Dallington tipped her head towards Mattie's plate. "Eat up, Child," she said. "We have loads to do this morning."

Chapter Seventeen

Winston sat at the dining table as the lively conversation flowed around him. Despite the cheerful chatter, his thoughts were heavy. The idea of Mattie having hordes of suitors lining up to meet her gnawed at him. How could she not attract them? She was unlike any young woman he knew. Mattie was undeniably beautiful, clever and full of wit. She was precisely the type of woman that he always envisioned he would marry. But life had a way of shattering dreams.

White stepped into the dining room and met Winston's gaze. "The constable wishes for a moment of your time, my lord," he announced.

"Very well," Winston said, pushing back his chair. He glanced at the ladies. "Excuse me."

Mattie looked over at him, offering a private smile that warmed his heart. He returned her smile, leaning closer to her, feeling an immense desire to be near her. "Do not let my mother's enthusiasm for the Season overwhelm you," he remarked.

"I won't," Mattie assured him.

"Good, because I have no doubt you will do remarkably well this Season," he praised, rising from his seat.

Winston departed from the dining room and headed towards the entry hall. There, he saw the tall, broad-shouldered constable with a scar that ran along his chin. Mr. Strunk held his hat in his hand as he acknowledged Winston with a tip of his head. "Good morning, my lord," he greeted.

"Good morning," Winston responded.

"I hope I did not come at a bad time," Mr. Strunk said.

"You did no such thing," Winston remarked. "Is Isaac in custody?"

Mr. Strunk shook his head. "Unfortunately, I went to the cottage where Mr. Blythe was supposedly residing, and he was not there."

"Where could he be?" Winston asked, frustration lacing his voice.

"It appears as if he had left in a hurry. The cottage looked as if it had been ransacked," Mr. Strunk informed him.

"Wonderful," Winston muttered.

Mr. Strunk grew solemn. "I have a few men looking for Mr. Blythe and I have no doubt that he will eventually turn up."

Winston frowned, his mind racing with the potential havoc Isaac could wreak before he was caught. "I want him found and punished for breaking into my home," he said firmly.

"And he will be," Mr. Strunk assured him. "Have some patience. Mr. Blythe will be in my custody soon enough."

Knowing there was little he could do but wait, Winston nodded in acknowledgement. "Inform me at once when Isaac is in custody."

"I will," Mr. Strunk responded before he departed from the manor.

As he went to turn around, he found himself face to face with Elodie. She smiled. "Hello, Brother," she said innocently.

"What are you doing here?" Winston asked.

"Nothing," Elodie replied with a casual shrug. "I was just

hoping to speak to my brother for a moment. Is that wrong of me?"

"It depends on what you wish to speak about," Winston said warily.

Elodie placed a hand on her chest, feigning innocence once more. "Shall we speak in the drawing room so others cannot overhear this conversation?"

The last thing Winston wanted to do was engage in one of Elodie's schemes, but he knew she would continue to pester him until he gave in. He might as well get it over with.

Winston gestured towards the drawing room. "After you, Sister," he said.

Elodie brushed past him and entered the drawing room. Once she stood in the middle, she spun back around and lowered her voice. "When are you going to make your intentions known to Mattie?"

Winston sighed. He should have known that Elodie would wish to talk about such a difficult topic. "I'm not," he responded curtly.

"Whyever not?" Elodie asked, her tone incredulous. "You care for her, she cares for you... the next step is a baby in the cradle."

Winston grinned despite himself. "You missed a few steps there."

"Did I?" Elodie asked, smiling mischievously.

Winston's grin faded as he met his sister's earnest gaze. "Elodie, it is not that simple. There are things you don't understand."

"What is there to understand?" Elodie asked. "Could you truly watch Mattie being courted by a myriad of suitors and just stand by and watch?"

Winston decided it was best if he just told Elodie the truth and hoped she would understand. "I wrote Mattie a letter, declaring my intentions, but she never responded."

"You gave her this letter?" Elodie asked.

"No, but I gave it to Miss Emma, and she assured me that Mattie would receive it," Winston said.

Elodie considered his words before asking, "When was this?"

"About a year ago," Winston replied.

"People change," Elodie insisted. "What if Mattie regrets not responding to your letter and is hoping you make another attempt?"

Winston placed a hand on his sister's shoulder. "I am not going to pester Mattie until she agrees to marry me. That wouldn't be fair to her, or me."

"So you just give up?"

He shook his head. "It is better this way."

Elodie's eyes grew wide with frustration. "Better for whom?" she asked, her voice rising in challenge.

Winston sighed, dropping his arm. "It is complicated, Elodie, and I hope that you will respect my choice in the matter."

"But you are wrong to do so," Elodie insisted. "You are denying yourself happiness. You must trust me on this. Just go speak to Mattie and tell her that you are madly in love with her."

He blinked, taken aback. "Who said anything about love?"

Elodie gave him a knowing look. "I can see it in your eyes whenever you look at Mattie," she said. "And, quite frankly, I have suspected it for quite some time now."

Winston looked away, the weight of her words pressing on him. "What if you are wrong?" he asked. "I will be humiliated once more."

"I used to think that love was elusive, like a unicorn…"

"Unicorns aren't real," Winston interjected.

"… we shall have to agree to disagree on that," she said, undeterred.

Winston gave his sister an exasperated look. "There is nothing to disagree upon. Unicorns aren't real."

The Gentleman's Miscalculation

"Aren't they?" Elodie's eyes twinkled with amusement.

"They are not," Winston responded firmly.

"Fine. Have it your way," Elodie said with a smile. "I used to think that love was imaginary, like a unicorn, but I was wrong. If you have a chance at love, you must take it, even if it means that your heart is ripped open. Because the right person is capable of making it whole."

Winston eyed Elodie curiously, wondering when she had gotten so wise. But despite the familiar amusement in her eyes, he saw the sincerity as well. Perhaps she was right. And, perhaps, despite everything, there was still a chance for him and Mattie. "Thank you, Elodie," he said softly. "I will think about what you have said."

Elodie smiled. "You might want to speak to Mattie now since Mother is holding her hostage in the dining room."

He chuckled. "That does not surprise me."

As he made his way to the dining room, Elodie's words echoed in his mind. With each step, his resolve strengthened. He would speak to Mattie. He would tell her everything and hope that she wouldn't reject him once more.

Winston stopped outside of the dining room door as he heard Mattie's laugh drift out into the corridor. Her laugh was his favorite sound in the whole world. He took a moment, savoring the melody of her joy and letting it fortify his courage.

Taking a deep breath, Winston stepped into the dining room and met Mattie's gaze. She smiled. A beautiful smile. With it, he glimpsed something far more beautiful than all the stars in the night sky.

"Ah, Winston," his mother greeted, drawing his attention. "Have you concluded your business?"

"Yes, Mother," Winston replied.

His mother shoved back her chair. "Good, because White just informed me that the musicians are setting up in the music room."

"Musicians?" Winston asked.

Rising, his mother responded, "Do you not recall agreeing to being Mattie's dance partner?"

"I do, but I just didn't realize that it would happen so soon," Winston said. "I thought we were waiting for the dancing master."

"I saw no reason to lollygag," his mother responded.

Mattie stood up, smoothing down the fabric of her black dress. "I feel as if I should warn Lord Winston that I am not the most accomplished dancer."

Winston gave her an encouraging smile. "I have no doubt that you are much better than you give yourself credit for," he reassured her.

"You are kind," Mattie said as she approached him. She came to a stop in front of him and lowered her voice. "I'm sorry."

Winston cocked his head. "Whatever for?"

"I am sure you have more important things to do than be my dance partner," she remarked as she lowered her gaze.

In a voice that he hoped conveyed his sincerity, he replied, "There is no other place I would like to be."

Mattie brought her gaze back up, uncertainty in her eyes. "Do you truly mean it, my lord?"

He puffed out his chest. "It is not every day that I can show off my extraordinary dancing skills."

A laugh escaped Mattie's lips and she brought a hand up to cover her mouth. "Well, I am most grateful to have such a skilled partner."

Encouraged by her laughter, Winston suggested, "Perhaps we could take a walk in the gardens after our dance."

Mattie's eyes seemed to search his, as if she were looking for answers. "I would like that," she said.

"Good," Winston replied, offering his arm. "Shall we make our way to the music room?"

She placed her hand gently on his arm, and they walked

together down the corridor towards the music room. The distant sounds of violins and soft murmurs of conversation filled the air.

As they entered the music room, Winston released Mattie's arm, but remained close by her side. A faint scent of lavender wafted off her person, and he couldn't help but take a moment to savor it.

His mother had followed them into the room and now clapped her hands to garner everyone's attention. "I believe we shall start with the waltz."

Mattie's mouth dropped. "The waltz?" she repeated. "I have never danced the waltz with a gentleman before."

Winston turned to face her fully, seeing the worry lines etched on her forehead. He leaned in closer and whispered reassuringly, "Trust me."

She blinked, and all the worry seemed to disappear from her expression, replaced by a look of quiet determination. "I do," she replied with conviction.

The musicians began to play a soft, lilting waltz, and Winston took Mattie's hand in his own, guiding her to the center of the room. He placed his hand gently on her waist, feeling the slight tremor in her body. "Just follow my lead," he said softly.

And with that, they began to dance perfectly in step with each other, as if they were made for this very moment.

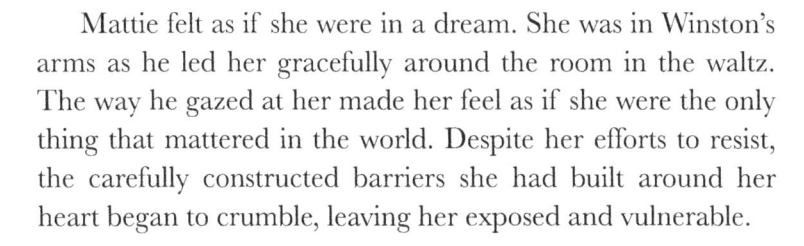

Mattie felt as if she were in a dream. She was in Winston's arms as he led her gracefully around the room in the waltz. The way he gazed at her made her feel as if she were the only thing that mattered in the world. Despite her efforts to resist, the carefully constructed barriers she had built around her heart began to crumble, leaving her exposed and vulnerable.

And that frightened her.

Could she truly risk letting Winston back into her heart, knowing what she did? He had kissed her and then treated her with cold disdain. Not that she planned to kiss him again. But heaven help her, she wanted to kiss him again. What was wrong with her? Her emotions were all over the place, and she couldn't grasp what she wanted—or needed—when she was in Winston's arms. His strong, comforting arms.

An overwhelming sense of panic washed over her. She couldn't quite seem to catch her breath and she needed to stop this dance at once.

Mattie dropped her arms and stepped back.

Winston watched her with concern etched across his handsome face. "Are you all right, Mattie?"

The genuine concern in his voice was her undoing. She felt her face grow warm and brought her hands up to cover her reddening cheeks. "I am… tired." Tired? Could she not have come up with a better excuse than that?

"Would you like to sit down?" Winston asked, his voice gentle.

"No, that won't be necessary," Mattie replied quickly. "I think it would be best if I returned home and rested."

Winston took a step closer to her, and she instinctively took a step back. She watched as his face fell, and her heart ached because of it. But it was better this way. If she let him back in, her heart may never recover when he inevitably left.

Mattie dropped into a curtsy. "Thank you for the dance," she said, her voice barely steady, before she departed from the room.

Once she was alone in the corridor, she let out a breath that she hadn't even realized she had been holding. How was it that she could long for Winston, knowing it was a terrible idea?

"Mattie… wait, please," Winston called out after her.

The Gentleman's Miscalculation

Mattie's steps faltered and she turned back to see Winston striding towards her.

Winston came to a stop in front of her but maintained a proper distance. "Did I say or do something to upset you?" he asked, his eyes imploring.

"No, you did not, my lord," she said, trying to maintain her composure. She couldn't tell him the truth. Not now. Not ever. It would be too humiliating.

He lifted an eyebrow. "My lord?" he repeated with a hint of amusement. "No, I am Winston. Just Winston."

Despite herself, she smiled at him. "My apologies," she murmured.

Taking a step closer to her, Winston's eyes remained locked on hers as he said, "I enjoyed our dance, and I look forward to dancing with you in Town." He paused. "Assuming you will have time for me when you are surrounded by your suitors."

"I will always make time for you, Winston," Mattie said softly, her heart in her throat.

"And I you," he replied, his voice equally soft and sincere.

Mattie held his gaze and she saw far more than she wanted to see. In his eyes, she saw herself—vulnerable, hopeful, and perhaps, just perhaps, capable of love once more.

Winston smiled, and all her defenses melted away. "It is a shame that you are tired because our gardens are quite beautiful."

She knew she should leave, but she wasn't quite ready to say goodbye to Winston. As much as she wanted to push him away, her heart was trying to pull him back in. "I suppose we could take a short walk," she responded.

"I would like that," Winston said, offering his arm.

Mattie accepted his arm and they walked towards the rear of the manor. A footman opened the door for them and then discreetly followed them onto the veranda.

As they started walking down the path, Winston gestured

towards the roses. "These are my mother's beloved roses. I do believe she loves them more than she does her own children."

She laughed. "I daresay you exaggerate. I have never seen a mother dote more on her children than Lady Dallington."

"What can I say? We are easy to love," Winston joked. He ran his finger along the stem of a rose. "I find it fascinating that something so beautiful as a rose grows on thorns."

"It is a way to protect itself."

"True, and that is where we are similar," Winston said. "I have fought so hard to prove myself that I feel as if I have surrounded myself with thorns."

Mattie reached out and touched the soft petals of a rose. "Thorns can be removed," she remarked.

"Yes, they can, but it can be a painful process," Winston said.

"Only for people that are afraid of being pricked," Mattie retorted. "But I believe that some things are worth a moment of pain."

Winston turned to face her, his expression unreadable. "How is it that you know precisely what to say to speak to my heart?"

Mattie shrugged, pretending that his words did not affect her. "I suppose it is because I am very wise," she teased.

"That you are," he agreed, hesitating. "Mattie… I am grateful for this moment alone… with you."

As he uttered his words, Mattie saw Matilda jump up on her bench, sprawling out lazily. She pointed to the goat, and said, "It would appear that Matilda is in need of a rest."

Winston followed her gaze. "Yes, I do wish that Mr. Warren wouldn't let Matilda roam free in our gardens."

"I just adore Matilda," Mattie said.

"Matilda is just a goat," Winston teased.

Mattie grinned. "I saw Matilda perched in a tree yesterday," she said. "She bellowed at me as I passed."

Winston turned back to face her, his expression growing

serious again. "Yes, well, I was hoping to speak to you, and it wasn't about Matilda."

Her heart raced as she sensed the gravity of what he was about to say. "What did you wish to speak about?"

He took a deep breath. "Mattie, do you ever think of that kiss?"

Every day.

But she didn't dare admit that.

She nodded. "I do, on occasion," she replied, attempting to keep her voice steady.

Moving closer to her, he said, "That kiss changed everything for me... for us. It made me realize that I cared for you, far more than I ever cared for another."

Mattie's heart swelled with emotion, but fear still lingered. "Winston, if that was the case, why did you treat me so terribly after?"

"It was because you ignored my letter, but I am willing to move past that—"

She furrowed her brows. "What letter?" she asked, interrupting him.

"The letter I delivered to your cottage," Winston replied. "The one I wrote the night we kissed."

"I received no such letter," Mattie assured him.

Winston pressed his lips together. "But I handed it to Miss Emma, and she assured me that she would deliver it to you."

"She never gave me a letter," Mattie asserted.

A look of palpable relief came to Winston's features. "For so long, I have thought the worst of you, but I was wrong to do so. I thought... you didn't care."

Mattie looked into his eyes, seeing the sincerity there. Her walls were crumbling, and despite the risks, she knew she had to take the chance. "Winston, I care for you, more so than I should admit."

Winston reached out and gently took her hand. "You don't know how happy I am to hear you say that."

She took a deep breath, feeling a mixture of hope and apprehension. "Dare I ask what was in that letter?"

As he opened his mouth to reply, the sound of slow clapping echoed from behind them.

Mattie turned her head to see Isaac standing a short distance away, a pistol tucked in the waistband of his trousers.

"That was beautiful," Isaac mocked, his voice dripping with sarcasm. "I have been waiting for the moment when you two finally succumbed to your feelings."

Winston moved to stand in front of her. "Get off my property."

Isaac retrieved his pistol and pointed it at Winston, his eyes cold. "You are not in a position to make demands here. It is my turn now."

"What do you want?" Winston asked, his voice steady despite the threat.

Taking a step closer to them, Isaac growled, "I want my wife and son back."

"Never!" Winston exclaimed.

"Then I shall be content with Miss Bawden," Isaac said. "Move aside, my lord."

Winston stood his ground. "Miss Bawden is going nowhere with you."

Isaac looked amused. "Did you think I came alone?" he asked. "If so, you would be sorely mistaken. I have taken the liberty of making the guard following Miss Bawden to be indisposed at the moment."

"Did you kill him?" Winston demanded, his eyes narrowing.

With a mock look of innocence, Isaac replied, "I am not a monster. No, he should wake up soon enough with a pounding headache."

Mattie turned her head towards the veranda where the footman was stationed and saw he was being held by gunpoint by a short, stout man.

The Gentleman's Miscalculation

"Miss Bawden, will you step forward, please?" Isaac asked, his voice dangerously polite.

Winston swiped his hand in front of him. "Absolutely not!" he exclaimed. "If you want Miss Bawden, you are going to have to kill me first."

Isaac cocked the pistol. "My pleasure, my lord."

Sensing the seriousness of the situation, Mattie moved to stand in front of Winston and put her hands up. "Do not hurt him."

"What are you doing, Mattie?" Winston asked, his voice filled with anguish. "You can't go with him."

She turned back to face him, her eyes pleading for him to understand. "I couldn't live with myself if you were killed because of me," she insisted.

Isaac's taunting voice reached their ears. "We can end this song and dance right now if you will give me Sarah and Matthew."

"No, I would die first," Winston said, his voice unwavering.

With a sigh, Isaac remarked, "We are back to you dying, then." He paused, and his voice grew stern. "Time is up. Give me Miss Bawden."

Winston took a commanding step towards Isaac, but Mattie placed a hand on his chest, stilling him. "What are you doing?" she asked.

"I won't let him take you," Winston responded, his eyes blazing with determination.

"He has a pistol," Mattie pointed out. "And I do not think it would take much for him to kill you."

Winston looked at her incredulously. "I can't lose you... not now."

Isaac stepped forward and grabbed Mattie's arm, yanking her back. "If you want Miss Bawden back, you know what you have to do."

Winston's voice grew thunderous. "If you hurt Miss Bawden—"

"That is entirely up to you, my lord," Isaac spat out. "It is your fault that it has come to this."

Mattie tried to remove her arm from Isaac's grip, but he held firm, his grasp tightening painfully.

"Please," she implored, her voice cracking. "Do not hurt him. I will go with you, just don't harm him."

"Wise choice," Isaac declared. "Now, let us be on our way before I lose my patience."

As Isaac started to lead Mattie away, Winston's voice rang out in a desperate shout, "No! You can't have Miss Bawden. I won't let you."

"He is rather stubborn, is he not?" Isaac muttered under his breath, his tone laced with irritation, before pointing the pistol at Winston and firing.

Mattie gasped in horror as Winston let out a pained groan and clutched his shoulder, blood seeping through his fingers. "What have you done?" she shouted as she tried to free herself from Isaac's unyielding hold. "Winston!"

Isaac dragged her towards a coach a short distance away and tossed her inside. He followed her in and sat down on the bench. The coach jerked forward, jostling them both.

"It is much more comfortable on the bench than the ground," Isaac joked.

She moved to sit across from Isaac and asked, "How could you? You promised you wouldn't hurt him."

"I lied," Isaac admitted callously. "Besides, you should be thanking me that I only shot him in the shoulder."

Mattie glared at him, her voice trembling with indignation. "Thank you?" she repeated. "What kind of man are you?"

Isaac's expression hardened, his jaw set firmly. "A desperate one," he retorted curtly. "I will do whatever it takes to get my family back."

"This isn't the way," Mattie protested. "Hurting people won't bring them back to you."

Isaac leaned back in his seat, his expression unwavering. "You don't understand, Miss Bawden. Lord Winston took everything from me. He will pay, one way or another."

Mattie's heart ached for Winston, who had been left behind wounded and vulnerable. She could only hope he would find a way to follow and rescue her. "Lord Winston is a good man—"

Isaac's bitter laugh cut her off. "Good men do not steal other men's wives," he shot back. "And now, you are my leverage. He will give me what I want, or he will lose you."

The coach continued along the rough road, the wheels rattling loudly and the pace relentless, jolting Mattie against the hard seat. She gripped the edge of the bench tightly, trying to steady herself as she took deep breaths to calm her racing heart. She needed to stay composed and find a way to escape.

Chapter Eighteen

Winston winced as the doctor examined the wound on his shoulder. He didn't have time for this. He needed to find a way to save Mattie and bring her back to him... alive. That was his first, and only, priority. He would do whatever it took, even risk his own life, to ensure she was safe.

Doctor Anderson took a step back, his expression serious but relieved. "You are very lucky, my lord," he said. "The bullet merely grazed your skin. It could have been a lot worse."

"Wonderful," Winston muttered.

"I do believe that stitches aren't necessary, but you will be left with a scar," the doctor explained, his tone matter-of-fact.

A scar was the least of his concerns, and he felt it was absurd to even remark on such a thing. Grimacing, he reached for his shirt and struggled to put it on, every movement sending jolts of pain through his shoulder.

His mother stepped forward, her eyes filled with worry. "You should rest," she urged gently.

Winston stared at his mother incredulously. "How can I rest knowing that Mattie is with a madman?" he demanded, his voice tight with frustration.

"I know it would be difficult…" she began.

"No, it would be impossible!" Winston exclaimed, his anger barely contained. "I have to find Mattie before Isaac harms her."

His mother's eyes softened with compassion. "I'm sorry. I don't know the right thing to say or do at this precise moment."

Winston took a deep breath, recognizing his mother's concern. He needed to stay calm, even though every fiber of his being screamed to act. "If I am to be honest, neither do I," he admitted.

Just then, Grady stepped into the room, his expression determined. "I sent word to Jasper about what transpired. He needs to know what happened."

"You knew where Jasper was keeping my aunt this entire time?" Winston asked.

"I did," Grady replied unabashedly.

Winston saw the dried blood on Grady's forehead and said, "You should have Doctor Anderson look at your wound."

Grady reached up and touched the top of his head, wincing slightly. "It is nothing," he said dismissively.

"It looks like more than nothing," Winston countered.

A pensive look came to Grady's expression. "This is just a reminder that I failed at my task, but I refuse to let Isaac win. He will pay for what he has done."

"My thoughts exactly," Winston responded, his resolve hardening.

His mother frowned. "What is it that you intend to do, Winston?" she asked, the worry evident in her voice. "You are a barrister after all. Not a Bow Street Runner."

Winston approached his mother and placed his hands on her shoulders. "I understand your concern, but I will do whatever it takes to get Mattie back."

"That is what concerns me the most," his mother remarked, her voice trembling.

Doctor Anderson reached for his satchel and spoke up. "I will be at my home. Please send for me if you are in need of my services."

Winston tipped his head. "Thank you, Doctor."

After the doctor departed from the drawing room, Lord Dallington stepped into the room, his face etched with concern.

"What did the doctor say?" his father asked, his voice tense.

Winston moved to place his waistcoat on. "He said I would live."

His father let out a sigh of relief. "What were you thinking?" he demanded. "You should never have aggravated Isaac."

"Isaac abducted Mattie," Winston stated, his voice rising with emotion. "I wasn't about to stand back and let that happen."

"You could have been killed," his father said, his voice breaking slightly.

Winston's jaw tightened as he fastened the last button on his waistcoat. "But I wasn't," he responded firmly.

Just as he uttered his words, a tall, slender woman with dark hair rushed into the room, her eyes wide with panic. Jasper followed closely behind her, his expression grim.

"Sarah!" his father shouted. "What in the blazes are you doing here?"

Her eyes were filled with desperation as she turned to Winston. "I had to come," she said, her voice shaking. "I couldn't stay hidden knowing what Isaac is capable of. He has gone too far, and I will not let him destroy more lives."

Winston had never formally met his aunt, but now was not the time for pleasantries. "Where is your son?"

"He is here, with me," Sarah said. "I will turn myself over to Isaac and—"

"Absolutely not!" his father shouted. "You will do no such thing. He will kill you, Sarah."

She shook her head. "No, he needs me to claim my inheritance."

"Is that any better?" his father asked.

With pained eyes, Sarah replied, "I can't stand around and do nothing. Your family has already done so much to protect me, and Isaac has been relentless."

Winston crossed his arms over his chest. "I agree with my father. We are not going to let you turn yourself over to Isaac."

"Then how are you going to get Miss Bawden back?" Sarah asked.

"I don't know," Winston admitted painfully, the weight of the situation pressing down on him. "But there must be another way."

Sarah approached him, coming to a stop in front of him, her eyes imploring his. "I know you are thinking you are doing what is best, but you do not know Isaac like I do. I do believe he is capable of killing Miss Bawden and anyone else that gets in his way."

Winston clenched his jaw. "Then we must stop him."

"How?" Sarah asked.

Melody stepped into the room. "I have an idea," she said.

With a shake of his head, Winston remarked, "I know you mean well, Sister, but this is not the time."

Undeterred by his lackluster response, Melody continued, "We set a trap for Isaac."

His father turned towards Melody, his voice stern. "This does not involve you, young lady."

Melody tilted her chin stubbornly. "I can do more than what is expected of me. I am an excellent shot and—"

"No!" his father shouted, his face reddening with anger. "Go to your bedchamber."

Rather than move, Melody held her father's gaze, the silence palpable. Winston had always known that Melody was strong, but he had never seen this determined side of her. It was unnerving, yet he had never been more proud of his sister.

White stepped into the room and held up a piece of paper. "A letter was just delivered to the servants' entrance."

Winston stepped forward and retrieved the note, his heart pounding in his chest. He read it quickly before crumpling the paper in his hand. "Isaac wants to trade Miss Bawden for Sarah and Matthew at the Wilsons' barn in one hour. He told us to come alone or else he will kill Miss Bawden," he revealed.

Jasper took a step forward, his expression serious. "We need to devise a plan, and quickly," he said. "And I think Lady Melody is right, we should set a trap."

His father pointed his finger at Jasper. "You keep my daughter out of this." He turned back to Melody. "It is time for you to leave."

"Why?" Melody asked defiantly. "I will just remain outside the door and eavesdrop, just as Elodie is doing."

His mother approached Melody and gave her a weak smile. "I know you are doing what you think is best, but I can't risk anything happening to you."

Melody met Winston's gaze, and her eyes flashed with a fierce determination, making him know that this wasn't over. "Very well," she conceded.

After his sister left the room, Jasper and Grady approached one another and started speaking in hushed tones. Their conversation, too quiet for anyone else to hear, only served to heighten Winston's irritation.

"Do you mind telling us what you two are planning?" Winston demanded, his voice tight with annoyance.

Jasper turned to the group and said, "It appears that Isaac has at least two other men working for him. We outnumber him, especially if we include Lady Melody."

His mother gasped, her hand flying to her mouth. "You cannot be in earnest."

Grady interjected, his tone calm but firm. "I have seen Lady Melody shoot, and she is an excellent shot."

"At targets!" his father shouted, tossing his hands up in the air in exasperation. "She shoots at targets, not at people. Find another way."

Jasper tipped his head. "Yes, my lord," he said. "Give Grady and me a moment to discuss another option."

As the two Bow Street Runners resumed their strategizing in low voices, his mother approached Winston and asked, "How are you faring?"

Winston huffed. "How do you think I am faring?" he asked. "The woman that I love is being held hostage."

"You love her?" his mother asked.

"Yes," Winston replied.

A smile spread across his mother's face, despite the gravity of the situation. "I am glad that you have finally come to terms with what we already know."

Winston ran a hand through his hair. "I can't lose her. Not now," he said, his voice breaking slightly.

His mother placed a comforting hand on his sleeve. "I know you want Mattie back, but you must think clearly and act decisively. Sacrificing yourself will do no good."

Aunt Sarah interrupted their conversation, her voice tinged with guilt. "I am sorry that it has come to this. I did not mean for anyone to get hurt."

"I know. But this is not your fault; it is Isaac's," Winston assured her.

"Yes, but he is my husband," Aunt Sarah said, her eyes filled with sorrow. "It was nice to be free of him, even if it was just for a short time."

The Gentleman's Miscalculation

Turning to face his aunt, Winston remarked, "I am not going to hand you over to Isaac."

"What other option do we have?" Aunt Sarah asked, her eyes widening with concern. "If Isaac even sees another person, he will make good on his promise to kill Miss Bawden."

"I don't know what the answer is, but we will figure it out together," Winston promised.

Jasper approached, his expression solemn. "Grady and I have devised a plan, but it is not without some risks."

Winston nodded, his resolve solidifying. "What would you have me do?"

The two Bow Street Runners exchanged a pointed look before Jasper asked, "Can you shoot, my lord?"

"I can," Winston confirmed.

"Good, because this plan could go awry very quickly," Jasper said.

Winston felt a surge of determination. "I will do whatever it takes to get Mattie back," he declared.

"All right," Jasper said. "Here is our plan…"

Mattie sat on a bundle of hay in the Wilsons' dilapidated barn, the rough texture pressing against her skin as she shifted uncomfortably. She had been here for what felt like hours, and her body ached from the rigid position. She longed for the comfort of her home and the luxury of a long, warm bath. However, her current reality was bleak, with the short, stout man standing nearby ensuring she did not escape.

The light filtered through the cracks in the barn's walls and roof, casting long, eerie shadows on the ground. Memories of playing in this barn as a child flooded back to her. That was a different time. A time when the barn was filled with laughter and life, not abandoned and grim as it was now.

The door creaked open, bringing with it a flood of light and a gust of fresh air. Isaac stepped into the barn, his presence immediately darkening the mood. He turned his attention to the short man. "Leave us, Thomas."

Thomas nodded curtly before departing, closing the door behind him and plunging the barn back into semi-darkness.

Isaac approached Mattie slowly, his footsteps echoing on the wooden floor. He sat down on an adjacent bundle of hay, his demeanor calm. "I hope you know that I did not want it to come to this."

Mattie huffed, her frustration bubbling to the surface. "I don't believe you."

"This is Lord Winston's fault, not mine," Isaac asserted. "He stole my family from me. You must understand that I would do whatever it takes to get them back."

She reached down and pulled a piece of hay off her black gown. "Perhaps you shouldn't have abused them, then."

Isaac visibly stiffened, his façade of calm cracking. "You know not what you speak of."

"I do," Mattie retorted. "I understand that you often would beat your wife and son."

"Only when they deserved it," Isaac countered, his tone defensive.

Mattie lifted an eyebrow, her gaze unwavering. "Does a woman or child ever deserve to be hit?"

Isaac rested his back against a column, his expression hardening. "You live in a gilded cage. You have no idea what others have to do just to survive."

"That didn't answer my question," she said.

He frowned. "I married Lady Sarah, and her father denied me her dowry. He knew I didn't have the funds to fight him in court, so we had to scrape just to get by. Do you know how humiliating that was?"

"I do not."

"Of course you don't," Isaac said bitterly. "You are the daughter of a viscount."

Mattie shook her head. "You seem to forget that my father only recently inherited his title. Before that, he was a vicar, and we lived on a limited income."

Isaac looked unimpressed, his lips curling in a sneer. "That is hardly the same, considering you had a housekeeper to tend to your family."

"You speak to me as if I have never experienced any struggles," Mattie said. "But I have. I have endured more than you know."

"Pardon me for not being impressed, but what do you know about struggles?" Isaac asked, leaning forward. "Do you know what it is like not being able to provide for your family, while your wife's family is living a life of leisure?"

Mattie crossed her arms over her chest. "Do you expect me to feel bad for you?" she asked. "You made your bed, and now you must lie in it."

Isaac chuckled dryly, his eyes glinting with malice. "You impertinent chit. I can see why Lord Winston has been so taken with you."

"He is not taken by me," she insisted.

Holding out his arm in a mocking gesture, Isaac said, "It was evident to me how he felt about you. That is why I knew abducting you would be the only way to get my family returned to me."

"You will be sorely mistaken. Winston won't turn over Lady Sarah to you," Mattie responded, her voice firm.

He smirked, leaning back. "We shall see."

"I won't allow it," Mattie declared.

The humor drained from Isaac's face, replaced by a menacing glare. "You won't allow it?" he repeated. "You hold no power here. You are only alive because you are serving a purpose."

Mattie knew she should bite her sharp tongue, but when had that ever stopped her before? "Winston will stop you, and you will be sent to Newgate to live out the rest of your pathetic life," she spat out.

In a swift, brutal motion, Isaac reared his hand back and slapped her across the cheek, the force of the blow knocking her onto the ground. Pain exploded in her cheek, and she tasted blood.

He rose and stood over her. "You will not speak unless you are spoken to. Do you understand?" he demanded, his voice cold and hard.

Mattie brought a trembling hand to her reddened cheek, the sting making her eyes water. She fought back the tears, not wanting to show any sign of weakness.

Isaac's nostrils flared with anger. "Do you understand?" he repeated.

"I do," Mattie said, her voice flat and devoid of emotion, masking the fear and anger boiling within her.

Holding his hand out, Isaac said, "Allow me to help you up."

"That won't be necessary—"

Isaac cut her off, his voice sharp. "I insist."

Reluctantly, Mattie slipped her hand into his, feeling the coarseness of his skin. He pulled her up roughly, yanking her towards him so their faces were inches apart.

"I'm sorry I hit you, but you left me with no choice," he growled, his hot breath against her face. "It is not favorable for women to speak their minds."

Mattie clenched her jaw, swallowing her retort. She knew she had to be careful, bide her time and find a way to escape. Isaac might have the upper hand now, but she refused to let him break her spirit.

Isaac released her and took a step back, a cruel smile curling his lips. "I recognize that look," he jeered. "It is hope. You think that Lord Winston is going to save you. Don't you?"

"I do," Mattie replied, her voice steady.

Isaac's smile grew. "How, pray tell, do you think he is going to do that?" he asked. "He is a barrister, or should I say a sheep farmer?"

Mattie bit her lower lip before saying, "He will find a way."

"If you believe that, you are a bigger fool than he is," Isaac declared. "If Lord Winston fails to bring Sarah and my son to me, then you will die. Make no mistake of that."

Mattie lowered her gaze, not knowing what else to do. She trusted Winston, and she knew he wouldn't leave her here to die. However, she hoped that he wouldn't sacrifice his aunt and her son, either.

Isaac removed a pocket watch from his jacket and studied it. "Your betrothed should be here soon," he said. "I suppose we shall see how truly important you are to him."

"He isn't my betrothed," Mattie said, her voice barely above a whisper.

"No?" Isaac asked. "I find that odd since you two have spent a considerable amount of time with one another since I have arrived."

Mattie brought her gaze up. "We are friends."

Isaac gave her an amused look. "You can tell yourself whatever you want, but you would be wrong," he said. "You'd think you would be pleased that you snagged a lord." He paused. "Unless you are disappointed you didn't turn Lord Dunsby's head?"

She pressed her lips together. "I have never been interested in Lord Dunsby, at least in that way."

"Not like how you feel about Lord Winston?" Isaac tsked. "I got tired of watching you two together. You two were so engrossed with one another that you failed to realize how often I came around."

"What is it that you want me to say?" she asked, tilting her chin.

Isaac's eyes held a sinister glint. "You can try to pretend to be brave, but we both know it is just an act." He took a step towards her, and she stumbled backwards, desperate to keep distance between them. "I promise that if I do have to kill you, it will be quick."

Mattie's eyes went wide as she stared back at Isaac, attempting to stay strong. But with every word that Isaac said, her resolve slipped further.

Isaac performed an exaggerated bow. "I will be back shortly, my dear. Until then, continue to make yourself at home."

Once Isaac departed from the barn, Mattie's eyes roamed the old structure, desperately seeking an escape route. She approached the walls, pressing against the old wooden boards, hoping to find a loose one. But they were all firmly in place.

The sound of rats scurrying along the rafters caught her attention, and she let out a shudder. Her situation seemed hopeless, but she knew she had to stay strong. Winston would come for her. She was sure of that. For now, she needed to find a way to survive until he did.

One thing was certain—if she ever had a chance to speak to Winston again, she would tell him how she felt about him. She loved him. She had tried so hard to fight against that revelation, but she could deny it no longer. And the fact that he told her that he cared for her gave her hope that he felt the same.

Furthermore, she needed to ask Emma why she had never given her that letter. Her sister was many things, but she wasn't forgetful. Had she kept the letter away from her on purpose? If so, why would Emma have done such a thing?

Mattie turned her attention back towards the wood boards and noticed a sliver of light coming from one in the back. She approached it and noticed that the nails were loose. Even if she were able to remove the nails, was that enough room for her to slip through?

As she debated what she should do, the barn door creaked open and Isaac stepped back in, his face twisted into a dark scowl. "What are you doing?" he growled, his voice laced with suspicion.

Mattie spun back around, her heart racing with fear. "I heard a rat," she lied, hoping her voice sounded somewhat convincing.

"Stupid chit," Isaac muttered, his eyes narrowing. "It is almost time to see if you are going to live another day or die."

Her heart sank at his words, but she summoned all her courage to stand firm. She truly hoped that this was not the end for her.

Chapter Nineteen

Winston sat across from his Aunt Sarah in the rattling coach as it jostled towards the Wilsons' barn. The old structure had been abandoned for many years, its once proud frame now shrouded in a tangle of weeds and overgrown bushes. Tall trees bordered the property, their branches looming over the dilapidated roof, threatening to further compromise its integrity.

Jasper and Grady had concocted a plan, but it was fraught with uncertainties and potential pitfalls. They had no clear idea of the number of men Isaac had under his command. Moreover, Isaac had made it clear that Winston was to bring only Aunt Sarah and Matthew. Any deviation, and Isaac would not hesitate to kill Mattie.

But Isaac had grossly underestimated Winston's love for Mattie. He would sacrifice his own life if it meant she could live another day. He had been on the verge of confessing his feelings to her when Isaac had abducted her.

Winston adjusted the cravat around his neck, which suddenly felt as constricting as a noose. What if their plan failed? Panic surged through him, a stark departure from his usual composed demeanor. As a barrister, he was adept at projecting an air of confidence, even when chaos surrounded him. It was a mask he wore well.

His aunt's voice pierced through the tense silence. "It will be all right."

Winston met her gaze. "Yes, it will be," he replied, attempting to muster his usual confident façade.

"I won't let anything happen to Miss Bawden," Aunt Sarah said firmly. "She is an innocent in all of this and it was terribly unfair of Isaac to drag her into his schemes."

"Isaac is a blackguard."

Aunt Sarah offered him a weak smile. "That he is," she said. "He wasn't always like this. I had once fancied myself in love with him."

Winston huffed. "That must have been long ago."

"It was," Aunt Sarah replied, her voice tinged with melancholy. "I fell in love with him the moment I first saw him, but I knew my family would never accept him because of his lowly station. But I chose love…" Her voice trailed off.

"Do you regret that?" he prodded gently.

Aunt Sarah shook her head. "No, despite everything that has happened to me, I believe in love. But sometimes, people change. And Isaac changed. Perhaps I did, as well." She sighed. "When my father wouldn't release my dowry, Isaac became irate and I realized that he had married me for the money, not for who I was."

"I'm sorry," he murmured, feeling inadequate in his response.

She waved her hand dismissively. "It was my own fault. I believed the lies that Isaac told me, and I chose to elope with him," she said. "I was complacent in all of it, and I understand why my father did what he did. But when my brothers turned their backs on me, especially Richard, I was devastated."

Aunt Sarah continued, "When I received word that Richard died, I was heartbroken that I could never make amends with him. I was determined to salvage some kind of relationship with your father since he was the only family I had left."

The coach hit a rut in the road, jolting to one side. Aunt Sarah steadied herself and shared, "When Isaac turned his heavy hand onto Matthew, I knew I had to flee and never look back. So I turned to Lionel for help."

"My father cares for you," Winston assured her.

"Lionel has been a godsend, and Matthew adores him," Aunt Sarah said. "I just wish it hadn't come to this."

Winston leaned forward in his seat. "This plan will work. You will be safe and reunited with your son soon enough."

Aunt Sarah didn't look convinced. "If something does happen to me, please watch over Matthew. He has done nothing wrong."

"I promise, but it won't come to that," Winston said.

"No, it won't," Aunt Sarah muttered. "Because I won't go back to being under Isaac's thumb. At any cost."

Winston saw his aunt fidgeting with the reticule around her wrist and could only imagine how nervous she was. But her eyes told him a different story: they were determined, if not slightly resigned.

He turned his head towards the window and saw that they were almost there. The dilapidated barn loomed ahead, its weathered boards and sagging roof standing in contrast to the overgrown field surrounding it. Jasper and Grady should be in position, hidden among the trees and underbrush. This ordeal should be over soon enough. Mattie would be back in his arms —where she belonged.

Aunt Sarah eyed him curiously. "Do you love Miss Bawden?"

"I do," Winston said, seeing no reason to deny it.

A small smile came to her lips. "I am happy for you. Love is a beautiful thing, especially with the right person."

The coach jerked to a stop a short distance away from the

barn. Winston exited the coach and reached back to assist his aunt out. Once her feet were on the ground, she withdrew her hand, her fingers trembling slightly.

Winston's eyes roamed over the field in front of the barn and saw no sign of Isaac. The tall grass and weeds swayed gently in the breeze, but there was no movement near the barn. A moment later, the barn door creaked open, and Isaac stepped out with an irate look on his face. "Where is my son?" he demanded, his voice echoing across the open space.

Aunt Sarah tilted her chin defiantly. "I am here to trade places with Miss Bawden. Let's leave Matthew out of this."

"He is my son!" Isaac shouted, his face reddening with anger.

"You don't treat him like it," Aunt Sarah declared. "You hit him."

Isaac took a commanding step towards her, his posture menacing. "It is my right to discipline him."

"As you do to me?" Aunt Sarah asked, her voice steady despite the danger.

His eyes narrowed. "You have, and always will be, a disappointment to me," he declared. "How else would I show you my displeasure?"

Winston spoke up. "Where is Miss Bawden?" he demanded.

Isaac smirked, his eyes glinting with malice. "You didn't think I was just going to hand her over to you, did you?" he asked. "I need to ensure that you came alone."

"We did," Winston lied, putting his hands out.

"And what of that guard that followed Miss Bawden around like a puppy?" Isaac asked, his gaze darting suspiciously around the field. "Do you expect me to believe that he isn't hiding somewhere, just waiting for a chance to shoot me?"

Aunt Sarah interjected, her voice cutting through the

tension. "This is between you and me. Let Miss Bawden go and I will come with you willingly."

"And what of Matthew?" Isaac asked.

"Let his uncle raise him," Aunt Sarah said. "Give him a chance to rise above his station and make something of himself."

Isaac pursed his lips together, his expression calculating. "With your inheritance, I can give him a better life."

"Not like my brother can," Aunt Sarah countered. "Lionel has promised to educate him and give him opportunities that you can only dream of."

"But not you?" Isaac scoffed.

Aunt Sarah shrugged. "As the daughter of a marquess, I was given those same opportunities, but I squandered them by marrying you."

Isaac's nostrils flared. "If your father had just released your dowry, then we would have been happy."

"Would we have?" Aunt Sarah asked, her voice tinged with sadness. "I truly doubt that."

Winston knew this conversation was going in circles, and he needed to ensure that Mattie hadn't been harmed. "Bring out Miss Bawden," he ordered.

"Or what?" Isaac mocked, a cruel smile playing on his lips.

Reaching into the waistband of his trousers, he removed a pistol and pointed it at Isaac. "I wasn't asking."

Isaac chuckled dryly, his amusement evident. "You may as well put your pistol away. I have men surrounding us," he said. "You didn't think I came here alone, did you?" He tsked, shaking his head. "You clearly have not done this type of thing before."

Winston's eyes roamed over the trees, hoping Jasper and Grady were safe. He kept his pistol aimed at Isaac. "I could shoot you," he stated, his voice unwavering.

"You could, but then you would be killed, as would Miss

Bawden," Isaac said, his smile widening. "Do you truly want to die this way?"

He lowered his pistol to the side, knowing he couldn't risk Mattie's life. "Give me Miss Bawden."

"You haven't said 'please' yet," Isaac jeered.

Aunt Sarah frowned. "This is ridiculous," she said. "Lord Winston and I will leave if you do not produce Miss Bawden."

Isaac's smile fell, replaced by a dark scowl. "You do not tell me what to do," he snapped.

"It is about time that I did," Aunt Sarah retorted.

Isaac glared at his wife for a moment before he turned back towards the barn. He disappeared inside of it for a moment and returned with Mattie. He was clutching her arm tightly, keeping her tucked next to him. Her face was pale, eyes wide with fear, but she was alive. And that was good enough for him.

"Are you happy now?" Isaac asked.

Aunt Sarah didn't respond to Isaac, but instead turned her attention towards Mattie. "Are you well?" she asked gently, her voice full of concern.

Mattie nodded, her eyes darting nervously between Isaac and Winston. "I am."

"Did Isaac hurt you?" Aunt Sarah pressed.

Mattie hesitated, then raised her hand to her bruised cheek and winced. "He did," she responded.

Winston tightened his hold on his pistol, fury boiling within him. The sight of Mattie's bruised cheek made him want to shoot Isaac on the spot, but he knew he couldn't risk Mattie's safety. He needed to be strategic, not impulsive.

"Release Miss Bawden," Aunt Sarah ordered.

Isaac balked, his grip on Mattie tightening. "And give away any leverage that I have?" he asked. "I think not. You come here first."

Aunt Sarah took a step towards Isaac and Winston quickly

put his hand out to stop her. "What are you doing?" he asked in a hushed voice. "This is not what we discussed."

"It is the only way to free Miss Bawden," Aunt Sarah responded, her resolve clear.

"How do we know he will do what he says?" Winston questioned.

Aunt Sarah gave him a sad look. "We don't, but what choice do we have?" she asked softly before brushing past his hand.

As she approached Isaac, he dropped Miss Bawden's arm and yanked his wife towards him. "You will pay for what you did!" he growled, his face contorted with rage.

Mattie rushed towards Winston, her eyes filled with relief and fear. He held his arms out to her and she ran into them, her body trembling. He embraced her warmly, murmuring, "You are safe."

Shifting in his arms, she looked up at him with concerned eyes. "What about Lady Sarah?" she asked, her voice quivering.

"We have a plan," he assured her, though he was certain his eyes betrayed the uncertainty he felt.

Isaac's voice broke through their conversation. "You may go," he said coldly. "And inform Lord Dallington that I will be back for my son."

Winston moved to stand next to Mattie, their hands intertwined. "I'm afraid I can't let you take my aunt."

"And why not?" Isaac asked, his eyes narrowing slightly.

"I won't let you hurt her, ever again," Winston declared.

Isaac scoffed. "I didn't want it to come to this, but so be it," he said as he turned his head towards the trees. "Kill them."

Mattie couldn't quite believe this was happening. Everything felt surreal and the tension in the air was palpable. Winston moved to stand in front of her, his broad shoulders shielding her from danger. Was this truly the end for her, for them?

Lady Sarah's voice broke through the tense silence. "Let them go, Isaac!" she ordered, her voice steely and commanding.

Isaac's cruel laugh echoed across the expansive field. "What do you think you are going to do with that?" he mocked.

Mattie moved out from behind Winston and saw that Lady Sarah had broken free from Isaac's hold and was now pointing a pistol at him. "What I should have done long ago," she retorted.

"Do you truly mean to kill me?" Isaac sneered.

"I do," Lady Sarah responded. "I'm tired of the beatings and pretending all is well. I'm tired, Isaac. So tired."

Isaac took a step closer, and she cocked her pistol, her finger hovering over the trigger. "If you kill me, then you are all dead," he threatened, his voice low.

Winston spoke up, his voice calm and authoritative. "That is not quite true," he said. "Two Bow Street Runners have accompanied me, and they have you surrounded."

Isaac's eyes flickered with uncertainty as he glanced at the nearby trees. "How do we know if my men haven't taken out your Bow Street Runners?" he asked, his tone more cautious now.

"I guess there is only one way to find out," Winston replied. "Jasper! Grady! Are you there?"

There came rustling in the trees before Grady stepped out into the field, his pistol drawn. "Isaac's men have been subdued and Jasper is keeping watch over them," he announced.

Winston smirked, a glimmer of triumph in his eyes. "Well, it appears that you lost, Isaac," he said.

In a swift, desperate move, Isaac lunged towards Lady Sarah and grabbed the pistol from her hand. "You were saying, my lord?" he mocked, pointing it at his wife. "We can still both walk away with what is ours."

Grady brought his pistol up and pointed it at Isaac. "Put the pistol down," he ordered.

Isaac yanked Sarah towards him and slipped his arm around her waist, pressing the pistol against her side. "Sarah is mine!" he exclaimed. "Leave us be."

Winston took a step forward, his eyes locked on Isaac. "No. I can't do that."

"You can't do anything to stop me," Isaac said. "You and I both know that in the eyes of the law, she belongs to me. And there is no way that Parliament will grant Sarah a divorce. She is nothing."

"She is the daughter of a marquess," Winston countered, his voice rising with indignation.

Isaac scoffed. "Who was publicly disowned by her own father," he jeered. "Or did you forget that little detail?"

Winston put his hand up. "Do the right thing, Isaac," he encouraged.

"And what is your definition of the 'right thing'?" Isaac asked, his grip tightening on Lady Sarah.

"My aunt clearly doesn't want to go with you," Winston responded. "You must let her go."

Isaac shook his head, his expression hard. "And should I also let my son go?" he asked. "Have him raised by a man who turned his back on his own sister?"

"My father is different now," Winston asserted.

Mattie's eyes caught some movement high in the trees near the barn, a flash of color. Someone was up there. Was it Jasper?

Isaac cocked the pistol, drawing back Mattie's attention.

"Leave us be, my lord," he mocked. "Sarah wants to be with me."

In a defiant move, Lady Sarah said, "No, I don't. And I suspect that you don't want to be with me either."

"I love you!" Isaac shouted.

Lady Sarah huffed. "I daresay you want my inheritance more than you want me."

"Those go hand in hand," Isaac responded.

"What if I give you the money?" Lady Sarah asked, desperation tinging in her voice. "And you just walk away from us."

Isaac's face grew hard. "No! I won't give up on us."

Lady Sarah shifted her head to meet Isaac's gaze. "There is no 'us.' There never has been," she stated, her voice cold. "You have despised me from the moment my father refused to release the dowry."

"That isn't true!" Isaac exclaimed. "You have just grown more disobedient with time, and you are teaching our son to disobey me now."

"I am teaching Matthew nothing. He sees you for who you are," Lady Sarah remarked. "A monster."

Isaac's eyes grew wide with fury. "I will show you a monster!" he shouted. He shoved the pistol into his wife's side, causing her to cry out in pain.

A shot rang out, echoing throughout the field. Isaac fell to the ground, dead.

Mattie's eyes turned towards Grady, but his pistol was still at his side. Her gaze immediately turned towards the trees and saw movement in them.

Winston put his hand out to shield Mattie. "Who goes there?" he demanded.

A few moments later, Melody stepped out from amongst the cover of the trees, a pistol in her hand.

"Melody?" Winston asked, his voice full of shock. "What did you do?"

The Gentleman's Miscalculation

Melody held a pistol in her hand, her voice calm and collected. "I wasn't about to let Isaac kill Aunt Sarah."

"So you killed him?" Winston asked, his eyes wide with disbelief.

"It was either him or Aunt Sarah, and I made my choice," Melody said firmly. "A simple thank you would suffice."

Lady Sarah rushed over to Melody and threw her arms around her. "Thank you, Melody. You have freed me from my prison."

Grady stepped over to Winston and remarked, "I told you that Lady Melody was a good shot."

Mattie looked down at Isaac's body, his face in the dirt, knowing that Melody shooting Isaac was the only way. Isaac wouldn't have given up his wife at any cost, and he would have most likely killed her, given the chance.

Winston approached his sister and crossed his arms over his chest, his face a mixture of relief and exasperation. "What were you thinking?"

Melody stepped out of Lady Sarah's embrace, her tone not the least bit repentant. "I was thinking that someone needed to save our aunt."

"What is Father going to say?" Winston asked.

Melody gave him a stern look. "Nothing, because you are not going to say anything about what I did here."

"Whyever not?" Winston pressed.

Taking a step closer to her brother, Melody replied, "We both know that Isaac needed to die but I was the only one that was able to do it."

Grady, standing nearby, tipped his head in agreement. "She isn't wrong, my lord."

Winston frowned. "I don't like this, not one bit."

Mattie reached for Winston's hand. "Melody is right. No one can know of what happened here today."

"And what of Isaac?" Winston asked, glancing at the lifeless body on the ground. "How do we explain his death?"

277

Lady Sarah stepped forward, her face set in determination. "Tell everyone that I killed him."

Grady stepped closer to Isaac's body, crouching down to examine it. "In my report, I will confirm that it was self-defense. That part is at least true."

"But what of your reputation?" Winston asked, concern for his aunt evident in his voice.

Lady Sarah huffed. "What reputation?" she asked. "I care little of what people think of me, especially now. It is not as if I will ever be welcomed back into Society."

Melody placed a comforting hand on her aunt's sleeve. "But you will always be welcomed in our family."

"Thank you, Melody," Lady Sarah murmured.

Winston glanced between his sister and aunt, his expression resigned. "Very well, I won't say anything to Father about this."

Melody beamed. "Thank you, Winston," she said, dropping her hand to her side. "I should be heading back before anyone notices my absence."

Gesturing towards the coach, Winston offered, "You can ride back with us."

"I brought my own horse," Melody responded. "But thank you."

As Melody walked away, Winston turned to Mattie, his voice filled with a newfound respect. "I daresay I have underestimated my sister."

"I think we both have," Mattie remarked.

"But it ends now," Winston said.

Mattie tightened her hold on Winston's hand. "I should go home. I have no doubt that my family is worried about me."

Winston nodded before leading her to the coach. Once she was situated inside, he assisted his aunt in, ensuring her comfort. Then he claimed the seat next to Mattie, his hand never leaving hers.

As the coach jerked forward, Lady Sarah broke the silence,

her voice filled with sadness. "Is it sad that I only feel relief now that Isaac is dead?"

"No, I do not think so," Winston responded gently.

Lady Sarah winced, her fingers nervously twisting in her lap. "I'm sorry I didn't tell you that I brought a pistol, but I thought you would try to talk me out of it."

Winston sighed, a heavy but understanding sound. "I probably would have, but everything worked out for the best."

"Jasper taught me how to shoot when he watched over us at the cottage," Lady Sarah admitted. "But do not get angry at him since I asked him to. I was tired of running from Isaac. I wanted to fight back, if I was given the chance."

Winston glanced over at Mattie, his expression softening. "You are both safe, and that is all that matters."

Mattie smiled at him. "Thank you for saving me," she said, feeling immense gratitude for the man beside her.

He returned her smile, his eyes full of warmth. "I will always save you, Mattie, now and forever."

She felt a blush creep up her neck as they stared at one another, the intensity of their connection making her heart race. This man was her future. She was sure of that.

Lady Sarah's voice brought her back to the present. "I am worried how Matthew will react to the news that his father is dead."

Winston met his aunt's gaze with concern. "Would you like for me to be present when you tell him?"

"I would like that very much," Lady Sarah replied, her words filled with relief. "Isaac was a monster, but he still was Matthew's father."

"My family will be there for you during this difficult time," Winston remarked with determination in his voice.

Lady Sarah nodded, a small smile playing on her lips. "I am pleased to get to know each one of you, especially Elodie," she said. "Does she truly eavesdrop on every conversation?"

"Just about," Winston responded with a chuckle.

"Lionel has told me about each one of you, and I can see why he is so proud of his children," Lady Sarah remarked.

Winston shifted uncomfortably in his seat. "I doubt he is very proud of me."

Mattie could hear the pain in his words and she was about to respond, but Lady Sarah spoke first. "Why would you say that?"

With a shrug, Winston responded, "I am just a barrister."

Lady Sarah's brow lifted, her expression one of disbelief. "Just a barrister?" she asked. "You have quite the reputation in London, and I hear that you are a landowner as well."

"Yes, but it is merely a sheep farm," Winston said.

Leaning forward in her seat, Lady Sarah held Winston's gaze, her eyes earnest. "For being such a clever man, you have failed to see what is right in front of you. Your father and mother are immensely proud of you, and the person that you have become. I can hear it in their voices and see it in their eyes."

Mattie turned her head, watching as Winston's eyes grow moist. She knew how he had fought for their approval, not realizing he had had it all along.

"Thank you, Aunt Sarah," Winston said softly before turning his attention towards Mattie. "If you don't mind, I think it is time that we finish that talk."

"Now?" Mattie asked.

Winston reached up and pounded on the top of the coach. In response, the coach came to a stop on the side of the road. He reached for the door handle and opened it. Once he stepped out, he offered his hand to assist her out. "Mattie?"

Mattie slipped her hand into his and exited the coach, her heart pounding in anticipation. Winston took her hand and placed it into the crook of his arm, leading her towards the direction of her cottage.

"Now, where were we?" Winston asked, his voice tender and full of promise.

Chapter Twenty

As Winston led Mattie towards her family's cottage, he tried to recall the speech he had rehearsed in his head countless times. He knew that Mattie cared for him; she had said as much. But his feelings went far deeper. He loved her with everything he was and everything he would be.

Despite his best efforts to recall his speech, he found himself at a loss for words, something he was not accustomed to. Mattie glanced over at him and smiled, making him remember what he was fighting for.

He stopped and gently turned Mattie to face him. "I know this might not be the ideal time to say such things, but I cannot remain silent any longer," he said, his voice steady with determination. "I need to tell you how I feel about you."

"I am listening," Mattie responded, her eyes encouraging him to continue.

Winston took a deep breath before saying, "When we were growing up, I despised you. You were always underfoot, and I used to hide from you. The more I got to know you, the more I was sure that you would always be my nemesis."

"Well, that is good to know," Mattie muttered.

"But it all changed when we kissed," Winston admitted,

his voice softening. "Everything I thought I knew changed in a blink of an eye, and I realized that there was a fine line between love and hate. And I crossed that line."

Mattie's eyes widened slightly. "What are you saying, Winston?"

Winston reached for her hand. "I love you, Mattie," he said. "Even when I thought I hated you, I loved you. I have tried to fight it, but I miscalculated my feelings for you. My whole life is you, and I know that now."

"You love me?" she repeated, her voice barely above a whisper.

"I do," Winston confirmed.

Mattie grew quiet, her gaze thoughtful. "Are you not worried about how different we are? We fight constantly."

Winston grinned. "I don't want normal and simple and easy. I just want you," he said. "Do you think you could come to love me?"

She lowered her gaze to the lapels of his jacket, and he feared that he had gone too far in his questioning. However, in a soft voice, she said, "I love you."

He brought his finger under her chin and lifted it until their gazes met. "Do you truly mean it?"

Her eyes filled with unshed tears. "Like you, my heart started turning the moment you kissed me. I tried to fight it, but you claimed my heart that night."

Winston moved his hand to cup her right cheek. "You should know that I am not a rich man. I intend to stop working as a barrister and focus on my sheep farm. That means we will have to live in a cottage that has a leaky roof, at least for now."

A small smile came to Mattie's lips. "I do not mind a little water."

"I intend to work hard and give you a home that you deserve," Winston said.

Mattie's smile widened. "I do not need a home like Brockhall Manor. I just want a place where we can raise our children and be happy."

"I promise that I will be the man that will always make you smile," he asserted.

"And I promise that I will always love you, even when you say the most idiotic things," Mattie joked, her eyes sparkling.

Winston lifted his brow in amusement. "You are a minx."

"That is not the worst thing that you have called me," she retorted.

"No, it is not," Winston said. "But I do believe our days of name calling are over. I would prefer it if I called you 'my love.'"

Mattie seemed to consider his words. "I will allow it."

"There is only one more thing that I have to do," Winston said as he lowered himself down onto one knee. "Miss Mattie Bawden, will you do me the grand honor of marrying me?"

"Yes!" Mattie exclaimed.

Winston jumped up and pulled her into his arms. "You have made me the happiest of men," he said. "But there is one more thing that we must do."

"Kiss on it?" Mattie suggested with a playful smile.

He chuckled. "I was going to say that I need to speak to your father, but I like what you proposed as well."

Mattie shifted in his arms and looked up at him, her eyes warm and inviting. He leaned forward and pressed his lips against hers, making everything seem right in the world. Mattie was his; he existed for her. And nothing would compare with this kiss, knowing that his love would last forever.

Winston was so engrossed in the moment that he barely registered the loud clearing of a throat behind him.

Mattie broke the kiss and turned her head. "Father!" she said, taking a step back from Winston, her cheeks flushed.

Lord Wythburn glared at Winston. "What is going on here?" he demanded.

Winston met the lord's gaze and replied with as much composure as he could muster, "I offered for Mattie, and she accepted."

"Without speaking to me first?" Lord Wythburn asked. "That surely is an oversight. Is it not?"

"It is, my lord," Winston replied, his tone respectful but resolute. "My apologies. I'm afraid the moment just got away from me."

Lord Wythburn shifted his gaze towards Mattie, his expression softening slightly. "We have been so worried about you since we received Lady Dallington's letter. I am glad to see that you are well and unharmed."

With a grateful glance at Winston, Mattie responded, "Winston saved me."

"And you rewarded him with a kiss?" Lord Wythburn asked, his words holding censure.

Mattie tilted her chin defiantly. "It is perfectly acceptable since we are engaged to be married," she insisted.

Lord Wythburn frowned. "I should have seen this coming," he muttered. "Come along, I need to speak to Lord Winston privately."

As they followed Lord Wythburn to the cottage, Mattie asked, "Out of curiosity, what was in the note that you delivered to my sister?"

"I confessed my feelings and I offered for you," Winston admitted.

"Did you offer for me because of your feelings or because it was the honorable thing to do?" Mattie asked, her eyes searching his.

Winston shrugged one shoulder. "A little of both, I suppose."

"And now?" Mattie pressed, her gaze intent.

With a curious look, Winston said, "If you are asking me if I am marrying you because it is the honorable thing to do, you would be wrong. I am marrying you because I love you and I do not want to go another day without you by my side."

A mischievous glint came into Mattie's eyes. "That was a good answer."

"I do not know why you sound so surprised," Winston remarked.

Mattie reached for his hand and intertwined their fingers.

Winston arched an eyebrow. "Are you not worried about upsetting your father more?"

"I love you, Winston," Mattie replied. "And I do not care who knows it. I am the happiest I have ever been."

They reached the front steps of the cottage and Lord Wythburn turned to face them, his stern expression unchanged. "Lord Winston, a word with you inside," he said, gesturing towards the door.

Winston squeezed Mattie's hand before releasing it. "I will be right back," he promised.

Inside, Lord Wythburn led Winston to the study and closed the door behind them. "I need to understand your intentions clearly," he began, his tone measured.

Winston stood tall, his expression sincere. "My lord, I have loved Mattie for longer than I realized. My intentions are to marry her, cherish her and build a life together. I know I should have come to you first, but my feelings got the better of me."

Lord Wythburn studied him for a long moment before nodding slowly. "Very well. I see that you are earnest in your intentions. But you must understand, Mattie's happiness is paramount to me."

"And it is to me as well," Winston replied. "I promise you, I will do everything in my power to make her happy."

Lord Wythburn sighed as he sat down behind the desk. "I hope you are true to your word. For now, we have much to discuss." He gestured towards a seat. "Let's begin with her dowry."

Mattie watched as Winston followed her father inside, and her heart pounded with a mixture of anxiety and hope. She believed in Winston, in his love for her, and she hoped her father would come to see it as well.

The door creaked open and Emma stepped outside, curiosity etched on her face. "Why is Lord Winston speaking to Father in the study?"

"He is asking for Father's permission for us to marry," Mattie replied, seeing no reason to keep the truth from her sister.

Emma's lips pursed into a pout. "That is hardly fair," she muttered. "Why do you get to marry a lord?"

Mattie frowned, her frustration barely concealed. "It hardly matters to me that Winston is a lord. I love him, and I would have married him regardless."

"Yes, but Lord Winston is the son of a marquess," Emma insisted. "At least my chances to secure a lord have been elevated by your advantageous marriage."

"Wonderful," Mattie remarked dryly. Why was it that her sister only seemed to think of herself, especially at a moment like this?

Emma stepped closer, her expression softening slightly. "I am glad that you are happy, Sister."

"Thank you." Mattie paused, taking a deep breath as she prepared to broach a delicate subject. "Winston informed me that he gave you a letter about a year ago with instructions to deliver it to me. Do you recall that letter?"

Emma grew silent, her face growing pale. "I do."

"Dare I ask why you didn't deliver that letter to me?" Mattie asked, her voice tinged with accusation.

With hesitation, Emma responded, "I didn't want you to marry Lord Winston."

Mattie reared back. "Whyever not?"

Emma sighed deeply, her shoulders slumping. "I knew if you married Lord Winston, you would leave me, and I wasn't ready for that," she confessed.

"So you made the decision for me?" Mattie asked, her voice rising with incredulity.

"I didn't think Lord Winston was the right man for you," Emma insisted, a defensive edge creeping into her tone. "After all, you two fought all the time."

Mattie tried to keep the frustration out of her voice, but she was failing miserably. "People can change."

"Yes, but Lord Winston was always kind to me," Emma said. "I thought we would be a better match than you two."

Her brow shot up in surprise. "You wanted Winston for yourself?"

Emma had the decency to look ashamed. "At the time, yes, but I have since realized that I can marry someone higher-ranking than a younger son of a marquess now that Father is a viscount."

Mattie walked over to the bench and sat down. She was trying to find the right words to say because she was growing increasingly upset with each passing word that came out of Emma's mouth.

"I can't believe you didn't deliver the letter to me. I never thought you would do something so awful," Mattie said. "I almost lost Winston because of it."

"Regardless, you got precisely what you wanted."

"That is beside the point. All you seem to care about is having an advantageous marriage," Mattie declared.

Emma shrugged her shoulders, seemingly unperturbed. "If I want to be anything in life, I must make a brilliant match."

Mattie stared at her sister in disbelief. "You can be more than that."

"Says the woman who is marrying a son of a marquess," Emma remarked as she came to sit down next to her.

"I am marrying Winston because I love him," Mattie said. "He is not rich, and we will live in a small cottage at his sheep farm for now."

Emma looked at her with disbelief. "That sounds awful."

"Does it?" Mattie asked, a wistful smile on her lips. "Because to me, it sounds perfect."

In a soft voice, Emma said, "I am sorry for keeping that letter from you. It was unfair of me to do so."

Mattie knew it had taken a lot for her sister to apologize since she was not one to do so, but she wasn't ready to forgive her yet. In time she would, but not now. The betrayal was too raw. "Thank you for saying so, but I am still angry with you. It is time for you to grow up, Emma, and start caring about others."

Emma grew contrite. "You are right. I will try to be better." She glanced over her shoulder. "Are you sure you would rather live in a cottage than Darlington Abbey?"

"It doesn't matter where I live, as long as I am with Winston," Mattie admitted.

The door opened once more and Mrs. Watson stepped out with a look of relief on her face. "Thank heavens you have returned home, Child!" she declared. "We were fraught with worry about you."

Mattie rose and embraced Mrs. Watson warmly. "Thank you, but Lord Winston saved me."

"To think that terrible man dined with you and your family," Mrs. Watson declared, shaking her head in disbelief. "Mr. Blythe seemed like such a pleasant man."

"It was all an act," Mattie replied.

"Well, I hope he is on his way to Newgate right now," Mrs. Watson said.

Mattie grimaced. "I am afraid he is dead."

Mrs. Watson's eyes widened before saying, "Well, I

The Gentleman's Miscalculation

shouldn't speak ill of the dead, but good riddance." She smiled. "I do notice that Lord Winston is speaking to your father. Is he asking for your hand?"

"He is," Mattie confirmed, a soft smile playing on her lips.

Clasping her hands together, Mrs. Watson declared, "What wonderful news!"

"We will be residing at his sheep farm," Mattie said. "Which means I won't be too far to come and visit you."

Mrs. Watson beamed. "That makes me so happy to hear."

As she uttered her words, her father and Winston stepped outside, their expressions solemn. Mattie's heart pounded in her chest as she looked at them expectantly.

"Mattie," her father began, "Winston has assured me of his love and commitment to you. You have my blessing."

Tears of joy welled in her eyes as she rushed forward to embrace her father. "Thank you, Father," she whispered, her voice choked with emotion.

Winston stepped closer, taking Mattie's hand once more. "Thank you, my lord," he said sincerely. "May I have a word with my betrothed?"

Her father gave him a curt nod. "Yes, but make it quick."

"I will," Winston promised.

Hand in hand, Mattie and Winston walked a short distance away. He broke the silence by asking, "Are you happy, Mattie?"

"Blissfully so," she replied.

"Good, because that was the easy part," Winston said, a teasing smile playing at the corners of his lips. "Now we have to tell my family."

Mattie laughed, feeling lighter and freer than she ever had. "That shouldn't be a problem."

Winston shuddered dramatically. "It will not be for the faint of heart. I assure you."

"Together, we can do anything," Mattie encouraged, giving his hand a reassuring squeeze.

Bringing her hand up to his lips, Winston kissed it gently. "Together… I quite like the sound of that."

"Oh, I did speak to my sister about the letter," Mattie began, her tone growing serious. "I'm afraid her reasonings were entirely selfish."

Winston nodded. "My only regret is that I didn't ask you sooner about the letter."

Mattie stepped closer to him. "To be honest, I don't know if I would have been ready then, but I am ready now," she said earnestly. "With all my heart, and all my soul, I will love you forever, and even then it doesn't seem long enough."

"I love you, Mattie," Winston murmured, his voice holding a promise.

Epilogue

One year later...

Winston exited the stables, brushing off a few strands of hay from his blue jacket. The scent of freshly baked bread filled the air, making his stomach growl in anticipation. A light mist hung around him, dampening his jacket from his morning ride. He took a deep breath, savoring the cool, crisp air mixed with the comforting aroma of home.

He entered the cottage through the back door, stepping into the warm, inviting kitchen. Mrs. Watson stood by the hearth, stirring a pot with practiced ease. She turned and greeted him with a kind smile. "Good morning, my lord."

"Good morning," he responded, returning her smile.

"Your breakfast should be on the table shortly," Mrs. Watson informed him.

"Thank you," Winston said. "I truly appreciate you coming to help us out during this time."

Mrs. Watson waved off his gratitude with a gentle laugh. "You don't need to keep thanking me," she responded.

"But I feel as if I do," he said, placing a hand to his stomach. "Especially for your cooking."

Mrs. Watson laughed. "Your wife tries."

"That she does," Winston agreed. "Speaking of my wife, is she still sleeping?"

Shaking her head, Mrs. Watson responded, "No, she is in the front room."

"Excuse me," Winston said before he headed towards the front of the cottage. As he approached, he saw Mattie sitting on a settee, her red hair pulled back into a low bun, focused on altering one of her gowns. The mere sight of her made his heart swell with love.

Winston leaned against the doorway, taking a moment to admire her. This past year had been the happiest of his life, filled with laughter and love, far removed from the burdens of his past.

Mattie looked up and smiled, her eyes lighting up at the sight of him. "Good morning, Husband."

He pushed off from the doorframe and approached her. "How are you faring this morning?"

"Not good," Mattie admitted with a sigh. "I am taking out the waist on yet another gown."

"That is to be expected in your condition," Winston said gently.

Mattie placed the gown down and rubbed her growing belly. "That is what the doctor said as well."

Winston sat down beside her. "I have a letter for you."

His wife's face lit up with excitement. "Is it from my father?"

"It is," Winston confirmed, pulling the letter from his jacket pocket.

"Will you read it to me?" Mattie asked.

Winston leaned in for a kiss before replying, "Of course, my dear." He unfolded the paper and read:

· · ·

My Dearest Mattie,

My time is short, but I want to inform you that Emma has found a match. She is marrying the Duke of Kinver...

Winston paused as he heard Mattie gasp. "Do you want me to continue?" he asked.

Mattie snatched the letter out of his hand and read the rest of it. When she finished, she looked up, her expression one of disbelief. "I can't believe it. The Duke of Kinver is four times her age. What is Emma thinking?"

"Well, Emma only seemed to care about titles and status," Winston pointed out.

"Yes, but I was hoping she would grow out of that and marry for love," Mattie said, her voice tinged with disappointment.

Winston took her hand in his. "Not everyone is as lucky as we are," he remarked. "Speaking of which, I have some good news."

"Good, I could use some," Mattie responded.

Shifting in his seat, Winston said, "Mr. Barker has agreed to sell his property to me."

A broad smile spread across Mattie's lips. "That is wonderful news."

"It is, because his property has a decent-sized manor on it," Winston revealed. "We can finally move out of this cottage."

Mattie tightened her hold on his hand. "But I love this cottage."

"I know you do, which is why you are the best of women," Winston said. "You have been so patient with me as I have expanded our holdings. Now we are the largest landowners in the county, and it has been much more profitable than I ever imagined."

"I had no doubt that you would be successful at whatever you put your mind to," Mattie said.

Winston placed his other hand on Mattie's increasing belly. "We will need the extra room when the baby comes."

Mattie nodded. "I suppose you are right, but I will miss the bleating of the sheep in the morning waking me up."

"And perhaps we could persuade Mrs. Watson to become our housekeeper," Winston suggested.

"She has been so kind to help us out since I am far too big to move about the kitchen," Mattie said.

Winston grinned. "I have enjoyed the more elaborate meals."

Mattie frowned playfully. "I warned you that I was a terrible cook before we were married."

"You did, and I would marry you a thousand times over, despite my bread always being burned," Winston teased.

She laughed, just as he had intended. "I am getting better."

"That you are, my love," Winston said, his voice filled with affection and pride.

Mrs. Watson entered the room and announced, "Breakfast is ready."

Winston rose and extended a hand to assist Mattie up from her seated position. "I hope you are hungry."

Mattie smirked, placing her hand in his as she stood. "I am increasing. I am always hungry," she quipped.

He chuckled. "Thank you," he said sincerely.

Mattie tilted her head. "For what?"

Winston gently turned Mattie to face him, his hands resting on her shoulders. "For always making me laugh," he said. "I don't know what I did right to deserve you."

Mattie went on her tiptoes and kissed him lightly on the lips. "You happen to be a very good kisser," she teased.

"So you married me for my kissing abilities?" Winston asked, raising an eyebrow in a playful challenge.

She shrugged with a mischievous glint in her eyes. "That, and other things," she retorted. "After all, everything between us started with just a kiss."

"Yes, it did," Winston agreed. He leaned in, pressing his lips to hers in a tender, lingering kiss.

The End

Next book in the series...

Protecting her was his duty. Falling for her was a risk he couldn't afford—but couldn't resist.

Next book in the series...

Lady Melody Lockwood deciphers enemy codes from the safety of her home. It is safe and predictable, allowing her to feel as though she is doing more than what is expected of a lady in High Society. However, when a leak at the agency suggests her cover may have been blown, she faces a danger she never expected.

Wesley Ainsworth, the Earl of Emberly, is tasked with protecting Lady Melody, a responsibility he takes very seriously—even when she insists she doesn't need his help. Having already lost one agent under his watch, he is determined to do whatever it takes to keep her safe.

As the threat looms closer, Wesley and Melody are forced to work together to uncover the culprit that is lurking in the shadows of Brockhall Manor. Their partnership challenges them to balance duty with the desires of their hearts. Will they unravel the mystery in time, or will their guarded hearts keep them from working together and discovering the love they both deserve?

About the Author

Laura Beers is an award-winning author. She attended Brigham Young University, earning a Bachelor of Science degree in Construction Management. She can't sing, doesn't dance and loves naps.

Laura lives in Utah with her husband, three kids and her dysfunctional dog. When not writing regency romance, she loves skiing, hiking and drinking Dr Pepper.

You can connect with Laura on Facebook, Instagram or on her site at www.authorlaurabeers.com.

Made in the USA
Middletown, DE
26 January 2025